Sherlock's Home
The Empty House

Compiled by Sherlockology
Edited by Steve Emecz

Paperback ISBN 9781780922256
ePub ISBN 9781780922263
PDF ISBN 9781780922270

Published in the UK by MX Publishing
335 Princess Park Manor, Royal Drive,
London, N11 3GX

www.mxpublishing.com
Cover design by www.sherlockology.com

Jeff Decker

Contents

About This Book

When we first started Sherlockology it was down to our personal love of what was at the time a remarkable three episode BBC drama, created by the enormously talented Steven Moffat and Mark Gatiss. Each member of the team had previous interest in arguably the greatest fictional detective of all time and varied knowledge of previous incarnations and the canon from which they were based. As time went on however, like Alice in Wonderland, we began to venture down the rabbit hole into the world of Sir Arthur Conan Doyle and Sherlock Holmes.

What we discovered on our journey was that Sherlock Holmes is a character like no other. He does not simply live on the pages of a book, nor is he only brought to life by the various and numerous actors who have portrayed him. He is a living breathing, flesh and blood person, who becomes more real and more relevant in the real world around us, regardless of the era, the longer the acquaintance you share with him. Sherlock Holmes, Dr. John Watson, Mrs. Hudson, Mycroft Holmes, and the rest of the Sir Arthur Conan Doyle's characters, have become far more than the invention of a talented author. To us and to many before, and no doubt after, they have become life- long friends.

Were it not for Sir Arthur Conan Doyle introducing us, both literary history and our own imaginations, would be much duller indeed. He gave us the most unique type of hero, he gave us someone to believe in, and for that, the very least we can do is to ensure the creator of such an individual, has a legacy to live on for future generation. They will discover, as we have, the joy of meeting Sherlock Holmes.

That legacy lives in the pages of the canon, but also in the bricks and mortar of Undershaw. This was the building in which Sir Arthur Conan Doyle, designed, built, entertained his fellow authors and most importantly wrote more cases for Sherlock Holmes. For the house to be lost, would be an unimaginable travesty, and this book is a product of the fight to preserve it. Those who have contributed to the contents fight, the hundreds who submitted entries fight and most importantly, you the purchaser of this book fight with us.

We would like to extend a huge thank you to all those who made this book possible. To Roger Johnson who went above and beyond and was an absolute rock throughout the short time period we had to put this book together; to Michael Cox and Sue Vertue for their help and support, the producers of two different but equally brilliant Sherlock Holmes television series; Nicholas Briggs, Douglas Wilmer, David Stuart Davies, Roger Llewellyn, Gyles Brandreth, Jeff Decker, Alistair Duncan, Stephen Fry and Mark Gatiss (Patron of UPT) for their contributions and sharing with us the importance of saving Undershaw; and finally The Undershaw Preservation Trust, Lynn Gale and Jacquelynn Morris, for bringing this to the public's attention and MX Publishing for making the book a reality.

Sherlockology
www.sherlockology.com

The Undershaw Preservation Trust

Towards the end of 2008, I had a very vivid dream about a Victorian family standing in the doorway of a huge house. From behind an old-fashioned camera I appeared to be taking photographs. On waking I tried desperately to place these people that had shared my dream, but nothing prepared me for the shock when I opened a book of Sir Arthur's several months later to find a picture of his second family, just as they had appeared in my dream.

Several months later I set out by car with my camera slung on the back seat with no clear journey in mind. The 'For Sale' sign at the entrance of Undershaw, which I had passed on many occasions before, seemed to jump out at me: a clear indication that I should descend on Undershaw with my camera held firmly in my hand to capture its history. The photos that were taken on that day of a decaying building formed part of what has lead me into a campaign that, over the years, has aroused the attention of people from all walks of life and from all around the globe.

I had no idea what was waiting for me behind the mass of tall trees as I slowly walked down the long driveway that meandered its way down to the red brick building. History appeared to seep out of its walls as I trod the same ground as many who had walked before me centuries ago. I had gone there in my teens and somehow it felt that I was walking back in time. There, underneath high-rise scaffolding and a protective roof, stood the former Surrey home of Sherlock Holmes' creator, Sir Arthur Conan Doyle, a much respected gentleman of the neighbourhood in his day and one of the greatest fictional authors of all time.

I was struck by the state of near ruin the house was in; clearly it had been abandoned to weather the elements alone over the years. Almost instantaneously I felt a strong urge to save it and, by so doing, return it to its former charm, character and elegance.

Save it? How does one achieve such a remarkable, insane feat? Was I just an irrational, over-enthusiastic woman who wanted to perform the impossible? But the urge was so strong that I felt propelled forward: if there is something you want so badly, it can always be achieved.

My fervent hope for Undershaw is that it will be resurrected as Sherlock Holmes was resurrected and that, like Sherlock Holmes, it will live on for many generations to come.

Lynn Gale

Undershaw has always been a place of hospitality…the stage having first been set by Arthur Conan Doyle who entertained many family, friends and literary luminaries in the home that was his inspiration …and then carried on by managements who ran it for decades as a welcoming hotel , with guests enjoying its cuisine and conviviality and oft times dining in the garden tree house. Amongst ACD's many talents, the pursuit of justice was paramount. And it is justice that must again triumph to free Undershaw from the grips of vandalism and to restore it to a meeting place of like minds, interests, intrigue and aspiration.

Sue Meadows

Co-founders of The Undershaw Preservation Trust
www.saveundershaw.com

Undershaw – A Brief History

For the benefit of those who don't know, Undershaw is the name given by Sir Arthur Conan Doyle to his former home in Hindhead, Surrey. He lived there from October 1897 until September 1907 when he married his second wife, Jean Leckie, and moved to Crowborough in Sussex.

Undershaw is unique amongst Conan Doyle's former homes as it is the only one where he had a hand in the design. Many of its features were designed specifically with Louise Conan Doyle in mind. She had been suffering from tuberculosis since late 1893 and the large windows, shallow staircases and doors that could be pushed from both sides were all features designed for her comfort. Sadly the house would be the site of her death in July 1906 when she finally succumbed to her illness.

It was in this house that many of Conan Doyle's works of significance were created (in whole or in part). For the readers of this book the most notable works produced during this time were *The Hound of the Baskervilles* and *The Return of Sherlock Holmes*. It is therefore perfectly fair to say that Undershaw was the site of Sherlock Holmes's re-birth. This was, of course, a cause for celebration by his many fans at the time and is something fans of today are equally grateful for.

After Conan Doyle left the house in 1907 it was briefly let to tenants. It is believed that he hoped to eventually give the house to his son Kingsley but when he (Kinglsey) tragically died just before the end of the First World War, Conan Doyle made the decision to sell Undershaw at a rock-bottom price. Some little time later it became a hotel.

In 2004, when its period as a hotel came to an end, the house was purchased with a view to redevelopment. An application was made to the local council (and approved) to convert the grade two listed building into a series of apartments and town houses with additional new structures to be built in the grounds.

These are the plans that The Undershaw Preservation Trust and its supporters (including you dear reader) are fighting against. This battle needs fighting not only for the sake of Undershaw but for the sake of historically significant sites worldwide. The people in power need to be shown that we will not stand by without protest while they attempt to rob us of our history.

Alistair Duncan 2012

'An Entirely New Country - Arthur Conan Doyle, Undershaw and the Resurrection of Sherlock Holmes'

Not Our Glory
Words and Music by Caitlin Obom

This room, it don't hold you now like I did
but I can feel your footsteps through the floor
the paper peels away, and I keep waiting
but your hands don't trail the hallways anymore

And they can't read the dust
where your feet they graced the ground
and they don't see this memory
that's keepin' you around

No, we ain't empty
these silent houses keep the time
the years, they wrote a memoir
on each floorboard's crooked lines
read the world the way you want
you've your methods, i have mine
each of us can write a different story
and time may take our lives,
but not our glory

These walls could never grow used to the silence
or filtered light run shattered through the glass
meant to be remembered and delivered
something that was made to last

And they don't know a heart
when it's breaking down the door
if they don't understand what keeps it
pounding anymore

No, we ain't empty
these silent houses keep the time
the years, they wrote a memoir
on each floorboard's crooked lines

9

Read the world the way you want
you've your methods, I have mine
each of us can write a different story
and time may take our lives,
but not our glory

Oh my battered beauty
oh this wasted bone
don't give up the ghost yet
erasure's writ in stone

No, we ain't empty
these silent houses keep the time
the years, they wrote a memoir
on these floorboard's crooked lines
read the world the way you want
you've your methods, i have mine
each of us can write a different story
and time may take our lives,
but not our glory

Supporters

There isn't room in a hundred books for the words of all the supporters of Save Undershaw – but here is a small selection from actors, writers, producers and historians which sum up the sentiments of the thousands of Sherlock Holmes fans around the world.

Mark Gatiss, Stephen Fry, Roger Johnson, Gyles Brandreth, Douglas Wilmer, Nick Briggs, Michael Cox, David Stuart-Davies, Roger Llewelwyn, and Alistair Duncan.

I would like to express my whole-hearted enthusiasm for the campaign to save Undershaw. It seems to me a very sad reflection on our times that the home of one of our greatest and most popular writers should be so neglected and in danger of unsympathetic redevelopment.

Sir Arthur Conan Doyle occupied several residences in his prolific and thrilling career, only Undershaw bears the stamp of his massive personality. Here the Hound of the Baskervilles first breathed spectral life and Sherlock Holmes himself was resurrected from the Reichenbach Falls. Here Stoker, Barrie and Hornung and many others were entertained. It's no exaggeration to say that Undershaw was the centre of Doyle's life during perhaps the most fruitful and fascinating phase of his career. It must be saved and take its place among the sensitively preserved residences of this country's other literary giants. This is certainly a three-pipe problem but not, I am convinced, an insoluble one.

Mark Gatiss
Patron, The Undershaw Preservation Trust

Actor, screenwriter, novelist, and co-creator with Steven Moffat of the BBC series, 'Sherlock'.

Conan Doyle has passed with flying colours whatever test is needed to guarantee an eternal, imperishable place in British cultural life. It may be that Harry Potter won't last a century (I am sure he will, but you can't always tell) but it is more certain than anything else in all literature that Sherlock Holmes will last, not just centuries, but for millennia. There is simply no other fictional character in the world who has endured so long and who stands for so much. As we have seen so spectacularly and successfully just in the past year and a half, Sherlock can be reinvented for every age. What would generations yet unborn think of us if we allowed the home of Holmes's creator to fall into decay and disrepair? What would they think of us if they discovered that we had knowingly bulldozed it for no better reasons than greed and laziness? They would be as appalled as the hundreds of thousands around the world are who are calling out, "No. Stop! Think!! This is a false economy and an act of philistine stupidity."

There is so much a living, thriving Undershaw could achieve. It could be a study centre, a visitor attraction, a leading museum and a focus of pride. I urge all those have the power, to think of themselves not as wrecking balls, but as people of vision and creative insight. Holmes will only get bigger over the ages, don't let Britain get smaller.

Stephen Fry
Actor and Writer

Once the youngest member of the Sherlock Holmes Society of London and most recently seen as Mycroft Holmes in 'Sherlock Holmes: A Game of Shadows'.

Despite the crass philistine statement of a former Culture Secretary, Arthur Conan Doyle's place in English literature - and in international culture - is secure. Like the works of many others, his writings are still, a century on, studied, dissected and criticised by students and academics. But Conan Doyle is one of a select few whose books are also still read for sheer pleasure after a hundred years or more. People read "The Lost World", "The White Company" and especially the various tales of Sherlock Holmes for the best reason of all: because they want to. (As Sir Christopher Frayling has said, you can assure a modern reader that the Sherlock Holmes books are entertaining, and there's no need to add, "Of course, there are some dull bits..." That's a rare distinction for a Victorian author.)

Undershaw, Conan Doyle's house at Hindhead, is of national - even international - importance in the literary landscape of Britain. This is where he wrote 'The Adventures of Gerard', 'Sir Nigel' and 'The Great Boer War'. This was the house he left to become a medical officer in the South African conflict. This was his home when he became Sir Arthur. This is where Sherlock Holmes was reborn.

The fact that Conan Doyle worked with the architect J H Ball in designing the house gives it a rare and precious personal quality. To adapt a sentiment from the website; www.scottsabbotsford.co.uk, dedicated to the home of Sir Walter Scott, an author whom Conan Doyle deeply admired, *'When you touch the bricks and mortar of Undershaw you are touching the soul of Arthur Conan Doyle.'*
The present state of the house, neglected by its owners and damaged by vandals, is deeply sad. Undershaw can and must be saved!

Roger Johnson
Editor of The Sherlock Holmes Journal

The Sherlock Holmes Society of London

Arthur Conan Doyle was a fine writer, a great story-teller and a remarkable man. His personal story is fascinating (impressive and moving) and he made his mark on the world in a way that only a few have. He belongs to that small band of writers who have created characters that live beyond the page. Sherlock Holmes, Dr Watson. Mrs Hudson. Professor Moriarty, The Baker Street Irregulars - these characters and their world are known across every continent - and are set to last. Conan Doyle's home is a house of national and international cultural, social and literary significance.

Gyles Brandreth
Writer and Broadcaster

It seems wanton and barbaric that the former home of Sir Arthur Conan Doyle, creator of the most famous literary character in the world, Sherlock Holmes, and depiction of such vivid late Victorian atmosphere should be allowed to come under threat. In this house were conceived and written many of Doyle's finest stories, including his perhaps most famous one: The Hound of the Baskervilles.

Whatever Undershaw's future, be it hotel or care-home, it should most certainly be preserved from breaking up into flats or commercial premises, which would utterly destroy its character for ever. Comparisons in Doyle's literary stature with Jane Austen or anyone else, are idle and entirely beside the point.

I have had the great good fortune to be introduced to the Sherlock Holmes stories many years ago And the further good fortune to have played the role in thirteen episodes of a BBC TV series, which caused me to study the character in much depth, a process I have found to be of endless interest and the greatest enjoyment ever since.

I have also had the honour to be made an honorary member of the Sherlock Holmes Society of London. I would therefore wish to append my name to the protests that have, quite naturally come about.

Douglas Wilmer
Actor, BBC television series, 'Sherlock Holmes' (1965)

I'm an actor, a writer and a producer who's had a passion for Holmes since I was a child... but I suppose it's a passion that came about because of Basil Rathbone, Peter Cushing... Christopher Plummer, Robert Stephens and yes, even Stewart Granger (William Shatner was in that one, too, wasn't he?).

But I came back to the originals via David Stuart Davies's fantastic one-man theatre shows, starring the superb Roger Llewellyn - The Last Act and The Death and Life. These featured so many tantalizing snippets of the Conan Doyle text that I went back to them. And that made me want to produce audio dramatizations that were as close to the originals as possible.

Previous to this... I'd had two other professional encounters with Holmes...

Back in 1999, when I was working like crazy to finish the post-production sound design and music for the first Big Finish Doctor Who release - I was also rehearsing and subsequently performing as Holmes in a production of Sir Arthur Conan Doyle's own play, The Stoner Case - which we retitled The Speckled Band, for the purposes of easier recognition.

As I'm sure you will know, the original productions of it suffered from a lack of authenticity when it came to the representation of the snake. The irony being that when they used a real snake, everyone thought it was a fake one, because it hardly moved.

We NEVER considered using a real snake. We handled the snake problem in two ways. Firstly, the Douglas Wilmer route... when the snake came through the grill, I whacked it with a cane before anyone could see it (YES, IT WASN'T ACTUALLY THERE), then, secondly, we went for high melodrama!

Rylott/Roylott (the name was changed in Doyle's play for some reason - anyone know why?) was heard screaming from outside the auditorium. Suddenly, the doors burst open, and he charged in, wrestling with a fake snake, screaming and howling, his chest bared, his hair in a crazy mess (don't ask me why, just blame actor 'over-enthusiasm'). And as he 'died', he flung the snake towards us. And I caught it with my cane and flicked it skillfully onto Helen Stoner's bed... And then

17

Watson and I immediately flipped a blanket over it, before proceeding to whack it to death with our canes. Like two madmen possessed! Then we stopped.

And, panting from our exertions, we gingerly checked to see if the snake was dead. Discovering that it wasn't, we embarked upon another frenzy of whacking, until we were satisfied that our fake snake had indeed shuffled off its mortal coil.

It was quite difficult to get through the lines of the final scene without further, genuine panting!

The play was performed for two weeks at the Drayton Court theatre (in a big room under a pub - don't know whether it's still going!) and after disappointingly small audiences, word of mouth started to bring the crowds in just as the run was coming to an end. With the rate of increase of audience size, if we'd had permission to stay on, we might still be performing it now.

But the bottom line for me was that I'd loved playing Holmes! Really loved it. I don't think I'm anything like him. Nowhere near as clever. Thankfully nowhere near as unhealthy in my habits (any more - I'm talking about the smoking!)

But I do at least recognize something of that single-mindedness of Holmes. The fact that I'm all afire with enthusiasm when I'm working on something that I utterly love (which is thankfully most of the time these days), but utterly destroyed when I'm inactive. In fact, I fear inactivity. I fill my life with too much work - as my wife and child will tell you - not just because I fear I won't have enough money to support them, but because I feel that dark cloud that descends over me when I don't have anything creative to do.

So I can, to some tiny degree anyway, identify with Holmes. And, of course, it helps that I'm not entirely unlike him, physically. Well. Not entirely...

My next encounter with Holmes was when I was asked to play him as part of a season of thrillers that I'd been involved in for nearly a decade at the Theatre Royal Nottingham.

As a change to the usual diet of Francis Durbridge, the producer had decided to do a Sherlock Holmes play... mainly because he knew Avengers creator Brian Clemens and mainly because he knew Brian had written a Sherlock Holmes play... Oh and REALLY MAINLY, because he hoped Brian would do him a good deal on the royalties.

Yeah, that was the MAIN reason.

My dear friend and colleague Maggie Stables (if you're a Big Finish fan...) recommended me as Holmes. She had the ear of the producer - and was terrified he was about to cast someone entirely inappropriate... I've no idea who.

So, I got the job.

The Deputy Stage Manager gave me the back-handed compliment of, 'Well, out of all the people they could get for this season, I guess you're the least inappropriate to play the part.' Praise indeed.

Brian Clemens's play was, of course, Holmes and the Ripper. Not the first piece of work to ponder on how Holmes might have solved that infamous, real-life case - and probably not the last.

The style was... interesting, with more than a dash of the Rathbone/Bruce feel to it... And even a hint at a past, lost love of Holmes. A woman who had ended her days in an insane asylum. The clairvoyant character who imparts this information to Holmes, through feeling vibrations from a broach, later fell for Holmes herself. And the play ends rather sentimentally, with the clairvoyant 'Kate' (for whom Holmes has abandoned his customary skepticism) heading off on a chaperoned trip round Europe with 'Sherlock', as she rather outrageously calls him... A trip which will take in the Reichenbach Falls.

It was a monster of a role in terms of the number of lines to be learnt, and Holmes was in almost every scene. And I had only seven days in which to rehearse it. But it was fantastic fun to do... and was staged with very simple settings, with lighting and sound being employed to great use.

As is always the way when you do weekly rep, there is always some terrible naughtiness going on. Silly really, when the pressure is so high and the potential for cock-ups so great... but actors seem to mess about EVEN MORE when there's more pressure.

And I'm as guilty as the next man.

As Holmes, Watson and Kate finally know who committed the crime and set off to get their man, in rehearsals, I always used to say, 'Come on! Let's really ***expletive deleted*** him up!' as my exit line. On the first performance, I very nearly said it.

19

And when Watson made his final farewell to me, as I went off to Reichenbach with Kate, he was required to whisper a final piece of manly advice in my ear before I left. Needless to say, I got various versions of... 'She's a lesbian' or 'I'm gay and love you' on every performance. So I had my work cut out for me not ending the play by guffawing.

The great success of this production led the Theatre Royal to plan a return for Holmes and me the following year.

In the meantime, I was lucky enough to see David Stuart Davies's aforementioned, superb plays. I immediately sorted out the rights for audio adaptations. And at some point around this time, the return match for Holmes at the Theatre Royal became The Hound of the Baskervilles.

Following Holmes and the Ripper, by the way, I'd asked Brian Clemens, who came to see the performance and loved it, if I could adapt his play for audio. He agreed, enthusiastically. So I had my first, somewhat eccentric, series of Holmes planned!

Anyway, the producer of Hound of the Baskervilles revealed that he was going to write the script. He was a writer of no note whatsoever. I asked him how he was going to 'do the hound'. He said, 'Oh, that'll all happen off-stage... or maybe we'll see a couple of red eyes through the French Windows.'

I grimaced, saying, 'There aren't any french windows in Hound of the Baskervilles!' (There are in almost every other thriller we ever do at the Theatre Royal - it's the law) 'Oh, do you have any ideas?' asked the producer.

I immediately re-read the great story of the Hound, made some notes and had a meeting with the producer. 'You're going to end up having to write this,' my wife warned me. I met with the producer... 'I think you'd better write it,' he said. The money was terrible. But I was writing The Hound of the Baskervilles, so I didn't care.

I knew the Theatre Royal Nottingham audience well. They come for a laugh, so, without heading for outright comedy, I did bear this in mind. I'd been a part of a couple of really spooky productions at this theatre, and seen how well the mixture of laughs and shocks worked well.

I made the Barrymores a little broad and overly emotional about the death of their master... hoping to get a few moments of Watson being stern with them and regretting upsetting them. The trouble is, the actor playing Barrymore took the comedy cues in the script far too far to heart, and ended up rather milking it.

I also had fun with comedy elements with a soldier leaping out at Watson's party as they approached Baskerville Hall.

But my solution to the whole difficulty of portraying the hound on stage (with no budget!) was to hit the problem head-on. My premise was that Watson was putting on a stage production of The Hound of the Baskervilles and had asked Holmes along to a final rehearsal to judge how accurate the play was.

This meant that Holmes could be in the story more... because even when he wasn't meant to be in it, he could pop onto the stage to quiz Watson about how things were unfolding. I remember I was particularly concerned that Watson, suspecting that Barrymore might be connected with the murder, went out and left Henry Baskerville alone in the house with the Barrymores for quite some time (allowing him to meet the Stapletons). Why would Watson leave Henry at risk like that? The way we played it, Watson hadn't thought of that... leaving Holmes looking rather smug and superior.

The other advantage of it being portrayed as a stage play was that I could have Holmes as concerned as the audience might be about the potentially rubbish portrayal of the hound. During the play, he keeps asking Watson how exactly the hound will be portrayed. Irritated, Watson keeps avoiding the question.

And as the play progresses, Holmes gets more and more involved in the re-enactment... at one point quoting Watson's famous narrative passage about the appearance of the hound. The idea is that Holmes is quite disturbed by the memory of the monstrous beast.

And finally, Holmes finds himself left on stage, with the lights fading and only the sound of the hound in the distance as company. Clearly caught up in it all, he draws his revolver and challenges the hound to appear. And for a split-second, it does - as an actor wearing a giant hound mask leaps out for a moment before the lights black-out. In the blackout, Holmes fires those famous five shots. Although, I'm afraid, one night, the back-up gun firer was a little too anxious and fired off a couple of shots as well, which made it sound a bit like Holmes had a machine gun.

When the lights come up, Watson and the rest of the cast come on to apologize for there not being a hound. 'It was too difficult to do. We thought that should just all happen off stage!'

Utterly bamboozled and really quite disturbed, Holmes turns to the audience and says, 'But I saw it. I saw... the hound of the Baskervilles.'

Curtain in. Thunderous applause.

My next Holmes experience was directing Roger Llewellyn in audio adaptations of David Stuart Davies's brilliant one-man shows. And this is the start of the audio journey...

In the case of the first releases of our second series - my dramatizations of The Final Problem and The Empty House hardly qualify as adaptations at all. They are very nearly just the original text with the 'said he's removed. The main adapting involved breaking the text up into new paragraphs, to emphasize changes of thought for the actors, and audio stage directions which gave hints at the emotional content - especially of Watson's decision finally to break the silence and speak out about Moriarty.

Hound of the Baskervilles needed more work, but only because it was over 60,000 words long and we knew our script had to be 20-odd thousand words to happily fit onto two CDs of drama. As much as we possibly could, we left Conan Doyle untouched.

I found that when you go back to the original texts, you think, why have people ever felt the need to mess about with this? Probably because Watson's narration is removed for the sake of dramatic variety... but on audio, your audience welcomes narration and you can keep Watson's narration in tact!

But the bottom line is...

Re-invent
Adapt
Change the context.

It's all fine... It's often brilliant.

But go back to the original and you'll have the best time.

Nick Briggs
Actor and Writer

Current Sherlock Holmes in the Big Finish Sherlock Holmes adaptations.

We all owe a great debt to the authors we discovered in our youth. They gave us endless excitement and an appetite for reading which lasts the rest of our lives. In my case they were Anthony Hope, Sapper, Dornford Yates, John Buchan, Leslie Charteris and, above all, Conan Doyle. Sir Arthur gave us a gallery of heroes - Holmes, Challenger and Brigadier Gerard - who have stayed with me into the 21st century. The least we can do in return is to try to make sure that his home is remembered and respected.

Michael Cox

Producer, Granada television series, 'The Adventures of Sherlock Holmes' (1984/5)

Don't Undervalue Undershaw. Sherlock Holmes, the detective created by an impoverished doctor in Southsea, is the most beloved of all literary characters, yet the author's home lies neglected and at risk. Since Holmes first appeared in print in 1887, hardly a year has passed without a play, a song, a film, a radio show, a pastiche, a television series or some other manifestation of Mr Holmes of Baker Street. Tourists flock to see his statue in London and Edinburgh as well as those in Japan and Switzerland. He is loved the world over. Quite simply Sherlock Holmes is the greatest Englishman who never lived. And he was the brainchild of one of the country's most remarkable men, Arthur Conan Doyle. This brilliant polymath had more strings to his bow than the omniscient Baker Street sleuth himself, but fate has decreed that he will be forever remembered as the man who brought Sherlock Holmes to the world. And, indeed, so he should be remembered, revered and cherished. Conan Doyle has brought great pleasure to and touched the lives of so many. The Holmes stories are the magic door for young people to pass through into the rewarding world of literature. A whole genre of fiction would not exist without the cornerstone of Sherlock. Doyle built on the foundations laid down by Edgar Allan Poe and created the template for the modern detective story. Without Doyle there would be no Poirot, no Wimsey, no Morse, no Rebus and others of their ilk.

Sherlock Holmes is a creation who transcends the printed page and is an integral part of the literary and cultural fabric of this this country. Tourists can visit the homes of Shakespeare, Austen, Dickens, and the Brontes but currently there is no focus for Conan Doyle. Yet the built heritage is integral to understanding an author. Conan Doyle not only lived at Undershaw for a decade, writing many of his best loved works here, and entertaining high profile figures, but he played a key part in the design of the house. The bricks and mortar express the essence of Conan Doyle: his passion, his politics, and his place in society. Undershaw is a microcosm of the transition between the Victorian and modern eras, just as Conan Doyle fixed it in his best remembered novel The Hound of the Baskervilles (1901), written at Undershaw.

Arthur Conan Doyle's Undershaw has the potential to be a focus for the creative arts, to interpret the life and works of this great man, to contribute to the wider understanding of the cultural landscape of the early years of the twentieth century and to celebrate the immortal Sherlock Holmes. For the nation, for culture, for posterity, for the people, Undershaw must be preserved, interpreted and made accessible for future generations to enjoy.

David Stuart Davies
Writer

Playwright to the award-winning one-man play, 'Sherlock Holmes - The Last Act' and 'Sherlock Holmes - The Death and Life', and also author of both fiction and non-fiction on Sherlock Holmes.

I first played Holmes in a major new adaptation of The Hound of the Baskervilles at the New Vic, Newcastle-under-Lyme, in 1997. David Stuart Davies, an experienced, successful writer, and a world authority on Holmes, who had reviewed the performance favourably, approached me with an idea for a solo performance — without Watson! My close friend Gareth Armstrong was touring the world very successfully with his own play Shylock, and the "solo bug" was buzzing around my psyche.

It was an ingenious idea: it allowed Holmes to reveal his deepest thoughts to the audience, and display elements of his personality previously unsuspected by his devoted readers. DSD was keen to write the play. Gareth was keen to direct it. I formed a small company to produce it, and Salisbury Playhouse generously presented it in the 90-seat studio, in 1999.

After a short tour, we played five successful weeks on the Edinburgh Fringe, winning five stars; and a placing among the Top Ten plays of the year. An immediate three-week transfer to The Cockpit Theatre in London (the closest one to Baker Street) was followed by nine years international touring, with over 800 performances — and counting.

At which point, I asked David for a second play, which he duly provided... and both productions continue to tour extensively.

Though never a particular Sherlockian myself, I recognised that I was good casting for the role, with the required vocal style, and a certain angularity of profile, and I was delighted that the Holmes David had written for me bore strong reference to the character I had found for myself in The Hound.

David had liked, and I had enjoyed, the dry, sardonic and not infrequently cruel humour that had developed in my interpretation, and which he expanded in his own original, contributions. Cleverly, from his encyclopaedic Holmesian knowledge, he abstracts "clues" and then develops them into entertaining and intriguing dramatic constructs.

Holmes, this super-intelligent, unemotional, insensitive, distant observer of everything, whose lack of social self awareness could occasionally appear very amusing, provided a wide and contrasting palate of options for any actor to pursue. I think that a case for Asperger's Syndrome could be made for him.

I had got to know him quite well in the nine weeks of rehearsals and performance of The Hound, and the lengthy process undertaken by Gareth and myself to create a solo life for the man rapidly opened many more doors.

David had adopted the premise that the friends had gone their separate ways for two years — Watson with his wife in London, and Holmes with his bees in Sussex. And then ... Watson dies!
Holmes attends the funeral, and is of course drawn once more to the dust-covered Baker Street rooms, where he is confronted with... what? His future, now totally alone.

The audience is cast in the role of Watson, and Sherlock unburdens himself of all the secrets, shames and glories of his life. Including the major role that the doctor had played in the detective's work — and, more than we suspected, in his life.

In this way, the actor is required to inhabit the famous character as generally perceived by the world, but also to open many doors into his previously unrevealed private nature ... almost as therapy.
A major challenge for me, as a classically trained "leading" actor, who usually sounded like variations of himself, was to discover a range of characterisations, to represent the large cast that David had created to people Holmes' retrospective revelations. I was not confident enough to replicate the characters as written, so we decided to invent our own versions, which we could then contrast sufficiently with each other for theatrical effect, and, in several cases, provide the broader humour required to leaven the darker realms of DSD's invention.

Therefore, for instance, Inspector Hopkins, obviously, becomes Welsh (check my surname); everyone knows all doctors are Scottish, so Dr Mortimer has a strong Highland burr; and the bookseller becomes Irish, to allow for a cheap gag involving the pronunciation of "three" . It never fails.

It is essential for me truly to identify with each of the thirteen individuals, as some of them have only two or three lines; and the audience must believe in them instantly, if they are to fulfil their function in the narrative. They are therefore, invariably, broadly and strongly drawn; leaving ample room for the hopefully more subtle expositions of the character of the protagonist.
As to this character, I have found over all these performances that the more ruthlessly I reveal the selfishness, the indifference, the cruel wit,

and most of all the final honesty of the man, the more the audiences warm to him, and, at the emotional end, forgive him his shortcomings.

In terms of what I attribute his extraordinary longevity and success I would say that apart from the obvious nostalgic appeal — pea-soupered, gas-lit, hansom-cabbed, cobbled Victorian London — Holmes symbolises the regular triumph of good over evil, and achieves heroic success by the application of his own moral form of justice, offsetting the frequent injustices of the official legal system. And he is the original "Super-Hero", pre-empting Superman, Batman, and all the others by displaying incomprehensible abilities, apparently beyond human endeavour.

On the subject of whether I based my interpretation of the role on Jeremy Brett's version, I don't believe any actor worthy of the title, would "base his performance" on anyone else's. For me, the rehearsal process involves addressing every character issue head on:
Is this thought truthful? Is he saying this for the obvious reason — or to achieve some other goal? What is the subtextual plot in this situation? What result is he intending to achieve with this statement or action or question...?

My metaphor is, cutting a way through a dense steep forest, branch by branch, step by step — i.e. thought by thought, and line by line, until the summit is achieved, at which point, you look back and see the shape of the path you have hacked, which is the character you have built.

To base your work on another actor's concept, would be to copy only the outside of his creation, and leave a hollow inner core for yourself. That would not last thirteen years of performance. And the longer you intend to play the part, the longer you need to take in cutting through the forest.

The privilege of playing Holmes for such a long time has allowed me to allow him to develop intrinsically in a way not possible in the more usual acting schedules. When he has been "rested" for a couple of months — essential for the health of the actor, and because of the structures of commercial touring — after a break of this nature, I have to re-rehearse the plays, to bring the thoughts and lines back to the front of the brain, and the tip of the tongue, and have regularly been surprised at the way it has developed on its own. Like a good casserole, it has enriched itself. Radical new ideas occur about thoughts and meanings.

My preference is to do one or two nights in different theatres. It is the answer to the question of keeping it fresh, and not being bored. Every performance is a First Night in many respects.

My preferred work schedule is to arrive at 10.00am, meet the tech. team, and check out the stage, auditorium and dressing room. They help me to unload my car and show me where they have hung the lamps, following my detailed notes and diagrams, emailed three weeks before. I lay out the set — two chairs and tables, three rugs and a hat stand — and dress them with the props ... books, glasses pipes etc. They focus the lamps under my direction, and colour them as appropriate; we then plot the cues into the Lighting Board. After a brisk canter through the play, I can comfortably leave them to rehearse technically on their own. On a good day, this takes three hours in total, so that I can relax, eat, sleep, shower, and return sixty minutes before curtain to settle any issues that may have arisen. I then do my vocal warm-up for about ten minutes, and with a little make-up and costume, begin to look more like the man on the poster. After the show, I get out of the dressing room as fast as possible; occasionally meet and greet friends or fans, then get down to the boring and exhausting business of re-packing all my set and props, and, with help from the staff, carry them out to the car and re-load.

The lighting and acoustic are slightly different in each theatre. The stage size, height, and facilities are very different, as are the access to the stage and the wing spaces. I have to rehearse entry and exit carefully in each new theatre. I might play to a 1200-seater on Tuesday and a 90-seat studio on Thursday.

The audiences decide by their reactions what sort of a play they are seeing. If they respond very early to the humorous elements, they are telling me to play the show like that; but if they do not respond in this way, they get a darker, differently timed evening. I enjoy both versions, and relish the chance to give them the one they have chosen. Recently, in a three-night run in York, the Tuesday house barely laughed at all, but the Wednesday and Thursday audiences hooted as if it were one of Ayckbourn's funniest. All nights were sold out.

I certainly hope I have not become like the character myself. I am a genial, sociable fellow — "GSOH" with certain culinary skills, which my many friends regularly enjoy.

For my assessment of him... read above!

Roger Llewelwyn
Actor, The Sherlock Holmes Experience

I have been asked many times to give information on Undershaw and the fight to save it. Very rarely have I been asked why I personally think it should be saved. So this is a refreshing opportunity to talk about the house from a very personal perspective.

I was introduced to Sherlock Holmes by my mother in 1982 (yes a long time ago now) and have been a fan ever since. I was fortunate to be around and interested when Jeremy Brett first took to the screen as Sherlock Holmes in 1984. They were good times and those coming to Sherlock now, courtesy of the BBC, know only too well how you can become passionate about a character very quickly.

Yet Sherlock's creator is often forgotten, lost in the shadow of his famous detective, as are the many other things of interest that he did. His house Undershaw represents a ten-year period of his life when much of significance took place. The most notable of these things for many of us was the re-birth of Sherlock Holmes in The Hound of the Baskervilles and The Empty House. For Conan Doyle the big events were his service in the Boer War, his attempts at standing for Parliament and the death of his first wife Louise.

With Conan Doyle long dead, Undershaw is the only physical reminder of those times and it is under serious threat. Back in March 2010 I got involved with the Undershaw Preservation Trust and we discussed the idea of a book on the ten year period during which Undershaw was Conan Doyle's home. The result of my labours was An Entirely New Country in which I attempted to illustrate what went on during those years and what Undershaw represents not only to me but to the world. It was a labour of love and the resultant book is probably my favourite of all I've written.

The book that you are now reading is another attempt by me and its many other excellent contributors to make clear what the house means to us and why it should be saved.

I hope that what you read within these pages proves to you that the plans on the table, which would see the house irrevocably damaged, are not only unnecessary but they are also a permit for an act of historical vandalism. The people in power need to be shown that we will not stand by without protest while they attempt to rob us of our history.

Alistair Duncan
Writer

Author of 'An Entirely New Country - Arthur Conan Doyle, Undershaw and the Resurrection of Sherlock Holmes'

Stories & Poems

Undershaw
by Caitlin Rose Bowles
Swindon, UK

There it stands, on sandy soils
Sheltered from bitter winds by an embrace of Firs
But not the violent hands of modern man
Within clenched fists a hatred stirs.

Dust has settled in the darkened rooms
Where the Hound of the Baskervilles played
The sunlight is strangled by wooden boards
Wallpapers peeling and walls decayed.

The grand façade, now an empty shell
All the splendor ripped and rent
Ghostly echoes of what it once had been
Join the Undershaw's lament.

Who knows what great things were penned
Between those book lined walls
Who knows what secrets will be lost
If the Beautiful Undershaw Falls?

Charlie Milverton

by Charlotte Anne Walters

Shropshire, UK

Todd Carter smiled a patronising smile and straightened the lapels of his designer suit. He was smug, superior, rich and about to have a little fun.

"Well Mr Gareth Lestrade, on paper you stack up very nicely. Twenty years at Scotland Yard, senior police officer with all the relevant qualifications, but that's not enough. Think you've got what it takes to look after my girls? Prove it..."

He flashed a playful smile of whitened teeth then barked across to the burly, black-suited security guard standing by the door.

"Take him down Peterson," Todd commanded, adding a playful wink. "This ain't Scotland Yard."

He shrugged off a pang of guilt; *well, if the agency does insist on sending these old men...*

The guard rushed at Gareth, sixteen stone of muscle bearing down on him like a speeding train. This was shaping up to be the most surreal job interview imaginable.

Gareth had always been fairly adept at self-defence, but understood that to work in private security he needed to enhance his basic skills. Twelve months of unemployment had given him plenty of time.

Gareth swiftly blocked his attacker; they grappled together before a final outburst of effort enabled him to send his opponent confidently to the floor. What he lacked in strength, he compensated for in technique.

Todd was momentarily stunned by this unexpected outcome, though a face-full of Botox made it impossible to show it. He was becoming reluctantly impressed with this understated man who was clearly not a fame-hunter, kiss-and-tell merchant or someone who would have designs on his most precious possession, his girlfriend Della. *But could a forty-seven year old ex copper with a damaged reputation and no previous experience really look after a high-profile girl-band? Well, at least Della wouldn't want to sleep with him...*

Sherlock Holmes wasn't a sentimental man, but he did get used to certain people being in his world, like a favourite jacket or armchair. Detective Inspector Lestrade had been one of those people and now that he had gone, it was surprisingly unsettling.

So to find Lestrade back in his sitting room was comforting, a restoration of normality – except for Lestrade's expensive suit and LA tan.

"How is Doctor Watson?" Gareth asked, trying to ease in with general conversation.

"He has abandoned me for a wife."

"My wife abandoned me for a Chief Superintendent,"

"Not the same, her decision made sense."

"Thanks," replied Gareth sarcastically, greatly accustomed to Holmes' direct honesty.

"Smoke?"

"I don't, not now. I've just come back from LA, no one smokes – they all drink green-tea and have perfect teeth."

"You stopped off on the way back though, somewhere in Europe, Ibiza. All-inclusive 5 star hotel?"

This was what Holmes did, observed everything at lightning speed and made highly accurate inferences that would elude anyone of inferior brain.

"Don't look so surprised, you should know my methods by now. Your watch is two hours behind so not long-haul, and your boss owns a club in Ibiza I believe? You're wearing a hotel wrist-band so must have been all-inclusive and celebrities don't stay anywhere less than 5 star."

Gareth smiled, same old Holmes. They had known each other professionally for years but were not exactly friends. There were no normal conversations about family, football or last night's TV, such pleasantries would bore Holmes' hyperactive mind. But take him a problem, a perplexing murder, an odd series of apparently unconnected events, and he would come alive with furious energy.

"Why are you here Lestrade? You said you needed my help, so elaborate."

It had been a hectic twelve months, a real baptism-of-fire into the music business for an ex copper with no previous experience. Gareth felt as if he had travelled around the world and back again at least twice. He had seen more drugs, assaults and weapons than in the whole of his career on the force. A career that now lay in ruins.

"I've brought someone with me; they're waiting in the car. I wanted to see you first, make sure this would be something of interest to you. I know how scathing you can be towards a client if you find their situation disinteresting. And she's fragile, my job is to protect her – not expose her to your own peculiar brand of pleasantries."

"Della, I presume?"

"How do you know? There are three girls in the band."

"But Della has the highest profile, and it would take something serious to bring you to my door again."

"Holmes, I don't blame you for what happened..."

At which point the sitting room door opened and Della walked in. Dressed down in comfortable shoes, skinny jeans and a t-shirt she still looked strikingly attractive. A designer bag was slung over her shoulder and a huge pair of shades was pushed on top of her head, holding back a side-fringe of baby blonde hair.

"I'm sorry," she said, in a warm Northern accent, "I couldn't wait any longer. I'm going out of my mind Mr Holmes. The police aren't interested and Mr Lestrade said you could be trusted, that you help people. I really need help."

Della settled herself on the sofa next to Gareth, nervously rubbing together her hands.

"As you probably know, I'm a singer in a girl-band. I've worked so hard to get this far – I did my first talent contest aged five and was sending off demo tapes by the time I was fourteen. I'm twenty-nine now, but the record company tell everyone I'm twenty-four. Thank God for Botox or we'd never get away with it.

"Soon after getting signed to my label, I started dating my manager, Todd Carter. I was flattered, felt lucky he was interested in me. We've been together five years, we're even engaged. We're like one of those celebrity couples everyone loves to read about, Todd markets it for all it's worth – 'at home' shoots in magazines, pictures of us on yachts smiling like we're a devoted couple. Truth is, he's a control freak – even installed a tracker in my phone so that he always knows where I am. I can't breathe without his permission. He's got me on diets constantly, he's obsessed about me not looking my age – he's thirty-five and thinks it makes him seem younger if I look good. He's obsessed with his own looks too, had loads of cosmetic surgery. I won't say I'm afraid of him Mr Holmes, but he's a powerful man, he made me and can break me just as quick. I don't have money of my own, he controls everything – I can't even buy a bagel without him knowing."

"I presume this is leading somewhere interesting?" Holmes asked impatiently.

"I'm seeing someone else Mr Holmes, who I care about a great deal - someone who makes me happy. I'm not proud of it but in private Todd is cold, it's like he doesn't really want me but won't let anyone else have me. If he finds out, he'll destroy us both. I've been so careful, but something has happened – this evil, manipulating..."

Her voice choked as big fat tears tumbled from her wide, blue eyes. Gareth fished out a tissue and handed it to her. She composed herself enough to continue, holding Holmes' attention with her earnest expression.

"His name is Charlie Milverton. He preys on celebrities by getting his hands on anything which he can sell to the tabloids or spread on gossip websites. Then he makes contact and demands a fee in return for his silence. He's got so much dirt that everyone's afraid of him so his name never comes out – remember the MPs expenses scandal? The phone-tapping allegations? That young pop-star who killed himself after the papers published pictures of him taking drugs? All Milverton.

"Now he's set his sights on me and I don't know what to do. He has a security tape of me in a hotel lift...kissing this other man. He's threatened to sell it unless I pay £200,000. I have nothing of my own; I can't pay Mr Holmes – not without Todd knowing. But if this comes out, my reputation will be ruined and that of the other person involved – who really doesn't deserve this. Please help me."

Doctor Watson enjoyed escaping normality to visit Holmes at 221b. But it was difficult now that he had commitments, tea on the table when he got home and Sunday lunch with the in-laws. However, he had received a summons from Holmes and obediently made his way round, while his wife was at Pilates. As instructed, he brought with him all the information he had found from the internet about Charlie Milverton.

Holmes always acted impassively when Watson returned to his old rooms, but the doctor knew that his friend was secretively pleased to see him.

"Well," Watson exclaimed, throwing a pile of papers down on the coffee table, "I've been busy doing what you asked."

"Though not busy at work,"

"How do you know? I could have done all this at home."

"The paper quality is too good, you only buy cheap paper for home – that is clearly office stationary."

Watson was never particularly busy at work. He worked for a private medical practice, mainly seeing a stream of wasters sent by their sister company, a firm of solicitors specialising in 'no-win-no-fee' cases. Watson's job was to sign the forms confirming the person had whiplash, stress, a breakdown – even if they didn't.

"Charlie Milverton was a tabloid editor," Watson began, hoping to impress. "But he was ousted over drink problems. He retreated into the shadows and used his vast media contacts for dark purposes. He is obsessed with celebrities. He's the go-to person if you have a tape, incriminating email, leaked document - he will purchase it from you then sell it on. He is believed to be behind several websites, mainly celebrity gossip but one which is more political and serious – though no one can prove it."

Watson sat back in his chair feeling hopeful that perhaps, for once, his friend might be impressed with his findings.

"A sterling effort Watson, though you have failed to discover the most important thing."

"Which is?" asked Watson, hurt, but not altogether surprised.

"The legalities man! You work with lawyers - I need to know whether he's breaking any laws."

"I work *for* lawyers Holmes, there's a difference."

"Well, fortunately I anticipated your deficiencies and have consulted someone myself – a Mr L Pike, a well-known celebrity lawyer who owed me a favour. Milverton acts fast, he makes sure the material is released before a Super Injunction can be sought – and the courts are becoming increasingly reluctant to protect self-serving celebrities. I have no choice but to negotiate with him on behalf of my client, he will be here within the hour. Do stay Watson, your wife intents to visit friends after Pilates - that's why she took the car and you came here in a cab. I can see the receipt sticking out of your trouser pocket, so useful for claiming expenses from those lawyers you slave for."

Charlie Milverton shuffled into the room. Overweight, ugly and short, clearly blackmail was his only way of getting close to the 'beautiful people' who had become his obsession.

Holmes tried to negotiate but the stubborn little man would not budge. A reduced fee or the promise of payments by instalments was not acceptable to him. Any attempt to play on his sympathies failed. Watson observed that Holmes became unusually flustered at Milverton's resolve, losing his usual cool in the face of such obstinacy. He finally rose from his seat and asked Milverton to leave, looking dejected and exhausted as the strange media-beast made his way to the door – smiling victoriously.

"Payment by Saturday Mr Holmes, or full disclosure will be my only option. Tell your client to pay up or face the consequences."

Holmes slammed the door behind him and sat back in his chair. Watson let the silence settle between them as Holmes' mind frantically worked over the problem. Eventually, knowing that his wife would be returning home soon, he stood to leave.

"My wife will flip out if I'm home late."

"Dreadful Americanism," grumbled Holmes. Then, suddenly, he rose and grabbed Watson by the shoulders. "America! Brilliant Watson! Yet again you have proved to be invaluable without even realising. See yourself out..."

With that parting remark, Holmes grabbed his jacket and rushed from the room – full once again of that furious energy which usually spelt doom for his foes.

Accustomed as he was to his friend's rapid concluding of cases, even Watson was shocked when he turned on the TV news Friday morning and saw that Milverton had been arrested. The ex-tabloid editor had been taken from his home during a dawn raid and was now in police custody. Watson didn't wait to hear the reporter's version of events and rushed straight to Baker Street. This was worth being late for work and risking the wrath of the ever-watchful lawyers.

"America Watson," Holmes proudly announced, looking like a man who had been up all night but was buzzing with victorious energy. "I owe you an apology, you're findings did prove crucial after all."

Watson was unaccustomed to apologies from Holmes. Usually his efforts were rewarded with criticism. After his first book had been published, Holmes was pretty scathing and described it as sensationalist, not focusing enough on his 'method'. But it was Gareth Lestrade who had suffered the most.

Holmes had always been happy for his name to be kept out of the papers and despite helping Scotland Yard solve high-profile cases, he never took the credit. As far as the public were concerned, Gareth and his colleagues had solved the cases themselves – their name and achievements lauded in the press. But when Watson's book was published, even though some years had passed, the public felt angry that the police had taken credit for the work of an amateur. Tax payer's money had been spent but it was an ordinary citizen who had saved the day. There was an outcry, an investigation, and ultimately Gareth paid the price. Though he hadn't been the only police officer to accept Holmes' help, he was made the scapegoat – which suited the Chief Superintendant very well considering his relationship with Gareth's wife.

There was a suspension, a disciplinary hearing, the option to remain at Scotland Yard if he took a demotion but the damage was already done. Gareth salvaged whatever dignity he had left and resigned – shortly followed by the departure of his wife and a very costly divorce.

"I looked through your notes," Holmes announced. "You mentioned that Milverton was behind a political website, www.ileaks.com. Interesting stuff - particularly the allegations of corruption in the White House. This was exactly what I needed.

"You see, though Milverton's activities were not illegal here, the Americans take a dimmer view of such matters – especially if there is any suspicion of risk to national security. I just needed to find something which would be a breach of American law and then I could by-pass our own legal system. The US has powers under the Extradition Act of 2003 to extradite UK citizens for offenses committed against US law or security, even though the offense may have been committed here. Only a low level of proof is required, suspicion is enough for the US to demand that the person is taken into custody prior to extradition being granted.

"Well, Interpol were very interested when I gave them the findings of my little investigation into ileaks. Our friend Milverton has been using information acquired from a White House mole and by publishing it he has stirred up the wrath of our American cousins. The police have impounded his computers, documents and storage devices, even his phone. But fortunately, thanks to a few remaining contacts on the force, I did manage to salvage some salacious bits and pieces – including..."

He held up a memory stick in front of Watson's startled face.

"Is that Della's lift footage?"

"I can't guarantee that there haven't been copies made, but no editor will now touch anything from such a risky source."

Several weeks passed before Watson was able to sneak away from domestic bliss and visit his friend again. Once installed in his usual chair, Watson pushed for more information about Della and what the future now held for her. If he was going to write this up for his next book, he needed a better ending.

"This solves her immediate problem but she's still stuck with that awful man controlling her life," Watson commented.

"Not so. An opportunity is coming for her to walk away with the public firmly on her side. She wasn't the only person to be caught on camera with someone else that night."

"Carter was with someone too? How do you know?"

"I managed to find the source of the tape, a member of staff at the hotel. Fortunately, after a quick check with the Home Office, I confirmed that he was working here illegally. The threat of deportation was enough to ensure his compliance and I got him to search through the security footage from the corridor outside Carter's room. Carter brought someone back and they most helpfully began their 'enjoyment' outside in the corridor. The images are now with every tabloid editor, a little gift from me. Your Sunday paper should make interesting reading."

"That's brilliant. But, I have to admit being surprised that you would go to so much effort to help Della - problems matter to you, not particularly the people involved. You'd already stopped Milverton, why go the extra mile?"

"To help a good man get his woman, I suppose. Perhaps I felt I owed it to him. And I had nothing better to do."

"You mean the man in the lift with her? So you did watch it? Who was he? Celebrity-type I suppose."

"See for yourself..."

Holmes pushed the memory stick into his laptop and opened up the file. Watson watched the screen intently. There, he saw Della walk into the lift followed by her protection officer. Once the doors closed, she flicked a switch which caused the lift to shudder and stop. She laid a hand on Lestrade's arm and pulled him close as he kissed her.

"Oh my God," Watson exclaimed, watching in disbelief. "Did you know?"

"Of course I knew."

"Did he tell you?"

"No."

"Then how...?"

"It was the socks. They were both wearing identical socks when I met Della, clearly men's. Pop-stars don't generally share socks with their security guards. They were wearing the same expensive make of watch too, and the insignia on her bag was the same as on his belt. Matching socks, matching brands, even you could have worked it out Watson. Besides, if Carter really was watching her that closely, the lover had to be someone around her every day who he didn't suspect – a middle-aged security manager matches that profile rather well don't you think?"

"So the good guy takes the girl," smiled Watson, "with a little help from his friends..."

The Case of the Crystal Blue Bottle
by Luke Benjamen Kuhns
London, UK

It was a windy April night in 1886 and Sherlock Holmes was reading through his papers, smoking a pipe. The fire roared while Watson sat in front of it, with a glass of brandy in hand and his eyes closed. The wind made a soothing, hissing noise as it passed through cracks in the Baker Street windows. The time was just after 10pm and the streets outside were quiet as the darkness of the night had settled in and the cool, windy air drove people inside.

There was a knock on the front door and Holmes and Watson could hear Mrs Hudson's feet race to answer. She soon was showing a young police officer into the study.

"Mr Holmes?" he asked looking at the detective who was slouched over and whose face was buried in his notes and letters.

"Yes," said Sherlock looking at the officer and standing upright.

"Lestrade asked me to come get you at once. There's been a murder."

"Where?"

"Kensington High Street. A young girl, name's Deseray Underwood."

"What's the cause?"

"We don't know, that's why we need your help."

Sherlock turned to Watson who, by this point, was open-eyed and standing.

"Watson, would care to accompany me?" he asked.

"I would!" returned Watson and the three men were out the door.

When they arrived at the house, there were police all around and the neighbouring public could not help but watch the events unfold. Sherlock and Watson were shown into the chambers of this young girl where she lay fallen on the floor. There was no sign of a struggle and nothing in the room seemed out of place.

"Thank you for coming Holmes," said Lestrade.

"What do you know?" replied Holmes.

"Her name is Deseray Underwood, age 27, she's a governess for local family, her father, Everett, and brother, James, both live on Healy Street in Camden. Other than that she's engaged to this man," finished Lestrade waving at the officer to bring someone in.

"Was engaged," remarked Sherlock.

A man was escorted in the room by another officer. He was tall about 6'1, well built, with dark black hair and vivid brown eyes. His face was covered with a beard and he wore tiny speckled glasses.

"This is Samuel Mortimer, the girl's fiancé. He found her body and called us," said Lestrade.

"When did you find her?" asked Holmes.

"About two hours ago," said Samuel Mortimer. His voice cracked, shaking from nerves and sadness.

"You had reservations tonight?" Holmes said.

"Yes, but how did you know?" he asked.

"I can't imagine anyone walking about in a suit, newly shined shoes, and wearing such precious silver cuffs and watch for a night in," said Holmes.

"I see, well yes. I was meant to meet her for supper tonight. We had reservations and I was to meet her at the restaurant at 7. I waited for over an hour and knew something had happened. It was unlike my Deseray to be late. So I left and came straight to her house. I pounded on her door and no one answered but I could see a light on. I went outside and tried to climb up and see in the window, to see if I could make anything out. When I did, I saw her on the floor. So I rushed in and broke her door to get to her but, I was too late she was dead," and with that the man welled up and tears fell down his face.

Holmes walked over to the body and began to looking at it.

"Her eyes are yellow," said he, "possibly kidney failure. Mr Mortimer, was your fiancé ill?"

"No, not in the slightest."

Holmes bent down and sniffed the woman's neck, "something's there," he said under his breath. "I want everybody out of the room apart from Watson and Lestrade," demanded Holmes.

When everyone had cleared out he picked up the fallen chair which she had clearly been sitting in.

"She smells of something," said Holmes sitting in her chair looking at her vanity unit. "She sat here, prepared herself, put her makeup on, and finally... her perfume."

On the side of the vanity unit was a blue crystal bottle. Holmes picked it up and sniffed the cap.

He violently jerked the bottle away from his face and stood up walking to the other side of the room.

"There's your killer. That's not simply perfume, it's a bottle of liquid cyanide masked to look like perfume."

"Someone poisoned her with cyanide perfume?" questioned Lestrade, "for what reason?"

"That's what we need to find out." said Holmes.

"What do we know of her fiancé?" asked Watson.

"He's a wealthy business man, no criminal past, no criminal connections and a well respected family. They own a large portion of office buildings in Central London," said Lestrade.

"What could he gain from her death?" Watson asked.

"Ms Underwood, her family is well off too. Her dad spent time in America as a gold miner and returned very rich. The live modestly but they have a lot saved up. I'd reckon her insurance would be rather large," said Lestrade.

"But surely he'd want to kill her after they got married to claim that if that were the case?" said Watson.

"Bring him in, I wish to speak with him," said Holmes.

Samuel Mortimer was brought in the room once more and sat in a chair. Holmes pulled another and sat across from him.

"When were you two to be married?" he asked.

"Next week, on the Friday," Mortimer replied.

"Can you think of any reason why someone would want her dead?"

"No Mr Holmes I honestly cannot!" he cried.

"Not even for her insurance?" Holme said raising his eyebrow.

"Mr Holmes if you are insinuating that I had anything to do with this you, are mistaken!"

"Where did she get this?" said Holmes, pointing to the blue crystal bottle.

"That? She got it from me, it was a gift."

The air in the room went stiff. Lestrade looked ready to pounce and Watson grabbed the butt of his cane tightly, but Holmes sat there cool and emotionless.

"Where did you get the perfume from?" Holmes asked.

"From a man named Whitaker, on Brick Lane, near Liverpool Street. He's got a perfume shop. I ordered a custom-made scent."

"Thank you Mr Mortimer. We will let you know what we find out."

Mortimer left the room leaving the three men alone with the body once more.

"This man is hiding something." said Lestrade.

"Don't be too hasty now," said Holmes, "Watson and I need to speak with Mr Whitaker. We'll see him in the morning and let you know what we find. For now keep her cause of death quiet, not even her family needs to know yet."

Holmes, reaching for the bottle, noticed a picture that was face-down on the vanity unit and he lifted it up. It was a picture of a Deseray with what looked like her father and brother. "I'll be taking this too," said Holmes and they retired for the night.

The next morning Holmes and Watson were on their way to Brick Lane where they found the perfume maker's shop. The outside of the shop was painted red, but the paint had begun to chip and fade. The windows were cloudy and clearly not been cleaned for some time.

Holmes and Watson entered the store and a small bell rung. The shelves were untidy with bottles all over them and on the floor. The sun shone through the dirty windows and onto the bottles, causing a display of lights to fill the room. On the floor Holmes noticed there were a dozen boxes filled with bottles, he peered through a door leading to the back and noticed someone coming. A moment later they were greeted by an elderly man.

"Hello gentlemen," said the man.

"Good day sir," said Holmes.

"I apologise for the store's disorder, but I am packing things up," said the old man.

"Packing for what?" asked Holmes.

48

"I'm moving - closing shop. Recently inherited a large sum of money and it's time to retire," said the man. "So what can I do for you?"

"Well all the best in your move" said Holmes before continuing, "Mr Whitaker, I have a bottle of perfume that I cannot discover the scent, would you mind?"

"Ah yes, I would be happy to tell you. Where is the bottle?" he replied.

"It's here," said Holmes pull it out and putting it on the blue crystal bottle.

The man's eyes widened momentarily as he gently picked up the bottle.

"Go on, I'm very interested to know" said Holmes.

"I – I," stuttered the man.

Holmes reached out and put it closer to the man's face and put his finger on the trigger of the perfume's bottle.

"Let me help you," said Holmes and the man pushed Holmes' hand away and fell back into the cabinet behind him.

"Whats the matter?" Watson asked.

"Get that bottle away from me!" cried Whitaker.

"Why?" asked Holmes.

The man picked up a large container and threw it at Holmes and the blue crystal bottle was knocked from his hand and shattered on the floor. Holmes and Watson covered their faces and saw the man run out the back. Watson started to run after the man but Holmes called him back. Behind the counter Holmes saw a picture of Whitaker with a face he recognised.

"Come Watson, there's no time to lose!" yelled Holmes.

"Where are we going?" Watson asked Holmes once they got outside and away from the deadly fumes trapped inside the shop. Sherlock handed Watson the photograph and pointed to the man.

"Who is that?" asked Watson. Holmes reached into his pocket and pulled out another photograph he had taken from Deseray's vanity.

"It's her father," said Holmes, "we need to find him right away."

Holmes and Watson called a cab and told him the address of Mr Underwood in Camden and they were off. When they arrived at the address Mr Mortimer was seen leaving in a hurry. As he walked down the steps they heard an angry voice yell out, "don't ever show your face here again!"

"Mr Mortimer!"

"Oh Mr Holmes, I'm sorry I didn't see you."

"What was that about?" he asked.

"Everett. Even now in the event of his daughter's death, he still hates me."

"Hates you?"

"Very much. He's tried to keep me and Deseray apart for so long. And now he's got his wish at the expense of great pain." Mortimer continued.

"Let us have a word with him," said Holmes.

"I wish you more luck than I had," Mortimer finished before walking away.

They walked up the steps to the door and knocked. A young chubby man with blonde hair answered.

"Can I help you?" he asked.

"I am Mr Sherlock Holmes and this is Dr Watson. We are looking into the death of your sister and would like to have a word with you and your father immediately. The man looked at the detective and doctor intently before widening the door to let them in. They were shown into a small sitting room where moments later they were greeted by a tall bulging man with thin grey hair.

"Mr Underwood?" asked Holmes.

"Yes, what do you want?" replied the man angrily.

"To talk to you about your daughter and Mr Mortimer."

"Mortimer that swine!" blurted Underwood, "he's done nothing but destroy my family!"

"You must understand he is suspect in the murder of your daughter... any information you have will be of great use" said Holmes

"Well I can assure you he is responsible for the murder."

"How are you so certain?"

"He destroys everything he touches."

"Will you explain yourself?" asked Holmes.

The man hung his head low before continuing, "They were meant to be married here soon in an unholy union! That man spoiled my girl."

"She was pregnant?" asked Holmes.

50

Underwood stared at Holmes and Watson, and his son fidgeted in his seat.

"Yes," came the voice of James Underwood.

"Son!" roared Everett.

"They'll find out anyways!" he shouted back.

"There's nothing to find out, I already know. I could tell from her body when I examined it and your father's choice of words made it clear that he knew and disapproved" said Holmes.

There was a fire in Everett Underwood's eyes that would have scared the devil out of hell, but he soon cooled and looked at Holmes and Watson and spoke.

"It's true. My Deseray was with child. It was the only reason they were getting married. Fact is, she was going to call off the wedding but caved in only because of this child. I told her I'd be happy to send her away, pretend she was on an extended holiday then do away with it. For a time she considered the idea but that infernal boy changed her mind. But I reckon he came to his sense and instead of letting her go he poisoned her, being rid of the whole situation!"

"Mr Underwood," said Holmes, "Do you know a Mr Whitaker, a perfume maker on Brick Lane?"

"No, never heard of the man in my life. What business do I have with a perfume maker?"

"Curious," said Holmes, "could you explain this then?" placing the picture of Everett and Mr Whitaker in front of him. Before he could continue an eruption came from the back of the house.

"They're on to it Everett, I'm getting out of town," said the man who rushed into the room.

"Ah, Mr Whitaker, so good of you of you to join us." said Holmes. The old man stood there baffled to see both Holmes and Watson in the lounge.

"Watson! Stop that man," said Holmes and the Doctor rushed over and grabbed the Whitaker.

"What's going on!" cried James Underwood.

"I am sorry to say, but it was your father who murdered your dear sister," said Holmes. "All in the name of honour."

"You would do the same if you had a child who is getting married to a fiend like Mortimer. His rich family buying up anything and everything. All he wanted was her money, and I 'aint having that!

51

That's what his attitude was with my girl and he ruined her, so I ruined him! I took away the one thing he wanted the most - her money!"

"Of that you are wrong Mr Underwood, the money had nothing to do with it," said Holmes.

"How did you manage to get the perfume in to her hands?" Watson asked.

"It seems that is my doing," said James Underwood, "Deseray had an engagement party this previous weekend and I knew that Mr Mortimer was getting her perfume. I asked my dad for the location of Mr Whitaker's shop and told Sam to go there."

"So you raced ahead of Mr Mortimer and bribed Mr Whitaker to sell a bottle of liquid cyanide and in return for this you would split Deseray's life insurance," finished Holmes looking at Mr Underwood.

Holmes reached into his pocket and pulled out a pair of handcuffs, James took his dad by the arm and Watson pushed the old perfume maker towards Holmes.

Lestrade was called in and Mr Underwood and Mr Whitaker were arrested, tried, and put in jail for the murder of poor Deseray Underwood.

James Underwood moved out of the once shared lodgings, sold all his father's belongings and never spoke to him again. Mr Mortimer, when told how Deseray died and her father's obsession, fell out of the lime-light of society and retreated into himself - a broken man never to be heard of again.

The Last Quiet Talk

by Cathrine Mathilde Louise Hoffner
Odense, Denmark

"Stand with me here upon the terrace, for it may be the last quiet talk we shall ever have."

Holmes took me gently by the sleeve and led me to the small terrace at the back of that beautiful house where so much evil had taken place. We left Von Bork tied up in the car, faced the other way, and Holmes lit both our cigarettes with the air of a man who is writing the final chapter of his life's work.

"What do you mean." I asked, trying a little not to sound too melancholy, which was almost impossible, for the night suddenly felt cold and unkind, with the light of the moon ruthlessly unveiling bittersweet memories of bygone days and the blurred vision of an unclear future.

"I mean you and I may never see each other again, Watson," he said, his grave tone resounding through the distance between us.

"You mean tomorrow?"

Holmes gave a quick smile, his eyes still fixed at the dark horizon beyond the gloomy waters. "I mean never, Watson."

"But surely, Holmes..."

"I am quite serious, Watson. You know that I always speak the truth." He gave me a quick glance, and returning to his cigarette, he made the night feel even more unkind.

"Except when you spoke to Von Bork only moments ago," I replied as sharply as I could manage, as I tried desperately to keep his eyes only a moment longer on me.

Sherlock Holmes shrugged his shoulders and made a dismissive gesture in the air, the long, white fingers waving a thick cloud of smoke towards the car. "That was different, and you know it."

He sighed deeply and shook his head in a manner I knew only too well from the days when he used to be engrossed in cases of serious crimes. "The truth of it all, Watson," he continued, his gaze still held somewhere far away, "is that before dawn, this country will be at war, and the peace and safety we know will have to yield to wickedness and death. A murder in Birlstone will become the smallest of drops in an endless ocean of inhuman crimes. Who knows what might happen to the two of us, Watson? With you rejoining the army, and me continuing to work for our government? It is not over with the capturing of Von Bork, you know. That was only the beginning."

We stood for a little while in silence. A painful feeling suddenly overwhelmed me, the very same feeling I had felt all those years ago, when I thought Holmes had met his death at the Reichenbach Falls in his fateful struggle with the late Professor Moriarty. The whole world seemed again to stop around me, if only for a brief moment.

The final traces of sunlight faded away into the realms of the night, and up above little stars twinkled down upon us from another world. It was with a heavy heart that I almost turned upon my heel to return to the car, when next to me, Holmes suddenly, and to my great surprise, chuckled mildly to himself. I observed him, remembering all those times I had done so in the past, and trying unsuccessfully to read his great mind as read others'. His thoughts appeared to be far away, somewhere pleasant, although where, I could not imagine.

"What is it, Holmes?" my voice was almost drained for hope, barely above a whisper, but still, there was nothing or no one upon this mighty earth who could stimulate my curiosity like this man beside me.

He smiled, a broader smile this time, and returned once again to this moment only to bring me with him into our shared past. "You remember the night at Stoke Moran, Watson? I know it has been many years."

The weight upon my shoulders seemed suddenly lifted, as Holmes reminded me of one of those adventures, which had once made out the whole of my life.

"Of course I remember," I ejaculated. "The first of our many stakeouts. I can hardly remember ever being so nervous in my entire life!"

"It was certainly a most novel and interesting case, that one," Holmes added, in his old professional voice.

"Hardly as novel as the affair of the red-headed league, surely," I answered warmly, suddenly feeling all the years of working together with Holmes vividly coming back to me.

Holmes burst into a violent laugh at the memory of his red-headed client and the mystery that surrounded him and his little shop for a while.

"Hardly that, Watson, hardly that."

Captured, I am sure, by the moment, Holmes suddenly spoke rapidly and in high spirits. As always I tried my best to keep up with him, and together the two of us remembered our old cases and our many thrilling adventures, as if they had happen only yesterday.

I could have sworn, then and there, that for a brief moment, it was no longer August of the year 1914, and I was not standing on some random terrace in a chaotic world on the brink of war. All of a sudden, I could feel the warmth of the cracking fire next to me, as I once again found myself seated, opposite Holmes, in our old rooms in Baker Street. Outside, the wind, the rain and the thick fog ruffled against our little windows behind the drawn blinds, while inside we sat quietly, having our tea, me behind the evening paper, and Holmes enthusiastically bent over his beloved scrapbook. Downstairs, Mrs. Hudson was preparing dinner, and the lovely smell of her English cooking slowly climbed each step of our narrow staircase and made me famished.

Then and there, on that summer evening in August, all my senses became overpowered by the everlasting memories of Baker Street: the tobacco smoke which always made my eyes sting in the evening; the sweet and calming sounds of the strings of the Stradivarius on Sunday mornings; the perfect view of the streets, shops and people from our sitting room windows; the thrill in my heart, whenever a new client with a new story to tell and a new case for us to solve would enter the front door and leave a mark upon our lives forever.

Holmes was right. It had been many years, but while the future might be unpredictable, no one could change the past. No one could take away those years we spend at 221b Baker Street right in the heart of the great city of London. Somehow, no matter what was going to happen, that place would always be home to me.

"We did have it pleasant there, Watson," Holmes suddenly replied, as in answer to my thoughts rather than my words.

He had turned towards me. It had been many years. I saw that now, standing only a few feet away from his moonlit face. I noticed for the first time the new, fine lines around his eyes and his mouth. I noticed, too, the deeper hollowness of his cheeks, the higher expanse of brow and the recent silver tinges in his raven hair. He was an old man now, I reminded myself, suddenly realising that for two whole years I had not spent a single moment with him.

"Times change, Watson, and I am afraid we have no choice but to change along with them." His voice was slightly hoarse, and his accent mildly influenced by the American.

Searching his face, I thought I traced the smallest hint of sadness in his dignified features, because there was truth in his words. Times had changed. The world he grew up in, a world that was his, no longer existed, and the lives we used to live could, for reasons over which we had no control, be no more. Gaslights had made way for electric lights, horse and trap for cars. The telegrams, which Holmes had sent and received daily, whenever he was on a case, were outdated and rarely used anymore, while his controversial and unique methods, which I had so often heard ridiculed and questioned by the official police, had now become a permanent part of every investigation at Scotland Yard.

Holmes used to be famous for his innovative mind and admirably energetic lines of action, singled out as the leading criminal agent in the world. Now, he belonged to times long past along with a series of humble, little tales that painted the slowly fading picture of the life of a remarkable man with remarkable powers. I flattered myself that they also spoke of friendship, loyalty and devotion in its strongest form.

These thoughts did not do me well, and I could not help but smile a little at myself in the mist of my endeavour to control my emotions, which, I had discovered, and not to my great surprise, grew more sensitive with the passing of the years.

Turning my face towards the silvery lane winding through the heavy, dark grass, which separated us from the blackness of the water's edge, I tried in earnest to convince myself that all this was past, and past for the best. No more stakeouts, no more cases. No more Mrs. Hudson or Baker Street. No more 'friend and colleague, Dr. Watson'.

I could feel the early autumn breeze, though warm it was, chill my very bone, as the reality of it all suddenly became as clear and true to me as the light from the moon far away over the rolling hills. We could never go back. Things would never be the same again.

All of a sudden, when clearing his throat, Holmes once again broke in upon my thoughts, and I was forced to return to the lonesome terrace and the chilly night air. I could feel my legs rapidly weakening under me as well as my head slightly spinning, which was of course perfectly normal given the day I had had.

"You alright, Watson?" Holmes' voice was very gentle this time. No doubt he could sense my despair, since I had never succeeded in hiding anything from him before.

"Perfectly," I lied. It was all I could say, but his continuous stare informed me that, indeed, he was not convinced.

It was then, in that minute moment, that the fog banks surrounding my heart evaporated, just as quickly as they had condensed. His grey eyes, eyes I knew so well, outshining even the stars above our heads, penetrated me with all the powers of the bond between us. He had not changed after all. Nothing had. I saw that now. He showed me. For the shortest of moments he looked his old, sleuth self, grinning mischievously with all the warmth, which his otherwise restrained body could muster.

I must have laughed heartily, for he did the same, as if he had been following my every thought this whole time. I saw once again before me the strong, young man of a mere 26 years of age turning upon his heal, test tube in hand, and with all the enthusiasm of youth, sparkling with boundless dedication to the work, which fortunately was to become his very existence as well as mine.

That image of our first meeting did not last very long, but it lasted long enough. God only knew how many years it had been since that fateful encounter in the laboratory beneath the hospital – and yet here we were, ever the friends and colleagues we had always been.

"Come what may," he said. And he was always right.

As they turned to the car Holmes pointed back to the moonlit sea and shook a thoughtful head.

"There's an east wind coming, Watson."

"I think not, Holmes. It is very warm."

"Good old Watson! You are the one fixed point in a changing age."

The Case of the Silk Parasol
by Jude Parsons
Corsham, UK

Gladys placed her cup back on the saucer and leant over the table towards her sister. "Mr Holmes? A singular man, my dear, and so clever!"

She nodded, picked up her cup again and wriggled her hips into a more comfortable position in the chair, as if staking her claim to that too. She took a delicate sip of her tea and continued.

"Oh yes, most respected. A little strange in his habits, perhaps... Now! His colleague, dear Dr Watson. Quite different. A most congenial gentleman." She blushed a little and a tell-tale hand strayed upwards to pat her hair. "'Always most polite."

She added with a tinge of regret, "Married of course. Not that I have ever met his wife. Goodness me, no. We don't move in the same circles, no indeed," she rallied and added crisply, "But I am sure she is very nice."

Marjorie nodded encouragement and sipped her own tea in a mirror image of her sister. She knew from experience that she would get more out of Gladys if she didn't interrupt her. The well-timed nod and the occasional raised eyebrow would be sufficient to keep the gossip simmering. She waited with an attentive smile for Gladys to rummage in her thoughts for the next titbit. But Gladys had lost her thread for the moment and had remembered her manners instead.

"How was your journey?" she enquired. "Not too arduous I hope?"

"Quite comfortable," replied Marjorie. "I had the carriage to myself most of the way. The view of the countryside was magnificent. Is it my imagination or are the daffodils out a little early this year?"

"Well, I hadn't thought. They might be. I don't suppose I notice them as much as you do, dear." Gladys glanced at the window as two laughing children ran past chasing a dog.

"Being on your own..." she began. "Well, it's hard sometimes. I thought at first when such a distinguished looking gentleman took lodgings with me... but no. Not my type; too brusque. Not that anything improper, you understand..."

"Goodness me, no," interjected Marjorie. "One does have to be so careful though, doesn't one?"

"Oh, there's no question of that sort of thing and people know it. I keep a respectable house."

"You certainly do," agreed Marjorie, "and you keep it lovely, too."

"It's nice of you to say so, dear. And your Frank? Is he well?"

"Oh, yes, quite well thank you," said Marjorie politely.

Gladys could never be sure if she was jealous of Marjorie's rather dull marriage and the security it offered or whether she preferred her widowed state and enviable position as landlady to the famous detective. She supposed that whichever position one was in, there were attractions to be had in the other.

"Is Mr Holmes home at present?" Marjorie offered the question more as a prod to Gladys' easy tongue than a genuine enquiry.

"No, dear," Gladys sniffed. "He's out on business," she nodded sagely, as one who was au fait with certain particulars. "A lady called this morning and asked to see him. Half past ten it was, because I had just set the kettle to boil for morning tea. Very genteel she was, too. Her cloak was handmade - the finest stitching, and her boots polished to perfection. Italian I'd say."

"Italian? Was she really? And she came all this way for a consultation!"

"No dear, the boots were Italian," Gladys corrected. "The lady herself was definitely English; her accent was of the highest calibre. And such an unusual case too," Gladys paused for the effect she knew this would have on her audience.

"You were present at the interview?"

"Well, no," admitted Gladys. "Not present *as such*... but you see the cabinet in the hallway was in need of a good polish, and naturally I couldn't help overhearing some of the conversation."

"Sound does *so* carry in these wood panelled houses," said Marjorie, to add substance to Gladys excuse for prying.

"Precisely. And, of course, Mr Holmes has such a distinctive voice. One really cannot help but hear it no matter how hard one tries not to."

Justification thus proffered and accepted, Gladys continued her story.

"It seems the lady's parasol had gone missing the day before; a very exquisite and expensive one, apparently."

Marjorie leant in a little closer, but Gladys was staring at the wall in reminiscence.

"Do you remember the parasol I used to have? The one with the yellow ribbons?" Gladys sighed. "I adored that parasol; I was *so* upset when I lost it."

"I remember." Marjorie certainly did. What a fuss Gladys had made about the loss of the silly parasol.

"And the missing parasol. Was it also yellow?" Marjorie prodded.

Gladys focused on Marjorie's inquisitive expression. "No! No indeed! This one was of the *finest* silk, a gift from the lady's aunt from whom she and her husband expect to inherit a considerable amount of money, it seems. Apparently the aunt would not take kindly to the young lady having lost it."

"Hmmm." Marjorie thought for a moment. "Is there more to the story then perhaps? Some subterfuge to disinherit the young couple?"

"That is one possibility," agreed Gladys.

Marjorie frowned. "But surely Mr Holmes would not be interested in the small matter of a lost parasol?"

"Oh, no!" countered Gladys. "Mr Holmes has a very good instinct for these things. Besides, he often says that things are seldom as simple as they appear."

"So, Mr Holmes suspects there is more to the story then? And that is where he is now? Investigating the matter?" Marjorie asked.

"Yes, he left earlier this morning. But what am I thinking of? You must be tired after your journey. And here I am chattering away and you have had no opportunity to tell me your news. Dear Marjorie, it is *so* good to see you," Gladys reached across the table and patted her sister's hand. "But shall we retire now, and in the morning you shall tell me how you, Frank and the children are managing?"

Marjorie's eyes flickered open in the dark. She was sure something had woken her. She listened carefully. There it was; a shuffling noise and the faint squeak of a hinge. Her bedroom door was silhouetted by a dim light coming from the passageway outside. She climbed out of bed and crept towards it. She could hear voices downstairs.

"Come on, my dear chap, that's right, sit down."

There was the soft creak of a body settling into a leather chair.

"My dear friend, you have rescued me again from my descent into weakness."

"Yes, well, I thought I might find you in that dreadful place."

"Amongst the devils and angels," boomed the cultured, slightly slurred voice. "That's where the solutions are to this case."

"I really think you should give this stuff up, you know. It's not good for you," said the second, softer voice.

"My dearest friend. Ever the doctor, eh? But it is good for me! It's my inspiration! My muse is in the smoke filled murmuring of the opium den. The delightful poppy growing so wild in faraway fields releases my mind to the wisdom of the Orient. The things I see. It all becomes quite clear."

"And tomorrow you will be nursing your head and cursing the same."

"You are such a steady fellow, Watson, and a damned good friend. Even when you are quite wrong. Have I told you how much I value your friendship?"

"At least a dozen times on the way here, my good fellow. Now, get some sleep. Tomorrow we must solve this case; the fee has been spent already, I suspect."

A brief draught against Marjorie's feet signalled the opening of the front door followed by a soft click. Marjorie moved to the window and caught sight of a short, dapper man disappearing along the pavement below. The dark house flooded with silence once more, punctuated only by the ticking of the grandfather clock in the hall.

When Marjorie opened her eyes again, sunlight was filtering into the room through the curtains. Gladys tapped the door for a second time and came in carrying a tea tray.

"I thought you might like tea in bed, dear. I don't suppose you get the chance at home, what with a husband and children to see to in the mornings."

Marjorie smiled and wriggled into a sitting position. "How kind, that looks lovely."

Gladys put the tray on a small table and poured out a cup of tea, which she handed to Marjorie before pouring a second cup for herself.

She sat on the bed.

"Did you have a good night's sleep?"

"Oh yes, thank you."

"Nothing disturbed you?"

So Gladys had heard it too, thought Marjorie.

"No, not at all," she replied, as she sipped her tea.

If Gladys had heard the conversation between Holmes and Watson last night, there was no need to draw attention to it now. Besides, a woman had her dignity to maintain, and Marjorie was loath to deprive her sister of the pride she felt in her position as landlady of the most famous detective in England. Some things were best left unspoken. Like her unhappiness in her own marriage. Frank's temper. Appearances must be kept up, dignity maintained. What else was there left to lean on in difficult times?

"Now," said Gladys, breaking into her thoughts. "Tell me all about Frank and the children."

Marjorie laughed. "Oh, you know. Frank works hard. We manage. The country is far less exciting than the life you lead here. And the children are growing up. Elizabeth is eleven now, you know, and helps out in the dairy. I don't know how I'd cope without her. And Geoffrey feeds the chickens every morning and helps his dad in the fields. The weather's been good so far and we expect a decent crop this year, which is a relief after last year's disaster."

Gladys nodded sympathetically. She kept her eyes on her teacup as she enquired, "And your arm, is it better now?"

"Better? Oh yes," Marjorie rubbed her right arm. "Much better now, thank you. Silly thing to do, fall over in the yard. You would think I would know better after living there all these years."

"Silly? Not really." Gladys raised her eyebrows. "Lucky that Frank was there when it happened. No lasting damage I hope?"

"No, the bones are quite mended now, so the doctor said. Like I said, just a silly accident," said Marjorie dismissively.

"Well then," said Gladys. "Once you are up and dressed, I fancy we might take a walk. There is a little errand I need to complete before lunch."

There had been no sign of Gladys' lodger at breakfast, or during the hour or so that Marjorie had helped Gladys with a few household tasks before leaving the house. The beds made and the kitchen floor washed, they set out with walking boots and umbrellas along Baker Street and turned into Marylebone Road.

"I'd forgotten how tall the buildings seem, and the awful smell of the drains. And the noise!" exclaimed Marjorie as a man holding a bundle of newspapers bellowed something unintelligible close to her left ear.

"You get used to it." Gladys peeked out from under her umbrella. "There, it's stopped raining."

The folded umbrella became a walking stick, tap tapping on the pavement as she marched along.

Marjorie tucked her own umbrella under her arm and kept pace. "The city is so busy. How fast people seem to live these days. Do you ever wonder, if you had stayed in the country, how different things might have been?"

"Yes." Gladys replied. "Quite often."

She had hated the country. She thought pigs were ugly and dirty, and the smell of them! She would rather have the smell of the city drains any day. At least you could go indoors and shut the smell outside. There was no such luxury in the countryside. The smell of pigs pervaded everything, until you were certain you must smell like a pig yourself.

"Where are we going?" asked Marjorie.

"To collect something." Gladys bit her lip. "Sometimes, Marjorie, people are so clever that they can't see the beach for staring at the pebbles."

The police constable showed the sisters into a tidy, well furnished office.

"If you don't mind waiting, ladies," he waved them towards two chairs set to one side of an expensive looking desk. "I'm sure Inspector Lestrade won't be long."

Drops of rain started to tap on the window. Gladys turned her head to see how hard it was raining and was about to remark to Marjorie that perhaps they had better take a cab home and never mind the expense, when the door opened.

"Gladys Hudson!" exclaimed the tall, well dressed man, his moustache puffing in rhythm to his words. "What a wonderful surprise! To what do I owe this pleasure?" he grasped Gladys's hand.

"My sister, Mrs Perriman." Gladys waved the other hand vaguely in Marjorie's direction. "The thing is, Inspector, Mr Holmes is a little under the weather today and he asked me if I would call in and collect something for him."

"Oh? I hope he is not suffering from anything serious?"

Gladys avoided the question. "He was certain it would be here."

"Well, whatever it is, I hope we can accommodate our good friend, Mr Holmes. I'm quite sure we owe him a favour or two. What was it you were sent to collect?"

"It is a parasol, a fine example of printed silk in shades of blue with lilac ribbons," said Gladys. "The handle is of ivory, and there is an inscription on it. 'Fortius quo fidelius'. It was left in a hansom cab on Tuesday morning and is certain to have been brought here to the lost property department by the driver."

"Well now, let me see if we have such an item." Lestrade opened the door and shouted along the corridor. "Gillings!"

Constable Gillings appeared and was given the description of the parasol. He saluted and set off to look for it.

The Inspector leant against the edge of his desk and took a cigar from a box.

"If you don't mind, ladies?"

"Not at all." Gladys waved the idea of objection away. "I'm quite used to gentlemen smoking."

He lit the cigar and took a puff. Pungent smoke seeped across the room. "Will you be staying long in London, Mrs Perriman?" he enquired.

Marjorie smiled. "Only a few more days, I'm afraid. My husband and the children will be missing me."

"Of course," the Inspector blew smoke thoughtfully towards the ceiling. He turned to Gladys. "Did you...?"

Constable Gillings reappeared holding out an exquisite silk parasol with an ivory handle.

The Inspector turned the parasol over in his hands. "Well, I never. How does he do it? How did he know this would be here? I mean, this precise one? Marvellous. I take my hat off to the man." He handed the parasol to Gladys. "Please tender my regards and convey my wishes to Mr Holmes for a speedy recovery."

"Thank you." Gladys rose. "Mr Holmes would be grateful for your discretion. The thing is... the young lady concerned... well, I'm sure I don't have to mention to you how delicate these situations can be."

The Inspector raised his eyebrows. "Well, well! Like that is it? Oh, yes I quite understand." He tapped the side of his nose. "You can rely on me, discretion is my byword."

"Thank you. Now we must be getting along, or I shall be late preparing lunch. Thank you so much, Inspector."

"Always glad to be of help. Shall I get you a cab? It's raining awfully out there, you know. Gillings!"

Marjorie frowned as the cab driver jiggled the reins and the horse trotted into a steady pace.

How did you know the parasol would be there? Marjorie lowered her voice. "I'm surprised the cab driver didn't take it and sell it. How did you know he wouldn't?"

Gladys smiled. "I didn't but, you know, there are still a lot of honest people about, Marjorie, even in London. A cab driver's reputation is worth a great deal to him if he wants to keep his wealthy customers. I suspected that the lady, not wanting anybody to know of her loss, had hired the cab herself in the street, instead of having a servant hail it. The driver wouldn't know where she was staying so couldn't return the parasol to her hotel. The only other safe option was the police station."

"Won't Mr Holmes be pleased that you have found the parasol," exclaimed Marjorie.

"I shan't tell him," said Gladys firmly.

"But… then how will you…?"

Gladys patted her sister's knee. "My dear, you are a married woman and I was too, once upon a time. We both understand how it goes with men, even one as clever as Mr Homes. He will not enquire too deeply because that would be admitting to a woman that there is something he doesn't know. A man's ego really won't allow that sort of thing. He will believe me, therefore, when I tell him that we went for a walk, it started to rain, and we took a cab home. Imagine our surprise to find somebody had left a parasol in the very cab we hired. I shall show it to him and tell him that, rather than leave it for the cab driver to steal, I have decided to take it to the lost property department at the police station."

"Whereupon," interjected Marjorie, "he will insist on taking it there for you."

Gladys smiled. "As you say."

"And the parasol's owner," Marjorie continued, "will be summoned and the fee shall be paid."

Gladys winked. "And I shall get my rent, and keep my reputation as landlady to the greatest detective that ever lived."

Distraction
by Ariane DeVere
Erith, UK

Sherlock hasn't had a case for eighteen days and is bored witless. On day nineteen John abandons him for over six hours; when John *finally* arrives home, his left shoe – still on his foot – is wrapped in a plastic bag.

"Right," he announces. "I've been all over London: took a taxi to six different places and stood in the soil at each place. Your task is to work out exactly where I've been, and in which order."

Sitting down on the sofa, he swings his left leg up onto Sherlock's lap and grins madly at him. "The game's a foot."

The Adventure of The Mad Colonel
by Evgeniya Zimina
Kostroma, Russia

"Well, Watson, you have been to war, haven't you? You know what it is like," said Holmes.

Although he said it with a smile, I could see he was upset. Our rooms were in a terrible mess. The air was thick with dust.

"My war was... er... different," I replied, picking a piece of broken china from the carpet. "No bombs. No raids. I feel a hostage here, in London. They are bombing us, and we are sitting doing nothing".

"We can't do much," said Holmes, examining the window shattered by the shockwave during yet another air-raid of the infamous London blitz. "So, we have to keep calm and carry on, as that new poster says. Have you seen it, Watson? That's the true British spirit!"

"Even the toughest of Britons lose their minds there days. Colonel Warburton, for example: a most tragic situation. You must have read – ah, I have forgotten. You never read anything except the criminal news and the agony column".

"So, what is it about Colonel Warburton?"

"He went mad after losing his son. A young officer, apparently, in charge of a bomb disposal unit. You know, the Royal Engineers. No experience. An unexploded bomb went off. The old colonel wanders about the city, calling him and asking people whether they know where he can find his son."

The doorbell interrupted our talk, and Mrs. Hudson, our housekeeper, announced that a lady wanted to see my friend.

"She is upset, poor thing", added Mrs. Hudson.

"Strangely enough, people don't come to me when they are happy," said Holmes, somewhat acidly.

A second later the lady entered the room. She was dressed with taste; her face would have been pleasant, had it not been for the look of total confusion and embarrassment in her eyes. Her lips were trembling.

"Do sit down," said Holmes.

"Mr. Holmes," she said, "I have heard you can help, and help is what I need most of all now. My name is Elizabeth Warburton; I am the wife of Colonel Warburton. You may have heard-"

"Yes," said Holmes, glancing at me with some surprise. "I was sorry to hear about the tragedy in your family. The loss of the only son-"

"Mr. Holmes," interrupted the lady, and her voice suddenly became firm, "that's why I am here. The problem is that we have never had a son".

I could see that Holmes, who was prepared to demonstrate his skills of deduction to the lady by giving her the information about her own life, was astonished.

"But. Mrs. Warburton, your husband, or, rather, his condition... Isn't it your husband who says he has lost a son, David Warburton-"

"Yes, he says it so very often. Sometimes, though," she hesitated a bit, "I don't think my husband is really mad. You see, Mr. Holmes, when James thinks I am looking the other way, his face changes. He looks perfectly sane. But then he starts talking about 'his son', and I don't know what to think. Isn't madness based on some true events? What if he had a son? An illegitimate son, of whom I knew nothing, whom he really lost and whose death drove James mad? I have already heard nasty rumours about it."

"Why don't you consult a psychiatrist? It seems the most reasonable thing to do," I asked.

"I have already done so. A family friend invited Dr Brown to dine with us a week ago. Dr Brown thinks my husband might be mentally disturbed, but admits that it is impossible to jump to conclusions so hastily."

'Well, the doctor and you could wait and see, couldn't you?"

"But the fantasy about the son could not appear out of nothing, could it? There must have been another woman and that boy, that young man. If his death was such a blow to James – Mr. Holmes, please, find out at least something about Lieutenant Warburton!"

"Excuse me," said Holmes, "but I usually do not take such cases. Unfaithful husbands, sane or insane, and illegitimate sons are of little interest to me."

"Oh, Mr. Holmes, please! I have nobody to confide in. Any information would help me to decide what to do next and how to behave. Just try to find facts about the son, this David Warburton."

69

"Very well," said Holmes. "I'll see what can be done".

When our visitor left, Holmes looked gloomy. "I call this 'degradation'," he said. "Me, and the case of an illegitimate son! The old colonel obviously had his secret; his madness opened the door of the family cupboard and the skeleton of his son-"

"It's black humour, Holmes," said I. "The woman is in distress, and we can help her."

"I have foolishly made a promise in the moment of weakness, caused by the condition of the room after the raid; I have given this woman some hope instead of recommending a good doctor for her husband!"

"It can't be difficult to find out about the young man and decide whether he really existed or has been invented by the mad mind of the poor old man. Besides, Holmes, you have never been worried about the mess our rooms are. Why bother now?"

"Well," admitted Holmes grudgingly, "it is still better than no puzzle at all. In the face of the enemy criminals forget to commit crimes, and if there is nothing more thought-provoking, I'll try to find the information about the son, if I can."

"Besides, there is something strange about the colonel's behaviour, according to his wife. One second he looks normal, another-"

"As a doctor, you know it is extremely difficult to diagnose madness. Human mind is a dark thing," said Holmes, yawning. "Not mine, though. But I am an exception, I am afraid. As for the lady, she, naturally, wants her husband to be sane and can't believe what she sees and hears."

The next two days brought us nothing new. The only thing Holmes managed to find out was that the colonel indeed behaved like a madman. He was walking near military offices, at the railway stations, asking each soldier and officer whether they knew anything about Lieutenant Warburton. However, he was harmless.

Many people recognised him and paid him no attention, although their faces grew sad when they saw the tall figure begging: "Can't you tell me anything about Warburton, David Warburton? He is my son. He can't be dead, I know he can't."

But the enquiries Holmes made failed to show that the Colonel had had any children at all, legitimate or otherwise.

I failed to understand anything at all about this strange business, because every time I tried to make a deduction, I was sinking deeper and deeper in the ocean of nonsense.

"So, to sum up, he wants to find a son whom he never had and whose imaginary death drove the old man mad? Holmes, it is absurd! It doesn't make any sense at all!"

"Of course, there is no sense – we are talking about a madman!" replied Holmes. "What are you reading, Watson? *Hamlet*? Another madman?"

"Holmes, if you don't like drama, it does not mean it is entirely useless. Besides, Prince Hamlet was not a madman, as every educated person knows. Just listen: *Though this be madness, yet there is method in't...*"

One day I came home to Baker Street and understood we had, had a visitor – the strong smell of favourite cigars of Mycroft Holmes was hanging in the air.

"You are right, Watson," said Holmes, watching my fruitless attempts to cope with the cough, "Mycroft left about a quarter of an hour ago".

"What did he want?"

"No more and no less than find a spy and, as he says, save the world. There is a leak. The War Office is worried. Some of our secrets are known to the enemy."

"There's a leak in the War Office?!"

"No, Mycroft thinks it to be most unlikely, and yet-"

"What are you going to do?" asked I.

"Well, the first thing to do is get rid of that Warburton business. David Warburton is a myth – I have made all the enquiries imaginable. He is the product of the Colonel's imagination. The most difficult thing will be to tell his wife that the person she needs to talk to is a doctor, who might be able to explain the cause of this unfortunate condition of the old gentleman.

"Mind you, Watson," Holmes continued, "when Mrs. Warburton came to us, it was you who told her that a psychiatrist is

71

needed. It will be kinder to the poor colonel to find him a place in a good mental home than let him wander about London in this state. If he is indeed up to something, as his wife thinks, there has been no proof whatsoever. She simply does not want to admit the unpleasant truth. It will be difficult for her. She is depressed because of the husband, and the financial position of the family leaves much to be desired. But the colonel needs special care, I am afraid."

"He is a curious person, this colonel," I said. "I'd like to have a look at him, out of professional interest".

"Excellent! You will be able to support my point of view when I talk to Mrs Warburton. Then I'll immediately set about resolving the problem Mycroft asked me to pay all my attention to. You said the other day that we cannot sit doing nothing. Here is a chance to improve the situation and do something useful for the country – and more challenging, too. Public-spirited. Now about Warburton. We may go and look at him now, and then drive to his wife to dot all the 'i's."

"But how do you know where to find him? We may spend hours looking for this weirdo!"

"There is nothing simpler than to find Colonel Warburton. He does exactly the same things almost every day. You could think he is some bank clerk who leaves home and goes to work at exactly the same..." Holmes stopped as though struck. His lazy expression, which appeared on his face every time he was talking about Colonel Warburton, changed.

"*Though this be madness, yet there is method in't...*" Watson, how many times have I told you that as a conductor of light you are unrivalled? Hurry up, or it will be too late!"

Grey airships in the grey sky were floating over the grey city. Holmes was almost running and I found it difficult to keep up with him.

"Holmes, half an hour ago you didn't know how to get rid of this case, and now you are running as though *you* were a madman, not the Colonel!"

"Method, Watson, method!"

"What do you mean, Holmes?"

"Right now I can only say that I was blind, so blind that if you ever decide to record the events of today, you will have to write about it without hiding my error, if you are a man of honour, Watson! I have made the same mistake I have so often accused you of, Watson! I was watching, but not observing!"

When we found ourselves at the station, the old gentleman was there, on the platform. He looked miserable, asking his usual questions. People were pushing him off their way. My heart was pierced with pity when I saw him.

"Why have we been running, Holmes? Is he in danger? From whom?"

"Watch him, Watson, and tell me what you think," Holmes said quietly.

As I was watching, the feeling of pity was intensifying. The sufferings of the man were unbearable to look at. A group of young officers came out to the platform; they were talking, laughing, and discussing something. The old colonel was standing with his back to them and we could see his profile.

"Well, Watson," said Holmes, and I heard triumph in his voice, "what is he doing now?"

The lips of the old man were moving, as though he was counting or repeating something to himself. In doing so he raised his head and I was astonished to see his shrewd and calculating expression. He slowly turned and saw us. His cold look was perfectly sane.

"Quick, Watson!" yelled Holmes. The colonel made an attempt to draw his revolver, but with the officers behind his back and with Holmes darting to him like a lightning he stood no chance at all.

Mycroft had just left, but the smell of his cigars was still in the air. He was in a hurry to interrogate Colonel Warburton.

"Two cases cracked in an hour," I said bitterly, "and I have to admit that I feel a fool. I still haven't understood what happened there, at the station, except that the colonel was arrested."

"You shouldn't be so bitter about it, Watson", replied Holmes. "Wasn't I a fool myself? Mrs. Warburton gave me the essential fact; she said that her husband looked sane more than often. But, as a woman, she was more interested in her theory about the colonel's possible affair, and

73

when I heard this theory I lost interest in the matter. I watched him several times and in my irritation I failed to see the pattern in what he was doing until you asked me how to find the colonel. He was talking only to the military, and he always looked as though he was memorising or repeating things. This case needed thorough observation, but my pride was hurt when I was offered such a trivial case, and I was a very careless observer. Besides, I ignored one important aspect that you, Watson, never ignore."

"What is it?" asked I in surprise.

"Feelings. I was trying to apply logic, and he banked on feelings."

"Whose feelings do you mean?"

"The feelings of people who surrounded Colonel Warburton. Some people were curious, in a vulgar way, about the colonel's affair, real or imaginary. Gossip-mongers, greedy for every bit of scandalous facts. Other people who met him felt sorry for the old scoundrel. You, Watson, did feel sorry, didn't you? People who lost their nearest and dearest sympathised with him. And he was manipulating these feelings, creating the combination of improbable facts, pretending to be mad, though there was method in his madness. People, however, thought him to be a victim, as he wanted it to be."

"And he was a spy. Why did he do it? The money? You said the financial situation of the family was bad."

'It must be so".

"It is disgusting, no matter what the motives were. But the disguise was unusual, wasn't it? You would think a spy is likely to keep a low profile, and he manifested his madness all over the city. Do you really think he managed to hear a lot by loitering around and talking to the military?"

"A word here, a word there. He was clever enough to assemble the whole picture, or its significant bits. But it is pleasant to think that we have put a stop to it and made a step, however tiny, towards the victory. By the way, Watson, have you seen the new government poster? 'Loose lips sink ships'."

"Mycroft's idea?"

Holmes shrugged his shoulders and smiled.

"I Walk a Path of Cyclicality"
by Katharine McCain
Rosemont, PA, USA

Sit, beside two men of note
Watch, as they dip hands –
Unfettered by locking joints
Unblemished by spots and stains –
Dip, into jars of honey
Golden and burnished by the sun
Sweetened through years of labor
Perhaps supplying them with more
Than nutrition and taste.

I can walk beyond the vibration of bees
And hail the man on the corner.

Beaten from his beat
He leans heavily against the smog
Asking if I'd share with him a cigar
But all I want is to know his name.

Are you Gabriel
George
Gary
Or Greg?

I walk on and see the men who are not seen
Those who sit, calculating in their webs
One, comfortably encased in leather
Wood paneling, fires,
Copious amounts of food
The other,
Sustained on a diet of coercion
And chalk dust.

Continuing on,
Trailing fingers over a familiar door
Until I find myself in an equally familiar hospital
Where amid the dying begins a relationship
With an inordinate amount of life
What can we
Deduce from that?

Farther still
And there's a student with his dog
(Not, it seems, named after a prime minister
or the synonym of a happy rock)
Who allows that mutt access
To another man's leg
The bite that leads directly
To words above.

Moving as far back as I'm allowed
I finally peep through a nondescript window
Situated in an unknown location
Where this faceless family gathers
I watch as a naming takes place
A decision of -
Thankfully, not Sherrinford -
But Sherlock

I can do all this,
Leaving footprints of ink
And still return in time
To share honey and tea.

The Beginning

by Annabelle Hammond

Norfolk, UK

John Watson hobbled into the classroom, only slightly leaning on his injured ankle. Lots of brightly coloured paintings glared at him from all sides of the room. He sighed in frustration. He certainly didn't feel all bright and cheery.

The class fell into silence. The teacher approached him. She was an elderly lady with short greying hair. She smiled at him sweetly. "You must be John, I'm Mrs Hudson. I'll be your teacher for the next year. Welcome to year 5," she said clapping her hands in delight. Her smile broadening like her face was going to crack. "Please go and find a seat, anywhere you like," she said giving him a little push on his shoulder. He stumbled slightly. The other children snickered and chuckled. "Oh, I'm ever so sorry, do you need any assistance? I didn't realise you have a bad ankle," she said with a frown.

John's face creased in annoyance. Just because he had a bad ankle didn't make him immobile, he could still look after himself perfectly fine. "I'm ok," he said but that didn't stop Mrs Hudson taking hold of his arm. He shrugged her off and moved away. "Really, I'm perfectly fine, I can do this myself," John said turning his back to Mrs Hudson. John's backpack was weighing him down. His parents had packed it full of books that he didn't need.

John looked around for an empty seat and there was only one. The other children whispered as he made his way over to it. The table was at the back of the classroom, its surface was clear. The boy who was sitting there didn't seem to be listening to anything that was going on around him. The boy was very tall and had dark curly hair, his fringe hanging in his eyes. He was pale and had high cheekbones. You could just imagine him looking down his nose at you in disgust. He wore a black shirt and trousers. He looked too mature to be in a class with John; after all they couldn't look more different.

John had blonde straight hair and a round face. At the age of 10 he already had frown lines on his forehead. He wore a knitted jumper which was a gift from his mother. His mother had made him wear it

77

today so he could make a good first impression to the class. He had only grumbled in reply and didn't argue. He had jeans on and some old brogues he had inherited from some distant relation. John actually felt like a child compared to the other boy. The boy's gaze flickered over to him, dark grey eyes analysed him then flicked back to the window.

John stepped around the table and sat down, chucking the back pack on the floor. He sunk down in his chair relieved to finally be off his feet. He wondered who the strange boy was sitting next to him. He seemed closed-off and unwelcoming. John coughed to get his attention. This rewarded him with a glare then nothing, once again.

At the front of the class Mrs Hudson began to talk about material properties. John didn't listen he was too busy wondering who this person was next to him.

"Staring at me won't solve any of your questions. That is unless you have my observation skills which I don't think you do. The names Holmes, Sherlock Holmes," the boy said finally turning to look at him. John stared quite gobsmacked. He offered his hand out of politeness. Sherlock just looked at it, and kept his arms folded across his chest.

"John-" he began.

"John Watson. You recently moved here because your father had been offered a better job at the local hospital. Your mother stays at home and it seems she spends a lot of spare time knitting. Your jumper is one of her experiments, I can see. Not the best she can do I'm sure," Sherlock said in a jumble of words. He spoke fast and serious, leaving John confused for a moment. John stared his mouth hanging open in shock.

"How...how did you know that?" he choked.

"Observation and deduction," he said as a matter of fact. "Don't worry you're all too stupid to understand, let alone learn the art. Watson please shut your mouth; I can already see that you have two fillings, one white and one grey. You ate too many sweets last year, that's obviously why your face is fat. You'll lose that weight in a few years. Oh and your leg, you hobbled in here like a lost soul. You never put weight fully on your left leg. I presume you recently twisted it while jumping from a tree. A grade II twisted ankle, the doctor told you. I bet you have a bruised ankle as well. Your horrible brown brogues must have been donated to you, why would anyone buy something so hideous?"

78

Sherlock paused. He offered an awkward smile despite all the criticism he had just given John.

"Umm, yes that's pretty much correct," John said, frowning down at the table. Sherlock made him uncomfortable.

"Sherlock, I presume you have something to say to the class?" Mrs Hudson's voice cut through the air.

"Ah, I don't wish to show off, Mrs Hudson," he said her name with distaste.

"I don't think that's possible Mr Holmes, give it a try by all means," she said with a false smile.

"Well then. Let's begin," Sherlock said both of his hands together now like he was praying. The whole class had turned around to glare at him. John felt even more uncomfortable. He had begun to sweat in his woollen jumper.

"You've been teaching the class that metals are strong, hard and shiny and good conductors. Which is incredibly boring, the dumbest elephant could tell you that," he said with a curl of the lip. His grey eyes were wide flicking back and forth, like he was viewing a map. "I can tell you that metals are malleable because they consist of many layers of atoms that can slide over each other when the material is bent or shaped. Metals also form giant structures where the electrons in the outer shells are free to move about. The free electrons and Metal ions can be forced together in a metallic bond. Is that enough Mrs Hudson or shall I continue?" Sherlock said looking away from the class with a smirk on his face.

John didn't have a clue what Sherlock had just said, his brain didn't understand words like malleable; he was only 10 after all. Looking at the rest of the class, John saw the shock on all the other children faces. Mrs Hudson stood at the front of the class, her hands on her hips. Her face was as red as a tomato, sweat dripped from her brow.

"Mr Holmes, maybe we can continue this discussion outside of the class room," she said through gritted teeth.

Sherlock stood, his lanky form towering over the class. He picked up a pencil from the next desk and stood waiting. The class watched in silence. Sherlock laughed and kept walking. After a few steps he threw the pencil. It missed Mrs Hudson's head by an inch. It was a perfect miss. Sherlock left the room, his laughter trailing behind him.

Voices rang out as the gossip began to spread. No one approached John instead he looked at the empty door. This other boy was incredible, no one could be that clever but he was. He was only 10 years old but he was extraordinary. John couldn't even begin to understand what had just happened.

Mrs Hudson was shouting outside the class room. She came back shaking and sweating. Sherlock didn't return. "Now class please can you all go and play for a few moments while I sort out some kind of punishment for Mr Holmes," she said only just containing her anger.

The class escaped her fury. The door slammed behind them. John hobbled down the mobile's steps and walked over to the playground. Again he was alone. He spotted a bench nearby on the field. It was empty while all the other children ran around playing tag. He walked over to it and eased himself down. He stretched his legs out in front of him. He ignored the pain in his ankle. It hurt but it wouldn't get better if he didn't exercise it.

He watched the other children run around and play. He thought the game was silly. You didn't gain anything from running around. John wasn't the healthiest person in the world, so he didn't see the point in being able to run around for hours. He would never need to run from anyone. Especially if he ended up being a doctor like he dreamed. He didn't need to run around a hospital at top speed.

"Silly isn't it?" a serious voice said from behind him. John turned and saw Sherlock standing there. He was now wearing a dark coat which looked too short on his lanky body. Sherlock came and sat down, crossing his legs and arms. John nodded. "People are too stupid for their own good, honestly this game isn't even fun," Sherlock said eyes flicking over people on the field.

"If it isn't fun what is?" John asked, finding courage in his voice. After all he was rather curious.

"Fun, only normal people think running is fun. Fun, is solving a problem that nobody else can. It's challenging yourself to be the best. To observe everything and never miss a clue, one day your life might depend on it," Sherlock said, his face glowing at his idea of fun.

"I want to be a doctor," John blurted because of his nerves. Sherlock glanced down at him, brows raised.

"One day John, you will be," he said. John shook his head, this boy couldn't possible know his future. They sat in silence thinking over each other's words.

Another boy ran over to them. He was average height and had brown hair. A smirk was spread across his face. There was something unsettling about him. John thought it was the way his blue eyes watched him.

"Got yourself a boyfriend, have you Sherlock? I'm sure the whole class would like to know," the boy said. Then he shouted "Sherlock's got a boyfriend," loud enough for everyone to hear and come running over. Voices rang out around them, fingers pointed and eyes glared.

The boy walked over to John, pushing Sherlock aside. "I'm James Moriarty, you shouldn't talk to Sherlock. He will fill your head with lies, he pretends to know everything to cover up how dumb he really is," James said and the spectators snickered. "You shouldn't be around people like him. They will only drag you down. Why don't you come with us now? We can show you how to be the best," He said stepping back, arms wide welcoming John to his little gang.

John didn't like this boy. He was too cocky. James slicked his hair back as he watched while flashing his pearly whites. He shouldn't talk to Sherlock like that, everyone was equal.

Slowly pulling his feet in, he stood, holding the bench to steady himself. Sherlock watched curiously. John put one hand behind his back, three fingers spread wide.

"I'm sorry but I'm going to decline your offer. There's nothing wrong with Sherlock. Of course he's rather self-centred, but so it seems are you," John said with a smile. He didn't like bullies and James was one. Confidence flooded through him. Sherlock stood up behind him. John bent one finger leaving two up.

"Are you sure? You'll be a weirdo like him if you decline. Nobody could want that," James taunted, with the same smile plastered on his face.

"Well, actually I'd rather be like him than you," John said, at the same time bending another finger.

"So be it," James said with a frown now. It seemed nobody had declined his offer before. James stepped forward coming nose to nose with John. John bent his last finger, his hand now clenched into a fist,

81

just as Sherlock stepped up beside him. Together they pushed Moriarty. He fell down in shock while John and Sherlock ran laughing together as they went.

It seemed John had made one friend after all. He'd also stood up to a bully who needed to be put into his place. Sherlock Holmes and John Watson made quite a team. Together they ran out the school gate, John lagging slightly behind, but he was having fun. They passed the Baker street sign a few moments later. John looked at his watch to see it was 2.21pm.

Mrs Hudson's voice shouted at them as they ran. "You boys, Get back here at once. You've already caused enough trouble, come back before I call the police!"

Sherlock laughed harder.

"What now?" John asked.

"My older brother Mycroft is one of the local policemen," Sherlock said panting from the run.

"Really? Is that what you want to do as well?" John asked, trying to imagine Sherlock as a policeman.

"Ah, I'm afraid not John. That's far too easy. Instead I'm going to be a consulting detective," Sherlock said with pride.

"Is that even a real job?" John asked. He'd never heard of it before. His brow creased in confusion, his brain trying to search for the words.

"No it isn't. I'm going to be the first. Sherlock Holmes, the world's first consulting detective," Sherlock shouted with confidence in his voice. An eccentric laugh pierced the air, and John couldn't help but join in. John thought Sherlock must be crazy but he kept his mouth shut.

Later that night, sitting at his cluttered desk John wrote:
Dear Diary, Today I made a new friend...

The Matchmaker of Furrow Street
by Aine Kim
London, UK

It was a cold, drizzly evening on May 17, 1895, when I was disturbed from my pipe by the sound of a hansom cab clattering to halt outside of 221B Baker Street. Minutes later there was a thumping noise from upstairs. Holmes darted past me to the window and pressed his sharp, eager face against it while casting about through the gloom, as though to draw the cab's passenger in from outside. Presently, the doorbell rang and my companion danced down the stairs to fling the door open and enthusiastically welcome our visitor.

Detective Inspector Lestrade had soon settled himself by the fire, while Holmes paced up and down the length of the room.

"Damned unseasonable weather, don't you think, Holmes?" remarked Lestrade.

Holmes' response remained unspoken as Mrs. Hudson swept into the room bearing a tea tray and a copy of the day's paper.

"Thank you, Mrs. Hudson. Lestrade, I suppose there's been some kind of grisly murder that you're here to ask me about," Holmes made a desultory swipe at the paper, but it was swiftly recovered by Lestrade.

"You won't find it in there, Holmes. The Yard is trying to keep this one quiet."

Holmes fell into his chair and leaned back, "Then, pray tell me about it yourself."

Mrs. Hudson took this as the cue to make her exit.

"Well," began Lestrade, "I trust you remember the case of the Putney Butcher."

"Watson, my file, if you please."

I passed him the brown manila file containing records of most criminals and crimes from the last century. "Hum! The Putney Butcher... Yes. Murdered 12 people and disguised their carcasses as those of animals for six weeks... Imprisoned for life at the Old Bailey in 1886. I suppose there's been another death that occurred in such a fashion so as to make you believe it was him? As I recall he escaped from Pentonville Prison at the end of last month," mused Holmes as he skimmed through the file.

Lestrade nodded, "Right on all counts but one."

It was too late. Holmes slammed the file shut and began to prowl about, waving his hands whenever Lestrade tried to speak.

"So... The Butcher returns, eh? But how can you be so sure that it is he? His recent escape from incarceration and the simplicity of the method of killing make him an easy target for impersonation. I expect you've already looked for the obvious signs - mark of a butcher's hook under the right ear, knife wounds to the ribcage-"

"Holmes," interjected Lestrade, "we already know he's not the killer."

My companion froze. "How can you be so sure?"

"Because," explained the Detective Inspector patiently, "he is the victim."

As we sat in the cab together, I watched as Holmes leafed through his ever-faithful brown file and listened to him ponder the killing.

"So the Boston Cannibal... there's motive there, I believe they met and came to blows in 1882... but I suppose this transatlantic issue might render it implausible. Walter Wilkerson - certainly motivated, but also deceased."

The cab drew up on a darkened side street, heavily populated with a crowd of police officers. Holmes made a swift exit and strode purposefully towards the body lying on the soot-encrusted cobblestones.

"Watson, what do you make of this?" he called to me. I approached the corpse and was surprised to see that the skin was mottled with dark, irregular bruises.

"This man has been stoned to death."

"Precisely. What else do you notice?"

I looked closer, and realised that what I had initially taken for a wizened old man was in fact a much younger and stronger specimen, as his thin head of white hair came away in my hand.

"Holmes, this man is heavily disguised, and to professional standard."

Holmes laughed bitterly. "He knew I would be searching for him - or rather assumed. I cannot be called upon to investigate every petty murderer who escapes from a moderate security prison."

I stood there as Holmes stalked about the crime scene, occasionally pausing to give away a cry of delight and pounce on some small element of our surroundings. Suddenly, there was the ringing of hooves upon stone and another police cab came into view. A young constable leapt out of it and ran to Detective Inspector Lestrade.

"Sir," he cried, "there's been another, sir!"

Once again, I found myself in the back of a cab with Holmes, who was growing extremely frustrated.

"Who could it be? None of these criminals came from a culture where stoning is practised, and the size and shape of the bruises tell us that the stones were all smaller and pointed, so the killer is either a very young woman or an elderly and infirm man. But now to say which of those it is..."

We again disembarked and Holmes noted the location of the corpse.

"Both of these deaths have occurred within one square mile of each other... Now what we may or may not infer from this will be confirmed by the next victim."

"Next victim?"

But Holmes had disappeared down the street and into the darkness, swinging a tiny, guttering oil lamp and taking the answer to my question with him.

The presence of a a trail of blood-spots on the ground caused Holmes to utter a great cry of "Aha!" bringing me to the end of the alleyway at once.

I found him stooped over the body of a young man, his cold, grey eyes alight with the joy of the chase, like those of a bloodhound. Held aloft in his long, bony fingers was a white card printed with the words, "Matches made in Heaven," and an address.

"You will observe, Watson," he said, "that this gentleman is a customer of Carhill's Matchmaking Service of Furrow Street."

"Yes, Holmes. Would I be right in thinking that this would be the very Furrow Street that lies not half a mile away from here?"

"Quite correct, my dear Watson. I would be honoured if you were to accompany me there."

Furrow Street was a small, dimly-lit stone-paved road that seemed to be solely frequented by balding, middle-aged men who gravitated unashamedly to a lone location. Carhill's Matchmaking Service was housed in a nondescript little building that squatted toad-like in the middle of the street.

Holmes and I ducked into an inn across the road and made our way to the window. My colleague whipped out his file and leaned forward.

"Both victims, we have established, were customers of this matchmaking service. The first victim's motive was obvious- having just escaped from prison, he needed to settle into a new life as quickly as possible, hence his compulsion to find a wife and also those dreadful side locks. The second... hum! He has been identified as Mr. Benson Forbes, who was happily married.

"Surely, he may simply have been searching for a new spouse?"

Holmes shook his head.

"A matchmaker does not cater to adulterers. An honest matchmaker knows that his customers will need to know anything and everything about each other, and if he cannot supply that information in the knowledge that it will appeal to a target market, he will not supply it at all. However, this does not appear to be your average matchmakers."

At this point, a small balding man scuttled out of the front of Carhill's Matchmaking Service and into the driver's seat of a cab, which began to slowly move away down the road.

Holmes tensed. He seemed about to leap out of his chair in excitement, but the moment passed, and he became still.

"Watson, I trust that you recall my two possible categorisations for the murderer?

"A young woman, or an elderly and infirm man. Surely you don't think-"

"I do, indeed, think, my dear Watson. I propose we make our way across the road and inquire as to the identity of our gentleman cab-driver."

The proprietor of Carhill's Matchmaking Service was a small, rat-like man, who bore a pungent stench of pickles about him.

"Well, gentlemen," he asked, "what may I do for you today?"

Without pausing for a reply, the man lunged at the cabinet against the wall and began foraging through one of the drawers.

"Miss Rachel Wilson, 29, slim build, black hair, father a banker, comes with a 'family car' and dowry of- no, let us perhaps consider instead, Miss Lily Curtis, 32, medium build, blonde hair, father unemployed at present, but left with an inheritance from a tea company, comes with small house and a-"

Holmes had become impatient at this point.

"I have no interest in any of these young ladies, however enchanting they may be," he said tersely, "but I would be most grateful if you were to give me the name of the man who has just exited your establishment."

I looked up to see that Mr Carhill's face had become sullen and overcast.

"I regret, sir," he spat, "that we are unable to share personal information of our clients with people who are not our patrons. Good afternoon!" With that, he slammed the drawer shut and vanished into the gloomy mire of his offices.

Holmes' features darkened and a grim determination overspread his face.

"What are we to do, Holmes?" I asked my companion. "Clearly the good Mr Carhill is unwilling to give us any of the information we require, but what of the cab driver?"

The shadow of the derelict cab was still visible as the weary horse drawing it plodded over the flagstones.

"Our cab driver, my dear Watson," he replied, "is the key to this investigation."

"Holmes," I cried, "surely we should give chase?" But my companion merely smiled and settled back in his chair.

Once the cab had completely disappeared from view, Holmes leaned forward and began to speak.

"That man is certainly a suspect, my dear Watson. He is an older man, incapable of killing in any other way than stoning someone to death with small, pointed rocks, and he has a motive-"

"Motive?" I interjected, "What motive could he have?"

"Watson, you perceive that most of the patrons of this establishment are wealthy, middle-aged men?"

I did.

"Our gentleman cab-driver is neither wealthy nor middle aged. He murders other clients in the simple, animalistic intention of easing the competition for a mate."

"Then why do we not detain him?"

"Because," smiled Holmes, "his guilt or innocence will depend on the identity of the next victim."

By this point, my patience was wearing thin.

"How can you be sure that there will be another victim?" I asked in exasperation.

"My dear Watson," he replied, "I am not sure that there will be another. I can only hope."

We sat in silence for a few minutes.

"All right," said my companion at last, "As no news of another victim appears to be forthcoming, I propose that we make our way to the victims' residences and look for clues amongst their personal effects."

The first victim's home was a squalid, wretched, little room filled with papers and containing no furniture other than a mat and a small brazier. When I had laboured up the stairs approaching it, I found Holmes, having arrived before me, rooting through a strongbox and flinging papers all about. At length, he emerged in triumph, holding a small envelope marked, "CMS."

"My dear Watson," said he, " this little envelope may hold the key to every one of these murders."

With that, he tore it open, and shook the contents out into his palm. Lying in his hand was a business card for M.Carhill of Carhill's Matchmaking Service, and a small photograph, which he raised between two fingers for further inspection.

"Hum! A fresh face indeed, Watson."

I joined him in his scrutiny. The photograph was of a young, unsmiling woman, staring almost aggressively at the photographer, and yet so captivating that I could barely take my eyes off the paper.

"Who do you think she is?" I asked.

"She is our link to the murderer," replied Holmes, as he placed the photograph in his pocket. "I can only hope that we will find her again at the second victim's house."

The late Mr. Benson Fforbes had resided in a double-story house in Chelsea, London, with a sizeable array of servants and a wife. I followed in Holmes wake as he made his way through the sea of wailing cooks, maids, charwomen and spouse, singular, until we reached Fforbes' room.

Widow Fforbes, a small, round woman with a mop of blonde hair, opened the door for us, bawling to herself as she did so. Thankfully, if somewhat insensitively, Holmes stepped aside to allow me in then shut the door in our host's face. Within ten minutes of searching, he had recovered both a CMS envelope and a photograph of the mystery woman, which he tactfully concealed in his coat as he left.

That evening, as we sat by the fire at Baker Street, Holmes dwelt upon the case as it drew to a close.

"So, my dear Watson, now we wait."

"How long do you think we shall have to do so?"

"How long will we have to wait until the next victim is reported? Oh, I should not say more than a few hours based on the killer's current rate. Then, it will be a simple matter of finding the photograph, detaining the cabbie and sufficiently intimidating him so as to produce a confession... Watson, I must say, although I have enjoyed this case it has proved disappointingly shallow."

At that moment, there was a tremendous crashing noise downstairs, followed by the thumping of feet, the door flew open with a bang, and Lestrade appeared, pale and drained. Holmes had started out of his chair. "What is it, Lestrade?" he cried impatiently.

"There's been another murder," came the response.

"Excellent. Now all we have to do is find the photograph and detain the cab driver."

"Holmes, I'm afraid that isn't going to happen."

My companion stopped short. "Why ever not?"

"Because," replied the Detective Inspector wearily, "he's been murdered."

89

Holmes and I sat in the police cab as it sped to the scene of the crime. Holmes' brow was furrowed and his eyes dark, and he spoke not a word.

At last, he exclaimed, "It's the woman, Watson! It must be! All this time, we've been on the wrong track, thinking she's the link to the killer when she is the killer!"

A search of the dead man's pockets produced the expected photograph and a complete change of mood in Holmes. Galvanised into action, he vanished for a few hours and returned in triumph.

"She's his daughter, Watson!"

I looked up to see a large and grubby porter making his way into the living room.

"Holmes?"

Holmes, for it was he, removed his moustache and sat down.

"The woman is Elizabeth Carhill, daughter of our matchmaker friend. She is also the murderer."

"But Holmes- how can you be so sure? Why would she kill her father's customers?"

"All of the victims were interested in her, and all of them were murdered the first time they met her. Victim 1, the Putney Butcher - he didn't suspect a thing. As a murderer himself, he was perfectly capable of self-defense, but his prospective bride discovered his past and decided that it was her responsibility to make him pay. Victim 2, Benson Fforbes- again, Carhill discovered his existing marriage and wanted revenge."

"And the cabbie? Why did she kill him?"

Holmes shrugged. "The thrill? The satisfaction she got from killing an innocent, the joy she felt in having the power to do so? Who can say? Probably not even the killer herself."

"And also," I continued, "how could she have killed them in the first place? Each of those men was at least 6 feet tall, and one was a murderer himself. It would take at least 20 minutes to kill a man with stones as small as those, and the victims would easily have overpowered their captor during that time."

Holmes laughed.

"Ah, this one was clever-clever! Herein lies the genius. She arrived early at the rendezvous, slipped a time-delayed narcotic into their drink, and removed her victims to a secondary location, where she killed them. Why she used stones is beyond me."

We were each lost in our own thoughts when Lestrade reappeared in the doorway.

"If you're ready, Holmes, we're going to make the arrest."

"Who are you arresting?"

"Why, Elizabeth Carhill, of course."

"And only her?"

"Yes. . ."

Holmes sprung from his chair.

"No, you're not. You're going to arrest her father as well."

Lestrade's face went blank. Holmes continued his monologue as he retrieved his coat and began to walk down the stairs.

"Elizabeth Carhill may have committed the actual murder, but she is by no means the only guilty party. I found some extremely incriminating evidence in Mr Carhill's desk, consisting of several letters addressed to him and negotiating prices for his daughter's murder of any given person. Hurry, Watson!"

"But, Holmes," called Lestrade after us, "who was the client who ordered the killings in this first place?"

Holmes stopped.

"His name is Moriarty."

"Who is he?"

"That is precisely what I intend to find out."

The Greatest Detective
by Amber Butler
Bonnieville, KY, USA

The sounds of Baker Street below
Pipe smoke drifts, languidly in the air
Hovering like the fog of London.

While sitting, folded in a leather chair
Deep eyes, incisive, look over crossed fingers
Seeing clues in everything.

Memories run deep at 221b
A woman's portrait on the desk
A painting of Reichenbach on the wall
And a blue diamond kept in a drawer.

Then, lifted, a violin is playing
Strings singing out Mendelssohn
Suddenly, those eyes ablaze, the violin's tossed aside
He's up now and at the hearth
Statuesque, he stands confident
The pieces are set.

All crime falls before Sherlock Holmes
And Doctor Watson takes up his pen.

The Adventure of the Black Feathers

by Julianne Ducrow
Normandy, France

John Watson knew he was about to die.

Under the blanket of grey cloud, John noted London had turned unusually quiet; the city's soundtrack muted all the while the man opposite him, held his right hand aloft. With an index finger flexing gradually, he began applying pressure to the trigger of the gun pointed directly at John's chest.

At that moment, it started to rain gently as if the very heavens were weeping in anticipation of coming events. Fine raindrops gradually darkening the concrete beneath their feet, as John waiting for death to finally take him this very evening on the rooftop.

It wasn't the first time John had found himself looking down the barrel of a gun. Nor would the feeling of cold steel piercing his body be a unique experience for him. They had described it as a miracle in Afghanistan. Had the bullet been a centimeter or so to the left and John would have been dead before he'd even heard the shot that killed him.

Only it hadn't. The sniper had either made his calculations incorrectly or somebody up there loved John very much, as he had not only survived the injury, but also made a full recovery, returning home to England on honorable discharge.

That was when he met Sherlock Holmes.

It was hard to describe John's first thoughts on encountering this strange, aloof but brilliant man. From their very first meeting, he had felt an instant and overwhelming bond between them, almost as if he were coming home. John was sorry to think he would now never see Sherlock again; never accompany him on a case, never watch him conduct some strange experiment in the flat they shared together, and it was thoughts of Sherlock than ran through his mind when he heard the gunfire and he knew his life was at an end.

It was a dismally overcast Sunday morning in late April when Michael Messenger had come to visit the occupants of 221B Baker Street. John

93

had gone out early to buy the morning papers and was sat reading them in his armchair opposite his flat mate, who was himself reading his favourite Edgar Allen Poe volume, when the door bell rang.

Mr. Messenger was a tall man, willowy built with dark hair and fair skin, not unlike Sherlock. They even shared the same catlike movements as he navigated his way around the flat and settled on one of the chairs after accepting a cup on tea from John.

"So how do you know each other?" John asked while pouring his own cup. Although it was commonplace for people to know Sherlock in certain circles, there seemed to be a familiarity between the two men. John would not like to term it as friendship, but it was certainly closer than a passing acquaintance.

The slightest flicker of a smile played across their visitor's lips, as he began to reminisce behind his blue eyes. Taking a breath as if to speak, he then paused for a moment before answering. Michael looked to be gauging how much Sherlock may have told his friend and indeed how much he would wish him to know about the particulars of their association.

When Sherlock made no move to speak, Michael informed John, "Sherlock and I once worked together, an age ago now it seems. Anyway, we had different ideas about things and so he took one path and I another."

He left the last word hanging in the air as if the sentence was not quite finished.

"And you became a solicitor and Sherlock a detective," John smiled sensing a sudden tension in the room and attempting to smooth it over as was his way. "So not very different paths after all. You both work to keep law and order."

"That we do," Michael agreed.

"So what can I help you with Michael?" Sherlock interrupted, "It must be something of great importance to bring you here."

"Always straight to business," the solicitor chuckled, and then cleared his throat to tell his story. "One of our important clients John Garrideb, has a problem, and someone with your skills I believe could help in the matter.

"Mr. Garrideb has two bothers. Howard is his business partner and their other brother Nathan, who both men are estranged to. I don't know the particulars, but when their father Alexander died, he left the family estate including Garrideb Hall in equal shares to his sons. The maintenance cost of a building of this size, as you can imagine, is quite considerable. A tycoon in Kansas, eager to purchase the property, has approached them. As none of them live there, they wish to sell it, however they need Nathan's consent, which once given will entitle him to a percentage of the sale upon completion. They cannot locate Nathan, which is why I come to you."

Sherlock's eyes narrowed on Michael as he steepled his fingers in a manner John had seen him do in thought a hundred times before.

"So you would like me to locate a missing person, in order to secure the sale of the Garrideb family estate," Sherlock simply stated.

"Indeed," agreed Michael, "That's the sort of thing you claim to do these days I thought."

"Among others," Sherlock concluded, "I'll take the case. If he is alive I shall find him and visit him on your behalf. I will not promise to reveal to you his location however, if after I inform him of why you wish to contact him, he still does not want to be found."

Michael nodded in agreement to the terms. "Fair enough. I should think he would be more than happy, as he will be a very wealthy man after the sale of this property has gone through. It has been valued at £15,000,000."

John wasn't surprised at the speed in which Sherlock found the missing Garrideb and the next day they caught a black cab across town and arrived at a newly built block of flats. John noted that Garrideb was not the name of the resident whose entry phone they pressed. Sherlock explained that Nathan had been living under a different name for some time now, even longer than when he stopped leaving his flat. One might suppose he might have died but regular deliveries of groceries had been seen by neighbours. After a few further enquiries he had discovered that the man was agoraphobic, terrified of even leaving his own front door.

Nathan Garrideb was clearly expecting them, and after the usual formalities, Sherlock passed on the information given to him by Michael Messenger, with regard to the sale of Garrideb Hall.

Although excited at first, the dawning realisation that he would have to leave his flat in order to sign away his part of the property, dampened his enthusiasm for his impending inheritance.

"But I can't leave the flat," he protested.

"I understand you have a condition which makes that problematic for you, but I assure you there is really nothing out there which will harm you," Sherlock told him in a soothing tone, reaching out to squeeze his shoulder in reassurance. Nathan seemed to instantly relax at this point and John wondered if Sherlock knew of some pressure point he might have learnt as a martial arts technique.

"So tell us what happened the last time you set foot outside this flat. What did you do that you shouldn't have, and more importantly, what did you see that you now wish you hadn't?"

Nathan was at first taken aback and stared wide-eyed and startled at the accuracy of Sherlock's deduction. He paused for a moment, weighing up his options and then made a sudden move as if to lunge toward Sherlock. John was there before that last thought had enough time to process, and he fingered his gun beneath his belt making sure the outline was clearly visible, as he warned, "I wouldn't do that if I were you. We just want to help, which we might be able to do, if you start by answering Sherlock's questions."

"I...I," Nathan began to stutter, "It was just for the money!" he finally exclaimed in a rush. "I didn't know anyone would get hurt, I really didn't want anyone to get hurt, but they still shot him! Right in front of me and I just panicked. I was holding the bag with the cash in it and I ran. They don't know where I live, we only ever arranged to meet in public places and I never gave my real name, not even the one I go by here. But I daren't go out. I still have all the cash, haven't spent a penny of it, it's still in the bag for God's sake. It wasn't all of it, they had a load too, but it's certainly more than my share. And I know they'll want it back. Not the type of men to be messed with, as the security guard certainly found out, and I don't fancy the same thing happening to me."

Sherlock said nothing to begin with, then leaned forward and again gripped the man's shoulder.

"This is what you are going to do," he instructed in hushed tones, "You are going to contact your brothers straight away and ask to meet them at your local pub tomorrow evening. You will give me as much information as you know on these men you have got involved with, and give me the key to this flat, that myself and John may enter it tomorrow night while you are out."

Sherlock and John finally left after Nathan Garrideb had fully agreed to Sherlock's requests, and John sat in the taxi home puzzled by the events, which was not uncommon for him while on a case with Sherlock.

"So Michael's Garridebs who are looking for him, are they who killed the security guard?" John asked.

"Oh no, they really are his brothers and he will undoubtedly inherit a fortune after the sale of his family home."

"That's sort of ironic then that he ends up in this situation, when if he'd held on long enough, he would have been a rich man anyway. So it's just all a big coincidence why your old pal Michael put us onto this case in the first place?"

Sherlock grinned a shark's smile, "There's no such thing as coincidence John."

The following evening they were back at the flats. They watched from across the road as Nathan did as Sherlock had instructed and left the building and went into the pub on the corner. John was amazed at the ease in which he accomplished this after being confined only to his four walls for so long. He had heard cases of agoraphobia, when the patient took years making even the smallest steps to recovery, and yet here, one word from Sherlock and the man appeared to be cured.

They entered Nathan's flat and waited for the men, who for reasons unknown to John, Sherlock was sure would break in that evening. Sure enough, within the hour they did exactly that, and after a bit of a skirmish, Sherlock took off after one man and John the other.

John followed in pursuit of the second man, up the stairs of the block of flats and through the fire escape on to the roof, but he realised his mistake too late.

The rooftop appeared deserted at first and John began to hastily look around for an alternative escape route and that was when he felt it. Cold hard metal pressed to the back of his head.

"Turn around, slowly," the red headed man ordered. John obeyed. "Toss your gun to the ground, then hands up in the air where I can see them." John followed the instructions edging backwards until he felt his heels touch the edge of the roof and abruptly stopped automatically taking a step forward again.

"Close enough," the man pointing the gun, warned. "Where's the money?"

"I don't know," John answered truthfully.

"That's a shame, looks like it's a bloody long way down, so hope you can fly?"

"Honestly, I don't know where it is," John said again, rising panic in his voice.

"Well that's too bad. I'll find it of course, not that you'll ever know, because by that time you'll be an ugly mess on the pavement down there."

John glanced over his shoulder to the street below. There was nothing to break his fall if he jumped of his own accord. He had no choice, there was no other way out of the situation and his chances of survival were slim, but he couldn't just stand there and wait to be shot.

John's sudden movement caught the other man off guard, but his finger was already squeezing the trigger and as the shot rang out, John felt a searing pain in his side. It was just a graze, John knew that instantly. The location where the bullet had impacted was nowhere near any vital organs and even without inspection, he was sure it had passed straight through him, but that was not what was to kill him. The impact of the bullet had propelled John backwards and unable to secure his footing, he was falling over the edge, gravity pulling him down to the waiting concrete below.

He fell facing skyward and suddenly felt grateful he would not see the ground rush up to greet him. The strange weightlessness felt surprisingly liberating despite his journey's obvious conclusion, but John's acceptance of situations was always one of his strengths, something he wondered born out of his days in the army. He had seen many men killed at war and now finally it was his turn.

Only the rooftop wasn't becoming further away, if anything, it was beginning to appear closer once again. John suddenly felt light headed. He wondered if it was the shock, but he had the distinct sensation of arms around him, supporting and carrying him back to the rooftop. Just before he blacked out entirely, he could see what looked like feathery black wings sweeping at the corned of his vision.

"It's okay John, I've got you," a familiar voice assured him.

When John awoke he was in a hospital bed. He could hear Sherlock talking to someone just outside his private room. The other voice in the conversation, although speaking in hushed whispers sounded familiar too, and it took a moment for John to identify it as belonging to Mycroft Holmes.

"That was not your main objective Sherlock," Mycroft growled.

"John's going to be fine. It's not the first time he's been shot and he recovered perfectly well before," Sherlock protested.

"Precisely! It's the second time he's been shot and Afghanistan was a close call too. That's two occasions when you have been quite sloppy. You know how important he is," Mycroft continued to lecture.

"You don't need to tell me Mycroft, I know how important John is," Sherlock indignantly spat back.

"Then you need to be more careful in future, this is your last chance Sherlock. You have been assigned to him; if he receives even a scratch, then you'll be recalled and your guardian status revoked! Do I make myself clear little brother?"

Sherlock glowered, "As ever, crystal clear, Mycroft."

"Good, wonderful," Mycroft concluded with a Cheshire grin as if everything was going according to plan and not the total disaster it might have been. "I'm engaging phase two, you see that woman over there?"

Sherlock turned his head to look in the direction in which Mycroft inferred.

"Nurse Morstan, yes she's been attending John," Sherlock informed him.

"Yes Mary, charming name don't you think?" Mycroft asked.

"Obviously," Sherlock agreed, "Can I assume she is part of phase two?"

Mycroft grinned a shark's smile similar to his brothers, "What do you think?"

Just over a week later John had been discharged from hospital and was sitting in his usual armchair in 221B reading the paper. Sherlock was out collecting more prescription pain relief for John, although he was making quite a speedy recovery as it turns out practice makes perfect when it came to this sort of injury.

Mrs. Hudson, their cleaner, was vacuuming the flat from top to bottom and fussing about the mess Sherlock's experiments made, making her job twice as hard as it ought to be.

"First of all it's tobacco ash," she grumbled, "then it's dissected who knows what, and for heavens sake, are these jars of mud? Not to mention the chickens! What is Sherlock doing with so many chickens? All I keep finding are these black feathers everywhere."

John wasn't listening as his mind kept wandering back to those strange events after his fall from the rooftop, which continued to replay in his mind on what seemed like a constant loop. He was sure it was delirium brought on by shock, but still, it seemed so real and there was something he just couldn't quite put his finger on.

Half an hour later and Sherlock still wasn't home, but Mrs. Hudson had finished for the day and was putting on her coat to leave.

"I'm off now John, I should think Sherlock will be back any minute now though. Will you be alright here by yourself?" she asked with more than a little concern present in her voice.

John put down his paper for the moment to answer her. "Yes I'll be fine. Sherlock's been taking good care of me and he's never out of the flat for very long ever since I've come home from the hospital, so I'm sure I'll be okay."

"Yes, Sherlock's been so good throughout all of this; an absolute angel," Mrs. Hudson agreed.

A sudden smile spread across John face, as if some vital fact that had for so long been eluding him, finally clicked into place.

He looked back at Mrs. Hudson and in all seriousness said, "Yes he is, isn't he."

221b for Undershaw

by Maria Fleischhack
Leipzig, Germany

Sherlock Holmes is a man of logic and deduction. While he is indeed familiar with every emotion a human being can experience and what their consequences might be, he ignores them in himself and normally focuses onthe problems at hand.

But when the great detective opened the evening paper one night in late spring, sitting on his chair in 221B Baker Street next to Watson, smoking, he found an article which touched him strangely. An etching of a beautiful house, abandoned and crumbling caught his eye and he found himself immersed in the accompanying article.

Ghosts were said to haunt the house; ghosts which did not scare those who visited the place, but which made it seem already occupied, and no one felt they had the right to move into it without being familiar with those spirits first.

Neighbours spoke of children's laughter which they heard from the terrace in front of the house; of conversing men, discussing politics and sports; of good night stories, whispered after dark.

And Sherlock Holmes felt, for the first time in his life, a powerful irrational tugging at his heart, which, after much contemplation, he defined as a violent case of homesickness. For a moment he was a ghost himself and tears shone in his eyes. And like the house, his heart was broken.

The Doctor and the Madman
by Cambria Trillian
San Antonio, Texas, USA

You may not have heard, but there was a man
In his mind he held Afghanistan
Coarse sands strained to blow that man away
As he doctored up bullet ricochets
But he was resilient, much fiercer than fear
His weary heart could not be commandeered.

Another gentleman, pipe wedged in teeth,
Stood as an emblem of mad caprice
His violin hummed at every hour
He was intellect and dry gunpowder
Garnet in his cold veins could be set aflame
Just say to him, "let's play a murder game."

It was unlikely but the pair did meet
Lived out their nine lives on Baker Street
Anchored soldier, mercurial friend
Each the other's improbable godsend
Through puzzling cases and cases of cocaine
The doctor and the madman, always strange.

The Impromptu Plunge
by William Warren
Moffat, Ontario, Canada

"No, I really don't see how I can be of any assistance to you," said Sherlock Holmes. "As far as I can see, no crime has been committed."

"No, there hasn't been," our prospective client agreed, "but we just want you to make sure." The old woman raised her hands in a motion of begging Holmes to stay seated.

He rose all the same, and headed for the stack of newspapers in the corner, running back as far as three months ago. "A man falls from a tightrope and dies: accident, case closed, so what? He made a mistake, two, in fact, one, misjudging the distance to the platform on the other side, and two, taking the job of being a tightrope walker in the first place. He fell off just before he reached the end of the rope. There was nothing of note in the event."

"He was blindfolded, Mister Holmes," the old woman added.

"Make that three mistakes, then." He waved the matter away. "Absolutely not; I can't help you in the slightest."

"I will pay you just to come down and take another look at the scene."

"Money is not my only desire, Missus Browner," he snapped. "My wish is to catch those people who think they can abuse the laws of nature and man, all at once, and get away with it. That, and to find diversions so my brain will not implode from boredom. No. Absolutely, positively, no."

"Now, Holmes," I protested, "really. She only wants some peace of mind about her son's death; surely we can give her that? And if it turns out to be merely an accident, then there's no harm done. Besides, it would do you good to get outside for a while."

"Will you please," Holmes screamed, "stop it! I don't have to go outside, I don't need to go outside, I don't want to go outside, you can't make me go outside. I will not go outside, and certainly not to investigate an accident."

"Well then," I announced. "If you won't, I will."

"Watson, don't you dare! Whenever you take up deduction, you always end up inside-out and backwards."

"I'll ask Mycroft, then. I'm sure he'd have more heart than you."

"Have you met my brother?" He scoffed. "I told you, he won't derail himself from his usual routines unless it is a matter of national security." His lithe form was quivering with rage. "And is an accidental death of a tightrope-walker a matter of national security? No, I don't think so."

"Then I'll go myself anyway!"

"If you do, I'll kill you."

"Then come along, and you will not have to arrest yourself."

He stood up, snatched up his hat, coat, cane and gloves and opened the door leading into the hall. "So let's go already."

When we arrived at the West End location where the circus was set up, Holmes dashed out of the cab and ran at top speed into the tent where the tightrope walk had taken place. When we caught up with him, he was already at the top platform, having scaled the long ladder in moments. He set about examining the platform while I looked around.

The tent was over two hundred feet tall, made of yellow material with wide red and blue stripes. Along the walls were arranged twelve rows of folding wooden chairs. The entire tent was empty, as it had been since the fatal event, though there were a few constables posted at the entrances.

"Ah, Mister Holmes," came the voice of our friend, Inspector Lestrade. "I thought you had declined this case?"

"And so had you," he replied. "But I see you are still here."

"Yes, well, there is something I should tell you about this case before you progress any further. Won't you come down?" The weasely-faced man cupped his hands around his mouth in a makeshift megaphone at the last.

"I think not, I'm much more interested by what I see up here, but I'll be down shortly, on my own time, thank you."

"I can't understand that man," Lestrade scoffed.

Lestrade is one of the most competent of the Scotland Yard officials, not nearly the oaf that many of my readers seem to have pictured him. Indeed, he could not have been an incompetent buffoon, or my friend Sherlock Holmes wouldn't have tolerated his company. But he did have an impatient streak to him, which was mainly the reason why his cases were often turned over to Holmes; he wanted instant results, and was not patient enough to wait things through and look carefully for clues.

"So I take it you had to convince him to take another look at the case, Doctor?" he asked, sidling up to stand beside me, both of us facing away from Holmes and at the audience's seats.

"Indeed, though it didn't take much."

"What did you do?"

"I threatened to leave him at home and come myself."

We shared a laugh for a moment before we both found ourselves gripped by the shoulder by a pair of long, thin, but incredibly powerful hands and Holmes' face appeared between ours, led first by the long, sharp nose, then the prominent cheekbones, then the intense, dark, beady eyes and thin lips. "Enjoying yourselves, are we?" he asked, the corners of his mouth turned up in a miniscule smile that was more akin to a sneer. His eyes held no warmth, and I had a feeling he knew what we were laughing about. "Having a friendly chuckle over the scene of a murder?"

"Murder, Holmes?"

"Yes, Watson. Murder."

"Well, what led you to believe that?" I turned to face him incredulously.

"Take a look." He turned me by the shoulder, which he still held in his firm grip, and pointed to the tightrope with his other hand, having let go of Lestrade. "Examine the distance between the platforms."

I looked, and found that they were closer together than I would have expected. I voiced my observation to Holmes, who chuckled in his throat.

"Indeed. Such a short walk is highly unlikely to be the scene of misjudged distance."

"But you can't base your theories upon only that," Lestrade protested.

"I'm not."

"Then what are you going on?" The inspector asked.

"What was that detail of the case you said you wanted me to know about?"

"Oh, yes, that. I just think you should know that this is a waste of time. We were just leaving; Scotland Yard has closed the case. They believe it to be a waste of time."

"And if I told you that I was really a chimpanzee," Holmes snapped, "would you believe that?"

"You know, that explains a lot," Lestrade muttered.

"Watson, please accompany me, I would like to see some of the other parts of the circus. Lestrade, please continue on your admirable work." He strode out the entranceway, and I followed close behind.

"Holmes, that was unkind back there."

"Perhaps, but it was also unkind when we won the Battle of Waterloo." He led me through the pavilions seemingly at random, peering into the tents as we passed. Suddenly, when I happened to glance behind, and then righted my gaze again, Holmes was nowhere to be seen. I returned to the spot of my distraction, and looked into all the tents from there to where I had realized Holmes' disappearance, when suddenly I heard, "Peepin' Tom, ah' wei?"

I whirled around with a shout, and saw a circus man standing there, four feet taller than I. He wore bright blue clothes and a frilly top hat with red feathers. His face was a mangled mess, with a many-times-broken nose, puffy eyes and a misshapen mouth. I realized he was wearing stilts.

"Excuse me, sir, I seem to have misplaced a friend of mine."

"Misplayced? Dee' mei, 'e mus' be small, fo' you 'o loose 'im so easy." His voice was unnaturally high, with a sharp edge to it.

"No, I mean I can't find him."

"Wehw ven, you'd be'ah go foind him. G'day." He spindled off down the hard-packed grass.

I searched for Holmes for an hour before I found him, on the other side of the carnival talking to a group of performers. I waited on the sidelines until he had finished. There was much laughing and exchange of quips and small-talk, and after a while, Holmes detached himself from them and came over to stand beside me.

"An interesting lot, these circus people," he said. "If ever I get tired of detective work, I might join up with them."

"What would you do?"

His reply completely took me by surprise. "I think I'd be a clown. A juggler."

106

We left the circus, and returned to Baker Street, after Holmes promised Mrs. Browner that he would devote the entirety of his attentions to the case. As soon as we got back to the rooms, Holmes dove for the settee, and curled up with his pipe.

"So this is what you call your full attention?" I asked.

"Yes, yes, most definitely." His eyes were closed, and his fingers were drumming on the bowl of the pipe.

"Well, I will leave you to your most engaging work, and go visit Mary."

"Who?"

"My fiancé. You remember." He often pretended to have no idea who Mary Morstan was, even though she had brought him that most remarkable case of the Sign of Four, and he had met her on many occasions since. I have never been able to figure out if his deliberate ignorance was because he simply did not like her, or if he was disappointed that I would be leaving eventually to marry her. Somehow I thought the former more likely; there was always a definite gap between Holmes and myself, and Mary was to him just another woman who had absolutely no connection to him after the Sign of Four case had been closed.

"Oh, right, yes of course." He didn't say another word, so I left.

Over the next few days, Holmes and I were rarely in the same room together for very long. This was not because we were avoiding each other, but because we were both very busy. Holmes said that he had a very pressing case, which he needed to solved quickly, and so rushed out of 221B at irregular, unannounced intervals. During influenza season, my practice nearly triples in intensity, and so I was out of the residence for most of the day, while Holmes' outdoor adventures usually began at night; I had grown used to the sight of a handwritten note in Holmes' meticulous scrawl stuck under the door-knocker reading *"Gone out. Food on dishes. Don't wait up. Breakfast at six-twenty-two exactly, please. Don't touch my cocaine syringe."*

On Saturday, I came into the living room to find Lestrade waiting in Holmes' preferred chair, an exasperated expression on his face and a dying cigarette between his fingers as he tapped his foot impatiently.

"Ah, there you are, Watson," he greeted me, standing up to shake my hand. "I had almost decided to leave and come back later. Do you know when Mister Holmes will return?"

"I have no idea, he's been in and out all week irregularly. What did you want to tell him? I can write a message down for him when he comes back."

"Oh, I can wait. Just another little problem I'm having with a case. Completely baffles me, I must say."

At that moment there came the sound of the front door slamming open and a violent scuffle downstairs making its way upwards and suddenly Holmes appeared at the door, dragging a man by the ear. He presently thrust his cargo down onto the sofa and pinned him there by the shoulder with one of his powerful arms.

"Holmes, what in heaven's name are you doing?" Lestrade babbled.

"I am presenting to you Mister Eugene Hailey, of the circus. Shake hands, Gene." He gave a violent shove against the man's arm. Mister Hailey reached out with his left hand and shook Lestrade's and my hand. He was a short man in a dirty suit with greasy, unwashed hair.

"And what are you doing with this man?" I asked, setting down my revolver, which I had drawn out of my pocket when I heard the struggle on the stairwell.

"I am arresting him for the murder of Abram Browner."

"The circus performer?" Lestrade groaned. "That case has been long closed, it was an accident." I confess, I had completely forgotten about it as well.

"Open your eyes, Lestrade, the evidence to the contrary is right in front of you." Sherlock Holmes shifted his grip to the man's throat, and Lestrade cried out.

"Holmes, you know I could have you arrested for the way you are treating this man," the Inspector cried.

"So you could. So arrest me. Go ahead."

"Oh, I, uh, realized I have an appointment at Scotland Yard," Lestrade turned around and walked out the door. "Goodbye, Doctor." I closed the door after him as he left.

"Now, Watson," said Holmes. "If I might borrow your revolver?"

"Holmes, surely you won't..."

"No, I won't, I just don't want to continue the entire interview in this position." He stood up and took the revolver, fixing it upon our guest's face. Holmes sat down at the table in the corner, resting the handle of the revolver on the table, pointed at his prisoner. "Now, Mister Hailey, conductor of the circus orchestra. Please listen carefully. And Watson, you should, too.

"Mister Abram Browner had loaned you quite a considerable sum of money, when your stock exchange debt had to be paid off. And he was a very good debtor, so I was told. However, when you didn't pay off the debt after three years, he began to pester you for the money back. After two more years, he threatened to bring this before the leader of the gypsies. Naturally, you would be thrown out of the circus, being an outsider in the first place, and so you could not risk that. It was then that your heart was filled with murder." He pounded his open fist against the table, knocking over the vase of flowers resting in the centre. "You murdered your only friend, did you not?" When Hailey didn't answer, Holmes pointed the gun at the floor and fired a round into it. "Did you not? Answer me!"

"Yes, I did," Eugene Hailey stuck his chin out in defiance. "But you'll never be able to prove it. And Scotland Yard will never believe you."

"We might," came a voice at the door, and Lestrade stood in it with two constables.

"Well, isn't this a merry gathering?" Holmes chuckled. "You were saying, Mister Hailey?"

"I killed him, sure enough. But the case will never be proved in court; they'll never believe it. The only evidence I left was purely circumstantial."

"Maybe if you explained it," Lestrade asked.

"No, I think I will," Holmes stood up. "Watson, take the revolver and keep it on our friend here. I'd hate for him to run off on us before I'm finished.

"You couldn't just take a gun and shoot him, for it is possible the clever gypsies might find the connection through your motives and convict you. Their methods of punishment are notoriously more medieval than the government's. So, you had to make it seem like an accident. How am I doing so far?"

"Exactly correct, sir." Hailey kept his defiant stance the whole time.

"So, what you did was organize an 'accident' for Mister Browner. Blindfolded tightrope-walkers rely on the music to know when they have reached the end of the rope, and so you ended the music just before he had got there. And you even made sure that should he decide to test whether he had indeed finished, he would fall, because of the loose wire; and you made a mistake that cost you your victory. You slightly loosened the screws holding the wire in place at one end with lamp oil. This convinced me that it was not an accident. You stopped the music just before he reached the end, and he fell. If you hadn't made sure the wire was loosened it would have seemed like a perfect accident, but you were not able to remove the oil entirely from the screws. The oil got me wondering. For motive, and a narration of the event, all I had to do was ask around at the circus, posing as a certain stilt-walker Watson met on the streets." He gave me a slight apologetic smile. "Then I became an expert on tightrope-walkers and how the events are coordinated. The music was the key. Am I correct in this?"

"Absolutely, Mister Holmes. But you still won't prevail against me in court with the evidence you have."

"Most likely not. But for your abuse of music, I can at least provide some entirely legal punishment. Watson, the gun if you please. No, I won't shoot him, just give it to me."

He took the revolver, held it up next to Hailey's right ear and fired two shots into the back of the settee, then changed over to the left ear and fired the remaining three. In the confined space of the room, the shots were extremely loud, and right next to Hailey's ear, it must have deafened him considerably.

"There we go, I'm finished with him. Lestrade, you may take him away." As they were leaving, Holmes asked. "Watson, please write a letter to Missus Browner about this. Oh, by the way, Lestrade, what was that case you wanted to bring to my attention?"

"Another irregular accident. I thought you'd like to make another murder out of it."

Eugene Hailey was carried away to the sound of Sherlock Holmes' braying laughter.

A Leap of Faith
by Emily Bignell
Brisbane, Australia

When clients came to 221B Baker Street, they weren't usually followed by paparazzi and autograph hunters. But those clients, weren't Aidan Crawley, celebrity author of a series of spy thrillers that were not only international bestsellers, but were also being made into blockbuster films.

Sherlock was expecting a visit from Aidan. Not so much from a process of deduction, but from seeing him interviewed the previous evening on the 9 o'clock news. Aidan had gone public about the breakdown of his marriage to his wife of 10 years, Melanie. He had been unable to contact her since she walked out on him, and announced, with tears in his eyes, that he would be enlisting Holmes's help to find her. "When it comes to finding my wife, I'll leave nothing to chance. Sherlock Holmes is the best detective in the world and if he can't find her, nobody can."

The tears were back in Aidan's eyes as he showed Sherlock and John photographs of Melanie, and told them how he had returned home six months before to find her gone. "Six months?" Sherlock repeated incredulously, "She left six months ago and you have only just come to me now?" Aidan looked embarrassed. "Well, I was hoping that I could find her, or that she'd come back to me. You see, our marriage had been in trouble for some time. Fame and success came at a price. I was away an awful lot, and when I was home I was holed up in my study writing most of the time. Melanie grew a little... irrational. She started accusing me of caring more for my work than her, even that I was having an affair with Caroline Cooley, which was utterly ridiculous." The casual mention of the beautiful lead actress in the film adaptation of his books raised both Sherlock and John's eyebrows. Oblivious, Aidan continued.

"She even began to threaten divorce, and that she'd take me to the cleaners. Anyway, I'd been in LA, overseeing the final draft of the script for the new film. When I came home, most of Melanie's things had gone and so was she. I sent a text asking her what was going on, and this is what came back." Aidan fumbled in his pocket and produced an iPhone, which he showed to Sherlock and John. The text message was brief and to the point: "I've left you. You will be hearing from my lawyers."

"And did you hear from her lawyers?" Sherlock asked.

"No," said Aidan. "I'm hoping that she's reconsidered. I just want to find her, talk things through with her."

"Have any of her family or friends heard from her?" asked John.

"Melanie didn't make friends easily, and she had no family, apart from me. She was an only child of older parents, no other living relatives. I was… it." Aidan looked sad. "I think that was why she became so jealous. She was afraid of losing the only family she had."

"So she made sure of it by leaving," Sherlock finished. Aidan looked at him, uncertain how to respond. John, seeing this, stepped in.

"Well, thank you for coming to see us, Aidan. We'll do what we can to help find your wife – although if she's hidden herself from you so well, I don't know how much luck we'll have tracking her down."

John saw Aidan out and came back to find Sherlock lying on the couch, staring at the ceiling.

"We won't have any luck tracking her down," he said as John entered. "We don't even know where to start looking for the body."

"Are you serious? You really think Aidan murdered Melanie?" John asked.

"I don't think it. I know it. Something just doesn't feel right." He leapt to his feet and went to the window, staring unseeingly at the street. "But where do we start looking?" he said, almost to himself.

John, in the meantime, was on his laptop, looking up Aidan Crawley. The top stories were from various gossip columns, linking him with Caroline Cooley. The accompanying photos certainly lent weight to the rumours – Aidan rubbing sunscreen into Caroline's back, Aidan and Caroline in a passionate clinch in the back of a cab, Aidan and Caroline leaving a hotel together…

"Looks as though poor Melanie had good reason to be jealous," John mused. "What a bastard."

"Excuse me, boys," Mrs Hudson knocked on the open door. "Sorry to disturb, but you have another visitor. This is Lucy Bennett."

She ushered in a rather good-looking woman, of around their own age. John stepped forward with enthusiasm to greet her.

"I'm John Watson, and that man over there ignoring us both is Sherlock Holmes. How can we help you?"

"Nice to meet you, John. This is going to sound weird but I'm here about Melanie Crawley."

That was enough to bring Sherlock back from the window.

"You know where Melanie Crawley is?" he asked.

"Maybe," Lucy replied.

"Maybe? You either do or you don't. If you're going to waste my time please leave."

"It's not as simple as that! Like I said, I might know where she is. But you will need to keep an open mind."

"I always keep an open mind," Sherlock replied loftily.

"Please tell us what you know, Lucy," John interjected, before things could escalate further.

"Okay. I was watching the 9 o'clock news last night and saw the story about Melanie. They showed a photograph of her, and for some reason I just couldn't stop thinking about her. And the word "Undershaw" kept coming to mind, although I had no idea what it was. I didn't pay much attention to that right away, but then when I was trying to go to sleep, I kept seeing this image." She stopped, as if unsure how to proceed. John, sensing Sherlock's scepticism, silenced him with a look.

"Go on, Lucy. What did you see?" he asked gently.

"It was somewhere in the country. It was as if I was lying under a tree. I was looking up, seeing sky between branches and leaves, and some sort of tower further away, an old crumbling tower. I have no idea where it was, but it was so clear, like a photograph. And again, the word Undershaw kept coming to mind. Next morning, I looked up Undershaw on the Internet. Turns out it's the ruin of a house out in the country that was once owned by a famous author. Completely abandoned now, and nobody goes next or near it."

"Are you trying to tell me that you think Melanie is buried somewhere in this place you dreamed about?" Sherlock demanded. Lucy looked at him, chin raised.

"I don't think she is. I know she is," she said, simply.

"Where have I heard that before?" John murmured.

Sherlock laughed. "Oh, you're one of these psychic people. How fun!"

113

"I am NOT a psychic!" Lucy's voice was like ice. "I don't know how I know the things I know sometimes. I just do. And I never usually tell anybody about them because of the exact reaction I'm getting now. Against my better judgment, I decided I would tell you, because Aidan Crawley said on the news that he was going to put you on the case."

"So you thought I'd go out to some old ruin in the middle of nowhere on the strength of something conjured up by your imagination." Sherlock was openly mocking now.

"So much for the open mind," Lucy said, getting to her feet. "Well, I've passed it on for what it's worth. I'll leave you to your nice, tangible, scientifically proven clues, shall I? Got many of those yet?"

"Lucy-" John got in before Sherlock could retaliate, but she shook her head.

"Don't bother. I'll see myself out." She went to the door, and turned back to them.

"Oh, and one more thing. Undershaw happens to be near the village where Melanie grew up. That was also on the internet, by the way, just in case you think I dreamed that too."

With that, she turned and went down the stairs. Sherlock caught up with her before she reached the front door.

"How do I know that you haven't made all this up?" he asked of her. She met his stare without a qualm.

"How do you know that I have?"

If the driveway leading to Undershaw was any indication of the condition of the house, it was in a pretty bad way indeed. Potholes and fallen branches made an obstacle course that required all of John's skills to navigate, but it was still a bumpy ride, and they were all glad to get out of the car at the end of it.

"What a shame it's a ruin," Lucy said softly, looking at the dilapidated building. "You can tell it was a beautiful house, once." She then started looking at the trees surrounding the house, before one seemed to catch her attention. She looked at it for a long moment before walking towards it, Sherlock and John following at a short distance. When they joined her beside it, she was looking towards a ruined tower in the distance.

114

"This is it," she said. "She's here."

John and Sherlock looked at the ground beneath the tree. They knew what they were looking for, so it was easy to see that there was a definite mound, and that the grass covering it was of a different shade to the rest. They looked at each other, and then John pulled out his phone and dialled Lestrade.

John did not think that Lucy needed to see the forensics team exhume whoever lay in that lonely grave, so he left Sherlock with Lestrade and his assistants and took her back to the nearby village, to the pub where they had booked rooms for the night. He found a table by the fire for them and went to get a glass of wine for her and a beer for himself. Returning with the drinks, he sat down and looked at her.

"You okay?" he asked.

"Yes," she said with a rather wan smile, and took a sip of wine. She looked at him. "What about you?"

John gave her an equally wan smile.

"A bit ... freaked out, to be honest with you. Sherlock can look at a person and tell you everything you need to know about them within minutes, but that's because he notices details and adds them all up. This is something else entirely. You really dreamed of that exact spot?"

"That exact spot," she confirmed, wryly. "Don't worry, it doesn't happen that often. And this is the first time it's been about a missing person. That's what I mean when I said I'm not psychic. I can't do it on demand, so to speak. Sometimes, I just know things. That's the only way I can explain it."

John nodded. He could see signs of strain in her face so he changed the subject to something a bit lighter. Soon they were so engrossed that they did not notice time passing until Sherlock appeared and pulled up a chair at their table.

"They found a body," he began. "They'll need DNA tests to confirm, of course, but they found a locket on it, with "From Aidan to Melanie" engraved on it." He glanced at Lucy and looked away again.

John could see that he was every bit as unsettled as he himself had been, more so, probably. Sherlock did not trust things that could not be proven, tested and measured. Even in his greatest leaps of deduction, he always had evidence to support his theories. The fact that dreams and intuition had led them to Melanie would not sit well with him at all.

"Oh, and Lestrade wanted to know what we were doing there," Sherlock continued. "I told him that Lucy was your latest girlfriend, John, and that you'd come down here for a break."

"And you just happened to come with us, is that it?" John asked in disbelief.

"Well, Lestrade didn't seem to see anything strange about it!"

"No, he probably didn't," John muttered. "Hope you don't mind, Lucy."

"I don't mind if you don't!" Lucy replied with a smile.

"So I told Lestrade we'd gone to have a look at Undershaw," Sherlock continued before John could respond, "and that we found the grave while we were exploring the grounds."

"Good story, Sherlock. If this Lestrade is anything like you, I don't think he would have believed my story." Lucy said.

"No. If anything, he would probably have taken you in for questioning,"

"Sherlock!" John's voice was a warning not to go any further.

"Are you saying I'm a suspect?" Lucy said, very quietly.

"No. He isn't," John replied, "He's just angry because you were right."

Sherlock and John were still glaring at each other when Lucy broke the uncomfortable silence.

"Look, Aidan Crawley's on the telly again," and pointed to the TV on the wall. The programme was a chat show, and the guest was indeed Aidan. It wasn't quite loud enough for them to hear, but Sherlock and John recognised the expressions and gestures, and guessed that he was telling the host the same story he'd told them. The camera went to a photo of Melanie for a moment, before returning to a close-up of a predictably teary-eyed Aidan.

The bartender noticed their attention and came over to join them.

"Sad, isn't it?" he said. "Melanie grew up in this village, you know. She and Aidan often came back for mini breaks, they'd always stay here, too."

"So you haven't seen them recently, then?" Sherlock asked.

"Well, Melanie was here about six months ago, but not Aidan. I did wonder if everything was all right, but then Aidan turned up and swept her back to town."

"Aidan came and collected her?" Sherlock asked.

"In a manner of speaking. He wanted to surprise Melanie, but she'd gone out. He went looking for her and found her up near Undershaw, she always loved to walk out there, and they decided to go back to London."

"So Melanie came back here and got her things, did she?" Sherlock pressed. The bartender looked a little surprised, but replied anyway.

"No, Aidan did, actually. He said Melanie wanted to stay at Undershaw a bit longer, so he left her up there and came back to collect her things and pay the bill. Excuse me, I must serve these customers."

He left, leaving a stunned silence behind him. John and Lucy looked at each other, then at Sherlock.

"When Aidan got her text, he guessed she was here," Sherlock said. "He came straight down and was lucky enough to find her at Undershaw. It's isolated, nobody around for miles, a perfect place for a murder and a hidden grave. No need to worry about an expensive divorce any more. He then made it known that she left him, pretended to look for her and then after six months referred the "case" to me! You heard what he said, "If Sherlock Holmes can't find her, nobody can." When I failed to find her, then all hope would be gone and he could move on to Caroline Cooley without suspicion. Even if foul play were suspected, who would know where to start looking? Oh, very clever!"

"But can we prove it?" Lucy asked doubtfully.

"Once the DNA tests show the remains to be Melanie's, and once the police hear the bartender's story, it will be very hard for Aidan to explain his way out of it," Sherlock replied. "By his own admission he found her up at Undershaw. He came back for Melanie's things, the bartender never saw her again. I'm certain an investigation of Melanie's bank accounts and mobile phone records will show that none of them have been used since the day Aidan came here. That's some pretty strong circumstantial evidence already."

"So now we wait for the DNA tests to come back," Lucy said.

"Yes. Now we wait."

The DNA tests came back positive. The remains were those of Melanie Crawley, and, as Sherlock predicted, once Lestrade heard the bartender's testimony, Aidan Crawley was taken in for questioning. Knowing there was no way out of it, he eventually confessed to Melanie's murder. It was one of the biggest news stories in ages.

"Poor Melanie," Lucy said. She had dropped into Baker Street at John's invitation, prior to their going to the movies, and they were watching the report on the news. "I'm so glad justice is being done for her. "

"If it wasn't for you, it might never have been done," John replied.

"Oh, Sherlock would have solved it eventually," Lucy said, looking over to where he sat at the table, glued to his microscope.

"No need for false modesty, Lucy," Sherlock answered, without looking up. "I might not like it, but your intuition, in this case, was correct. "

"And so was yours," Lucy responded. That did make Sherlock look at her, and with some displeasure.

"Explain," he said.

"John mentioned that you thought Aidan had murdered Melanie. There was nothing that had suggested that to John, but you knew. Just like I knew Melanie was at Undershaw."

"It was obvious," Sherlock said, tersely.

"But you couldn't explain why, could you? Any more than I could explain how I knew where she was. Maybe that's why you were so scathing when I first told you about it. Your intuition was no more provable than mine. You knew it and you hated it. Was that why you took a leap of faith and actually went with me to Undershaw?"

"No. I was hoping to prove you wrong," Sherlock said, returning to his microscope.

"Of course you were," Lucy said drily. "How silly of me to think otherwise. We'd better go, John, or we'll be late for the movie."

A Detective Worth Your Money

by Jacoba Taylor
Albany, New York, USA

So you're looking for a detective
One who's not ever been beat?
I'll tell you where to look, mate
Try 221b Baker Street.

He's the finest on the planet
Yes sir, he's mighty good
He solves crime better than the others
(Though Scotland Yard wishes they could).

His intelligence is truly astounding;
I never met a man so smart
He knows everything there is to know
From violin, to bees, to art.

But he's at his most incredible
When he applies his knowledge to crime
He can deduce from the subtlest of clues
Your riddle will be solved in no time.

And he also comes with a bonus;
A helpful doctor friend
While your man does all the thinking
His assistant sees you through to the end.

You need him to keep a secret?
Just tell him so at the start.
He'll swear his live to secrecy
He'll never tell any part.

This man is also agile
He boxes, fences, and shoots
So he isn't *only *smart
But he's also fair in riding boots.

He enjoys his job quite thoroughly
With his Doctor at his heels
Together they solve all the criminal
And at very reasonable deal.

You have just one question:
Who are these men, you say?
Sherlock Holmes and Watson
Are here to save the day.

The Blind Violinist
by Amy White
Hampshire, UK

Several times I have heard Holmes scraping upon his own violin, often to assist his own thinking upon a case. Tuneless musings, however, were often followed by excellently played and well-known pieces, as if to apologise for the tuneless playing of before. Therefore, when a case arose at the centre of its murderous plot was this instrument; it was only natural for Sherlock Holmes to take it up.

It was around a year after my own marriage, the time when I was least in touch with Holmes. I had received a telegram requesting me at Baker Street. When I arrived, Holmes was curled up in his armchair, wearing a blue silk dressing gown, and sitting opposite him was one of the most prestigious violin players in Europe, Joseph Tsaikov. His long, agile fingers were tapping impatiently on the arm of his chair, and when he entered, he looked up sharply; despite the fact his eyes were a milky white colour. Tsaikov had been blinded by carbonic acid at the age of seven, and the scars still showed.

"I take it this is what we were waiting for, Mr. Holmes?"

"Dr Watson has proved invaluable to me in many cases, maestro. I am hoping he will do so again."

The agitated finger tapping stopped. "In that case, I shall tell you my story. I was sent here by an Inspector Lestrade, who seemed to believe you would handle the case better than he would.

In my house, my study is dedicated to practicing my violin. I leave my Stradivarius locked safely in there each night, and the only keys that exist are in the possession of me and my housekeeper, whom has been with me for twenty-two years and I trust absolutely. Last night, around eleven o'clock, I was aroused by the sound of a sudden cry from my study. I sleep lightly, so I was the only one awake as I rushed to the source of the sound. Fumbling with my keys, I unlocked the door and my foot knocked against something warm. Walking along, I heard gargling, and after about a minute, I realised it was my butler, Worcester, lying on the floor with the Stradivarius in one hand, the bow in the other and an ugly slit at his throat."

Holmes smiled. Whenever this happened, it was rarely good news for everyone. He put his fingers together and rested his chin on top.

"How long has your butler been with you?"

"Since I was a young child. When I moved here, he was the only member of my old household to come with me?"

"What of the rest of them?"

"They chose to stay in their home country."

"Is it definite that the violin and bow are yours?"

"Most certainly. I have had them engraved with a specific pattern so I can recognise them with one touch."

"Who did this work?"

"A good friend of mine, Hans Bolkov. I have known him many years."

"Has your butler been behaving oddly at all?"

"No more than usual?"

"What do you mean?" asked Holmes sharply.

"Worcester has always had a… odd temperament as long as I have known him. I think he had an argument with my parents when I was just starting school, and as such has no warm feelings towards me."

"And yet you still employ him?"

"He is an excellent butler. He is the best of his kind I have ever had."

"I see. Well, Watson, I perceive it is time for us to have a look at the crime scene."

Before we left, Holmes took his own violin case from the table. I didn't ask him about it, knowing he most probably wouldn't answer, so the cab drive to Tsaikov's manor house was in silence. When we climbed out, we were greeted by Lestrade, who rubbed his hands together, partly out of excitement, partly because of the freezing temperature.

"I thought this would be right up your street Mr. Holmes," he wheezed, "what with the violin and everything. Well, it's a neat enough little murder, very well planned too. The butler, Worcester, is in his late sixties, and joined the Tsaikov residence when he was twenty-one. That's the little information I've managed to gather, so I'd be grateful if you'd have a look."

The late Andrew Worcester was killed by a thin but fatal slit to the carotid artery, and the amount of blood loss meant he was dead before any medical help arrived. His hair clotted together in a pool of blood as Holmes swarmed around him, bent double. Using his lens, he examined the wound, the victim's fingers and face, before moving onto the violin and bow still in the dead man's hands. He tested the weight of the instrument, before comparing them with his own violin he had brought along with him. When he lifted both his bow and Tsaikov's up to the light, his face lit up just for a moment before returning expressionless again. He had solved the case.

"Lestrade, I have your men."

"Men?"

"Indeed. Call round to Baker Street in an hour, and I shall hand them over."

"It may please you to know, Watson, that I was definite of the murderer before we even finished our interview with Mr Tsaikov."

"My dear Holmes!" We were sat opposite each other in our apartment, awaiting the arrival of Inspector Lestrade and the men who had caused the death of Worcester.

"The violinist let on far more than he should have."

"You don't mean to say…"

Before I could finish my sentence, we were interrupted by the arrival of Lestrade, Tsaikov and a frail, white haired man who looked as if he had seen no more sun than I had of him. Holmes stood up and gestured to him.

"Gentlemen, may I introduce Hans Bolkov, the accomplice in this dastardly plot of master and servant, where the blinded murderer determined to set up the murder of his butler who blinded him as a child with his cleaning agent, at the cause of an argument with the boy's parents."

"I will not stand here and listen to this preposterous tittle tattle!"

"Hang on a moment, sir!" Lestrade laid a hand on the maestro's shoulder, who had just risen from his chair in a fit of rage.

Holmes ignored this outburst, and turned to the official detective. "Lestrade, I believe you brought along Mr Tsaikov's bow?"

"Indeed, although I can hardly think why you wanted that and not the instrument itself," he handed over, and Holmes lifted the latch which normally released the taught horsehair from one end of the bow. Instead, the tip popped off of the wood about an inch or so, revealing a sliver of shining metal. Holmes slid it out to reveal a long, thin, beautifully crafted sword that was almost invisible when turned sideways. "I give you," he said softly, "the murder weapon. Tsaikov lured his butler into the study, slit his throat, placed the Stradivarius in his hands and raised the alarm as if he had just found him there?"

"But why?" I asked. "You alluded to it earlier, but I confess I am still rather in the dark."

"Aye to that," said Lestrade, nodding gravely.

"Tsaikov told us himself that Worcester had argued with his parents. He also told us that around the same time he had carbonic acid thrown at him. It would not, even as a child, to realise this was the acid his butler used to clean with."

Tsaikov sat down, spluttering with rage. Bolkov, on the other hand, was looking at Holmes with awe and respect.

"You must be magical," he uttered, "to realise such a thing. That, or in league with the devil. How in the name of all that is holy, did you figure it out?"

"With great ease," said Holmes, smiling. He was always flattered when someone noticed his genius, no matter how often it happened. "I first realised that it would have been impossible for Worcester to steal the Stradivarius himself. Firstly, he did not have a key, and secondly, why wait until now to steal it? I have often said that once you have eliminated the impossible, whatever remains, no matter how improbable, must be the truth. The only option left open to me was that the violin had been planted on him. It must have been someone with a key, and the only two in existence were in the possession of Tsaikov and the housekeeper, who had no motive. It must have been him, then. But how to kill him? The method was obvious, and yet there was no murder weapon. I brought my own violin along simply to see how it compared to a Stradivarius, but when I held the two bows two each other I saw that they were not only unalike in craftsmanship and the engravings which made it recognisable to its owner, but due to weight, mass and the sounds it made I foresaw there was a slender piece of steel inside the wooden stem that would match up perfectly to the cut in the butler's neck. The only person who could have added this in was the man who created the distinctive engravings upon it, and so I caught Bolkov in my net as well. I have no doubt that Tsaikov would have liked to have got rid of this weapon, but it would have been no use swapping it with another, as the marks upon the first would be too distinctive to miss. Oh, and my suspicions about the butler throwing the acid were confirmed when I noticed an acid burn on his right cheek, by the ear."

"But he could have got that by cleaning with the stuff," Lestrade pointed out, although he was evidently impressed.

"No, no; the splash pattern on the burn could only have been sustained by it being thrown and a tiny amount, as it always does, flying in the wrong direction."

"Well, Holmes," I said later that day, when Lestrade had carried off the murderer and his accomplice, "that was a rare find. A unique case both in the grotesque circumstances, and the remarkable way in which you solved it."

"I don't doubt," the consulting detective settled back in his armchair, and blew blue smoke rings from his old pipe, "the cases I accept are rarely the mundane. And now, back to the centre of this dastardly plot, but this time in entirely innocent circumstances." And with that, he picked up his own violin and, pipe still in mouth, began to play.

The Constant First Meeting
by William Maulden
London, UK

==IM/2185AD/03/04/21:06GMT==

==IM/FRAGMENT RECOVERED==

Back in training, our instructor said that the only constant is war. I disagree. The other is Sherlock Holmes, my friend.

==IM/CORRUPTED/BOOT INITIAL/SEARCH STRING: FIRST MEETING==

==IM/2183AD/05/23/15:32GMT==

I am still feeling my way around everything. My name is John Watson, I am thirty four years old, and a Doctor. Or rather, I was an Army Doctor.

My experience is an odd mesh of what happened to one person and what happened to another, and it's currently a struggle to align them both, like they are meeting each other for the first time. So it's been suggested I reactive the IM and use it to record thoughts and feelings while I recover from the surgery, and attempt to "rectify both halves of your personality John" according to the Criterion staff. Though they call me 'John' as if it isn't really my name. I guess it isn't.

There is a hazy recollection of a face when I close my eyes sometimes, lingering like the shadow of a bright light that you've stared at too long. Yesterday I felt the face was standing over me, then gone.

This is going to take some getting used to. Especially as I can't sleep at the moment.

==IM/2183AD/05/26/10:04GMT==

So yeah, the last two days have been a learning curve. The IM has had the tactical function I was used to removed, which is good I suppose. No constant bombardment of information anymore, which part of me almost misses. The doctors have told me the surgery should be a complete success, but at the moment I am limping like mad. Anyway, they have set me loose into London, a city I have never visited, in a country I have been before, on a planet I have never set foot on.

Except I have, and I know where landmarks are, and how to get to them by taxi and Mag Lev, while the rest of me marvels like a small child at the place. Oddly the first thing I did was head for the Thames, in the World Heritage quarter, and stand and stare at the Tower of London, Tower Bridge, and The Shard, all built when humanity stayed planted to this world, and now all dwarfed by the Greenwich Sky Hook down the river, disappearing up into the clouds, through the atmosphere, and meeting space. Extraordinary, and so much history. And a constant wrestle, feeling like a tourist when I know it all so intimately and have seen it before, but not with these eyes.

Stamford, who is in charge of my post psyche care, told me to meet him at Saint Bartholomew's Hospital tomorrow. He says he has someone in mind that could help with living arrangements, which is something I know I need to do but am also surprised about. The 'wrestle' doesn't seem to go away. Though at least I am getting tired now, which never used to happen. A few more days and I might actually be able to sleep, and I guess a bed is the best place to do that. As for now, I'm just going to enjoy the city again for the first time.

==IM/2183AD/05/27/09:46GMT==

I got to St Bart's very early to meet my new flatmate. Stamford was waiting already, and took me inside. This is by far the oldest building I've ever set foot in, amazing that it is still standing after all these hundreds of years.

I first met Sherlock Holmes in a laboratory in the basement of the old hospital. He was stood with his back to us, a slim tall man dressed in a two piece suit, in his mid forties, dark hair down to his neck, holding one of the old HL Tesseract Slates. I hadn't seen one of those in about fifteen years, the things used to be all the rage before the IM chips came in. But there he was, using old technology to study something on the desk before him.

Without even turning around, he said "Hello Doctor Watson, how are you?" His slumped shoulders seemed to lift with the words.

Stamford had apparently told him in advance about me, though he had disclosed very little of him to me apart from his name. I limped a little closer. "Not too bad, thank you Mr Holmes."

And then he turned, and the first thing I noticed was a tight smile and twinkle in his eye, which then seemed to harden and disappear almost as quickly as the curious flicker of recognition I felt.

"Welcome to Earth. Quite a change from New Kabul I imagine."

I turned to Stamford, who simply smiled and shook his head. He hadn't told him anything after all.

"How did you know where I was from?"

"Relatively simply. I could make a show of the military bearing you hold, or the slight limp you have from the Hard Light replacements, but mostly the tiny bar code you have on the back of your neck is a giveaway that you have recently been discharged as military property.

Quite a rare and unexpected honour I imagine. The only recent fighting off planet, so I am told by my brother, has been in the main asteroid belt in the Piazzi sector between Mars and Jupiter, where one particular slowly spinning rock that our military are currently fighting idiotic extraterrestrial-believing-cultists for is named New Kabul."

I was speechless. I had a bar code on the back of my neck? I would need to have words with Stamford later. Holmes obviously realised he had told me something about myself that even I didn't know.

"I am a show off. Call me Sherlock, please, if I am able to call you John."

"Of course", I managed to stumble out.

"Now, since we are obviously getting along so well as both of us have need of somewhere to live, you should know that I am messy, occasionally belligerent, and definitely what others perceive as 'rude'. I am stuck in my ways and prefer old technology to new, as you may have seen when you came in the lab. I own a three hundred year old violin and occasionally play it, loudly, at odd times when my brain has no information to process. I am also called on throughout the day and night by the City Police in an advisory capacity, and thus in sum total you may find life as a flat mate less quiet than you may have imagined when you left the hospital a couple of days ago."

"How did you know it was a couple of days ago?" I blurted out.

"Again, those Hard Light Limb replacements you are fitted with. Initially quite difficult to adjust to I'm told. You still feel the itch of the old limb even though the new one exists in the same space, and the adjusted rhythm of your heart to produce the Myocardic Field that generates the replacement is also a counterpoint to normal equilibrium. It's said that it will pass with normal or elevated use, or so the standard copy in the manuals says."

His eyes flicked to Stamford at the last part, then back to mine. I remained slightly open mouthed at the sheer speed of the information he had just spoken. Sherlock turned and picked up a dark brown coat, about ten years out of fashion amongst civilians.

"Since I don't think an extra night awake on the streets is productive for you, I'll meet you over at Baker Street this afternoon, about three o'clock? Number 221, flat B." I nodded, and Sherlock reached out to shake my hand – my real hand. "See you later."

And with that, he was out the door and gone. I turned to Stamford, probably with a slightly accusing expression on my face. "I didn't tell him anything," he said, "though he did request to meet you when he heard you were on-planet." I nodded, slightly stiffly. This is very odd. Now I just have to find my way to Baker Street.

==IM/2183AD/05/27/16:02GMT==

I caught a cab, easy enough really. I can imagine it'll end up expensive if I keep doing it, but I felt in a rush to get to Baker Street and meet Sherlock. When I first arrived I was shocked. After all that polymer and glass off-planet, the simple old brick work of the street was glaring but also slightly comforting. I touched the admission alert pad by the door, and was surprised when the door unbolted and automatically swung open. As soon as it shut behind me, an elderly yet oddly homely female voice seemed to warble from the walls.

"Hello John dear, Sherlock is upstairs waiting for you."

"Thank you" I managed to stammer out in my surprise. Entering the main room of the flat, I found Sherlock seated at a table looking at a sample dish through a magnifier generated by his old HL slate. He looked up immediately, a broad smile creasing his face at once.

"Ah, hello again John."

129

"How did the AI know my name already?" I asked him without further nicety.

"Oh, I took a sample of your skin cells when we shook hands and programmed the admission allowances for Mrs Hudson. Thought it would speed things along. Plus I couldn't be bothered to get up if it wasn't you at the door."

"I see. Mrs Hudson?"

"The building's Artificial Intelligence. I'd imagine you're more used to them being simply functional, but I've found allowing software to go to seed a bit brings in greater free thinking and personality, even if she is only a glorified house keeper."

From the ceiling, or maybe the walls, came "I'm a bit more than that Sherlock" in a kindly yet slightly petulant way.

"As long as you keep the heating on in the winter, that's all that matters Mrs Hudson," said Sherlock to the thin air. He was right, I was used to AI simply being another tool, not something you have to talk back to. I looked around the space of the room, full of clutter and odd random objects and technological antiques.

"You seem to have been here a while already" I said to Sherlock.

"Yes, several years actually. My previous flatmate had to leave, no fault of his own."

"Stamford told me you asked for me specifically."

"Or someone like you," Sherlock replied defensively, "not you specifically. I am used to having a counterpoint view around to my own. Military has proven a good match in the past."

"This is for the crime solving thing?"

"Correct."

"Why on Earth would the Police think to come to someone outside the force for help?"

Sherlock smiled that thin smile again, as if he had been asked this many times before. "You have a military grade IM Imprint Chip implanted in your hippocampus John, as does every member of the Police. I lack one."

"Ok, so they can pull up instant information on anything ever, anywhere."

"Exactly, but reliance breeds laziness. They may be able to access whatever information they need in seconds, but often they lack the intelligence to put two and two together. My ability to think freely and collate data on my own terms gives me an invaluable edge."

"So why do the Police bother to implant the things in their officers then?"

"Oh it's perfectly adequate and even useful for normal, bog standard and trifling street crime. The things the Police come to me with are not normal, bog standard and trifling street crime."

"What makes you think I would even be interested in living here, helping you with this?"

"I never mentioned anything about you helping me, but since you have brought it up yourself, excellent. You are used to being useful, it was what you were bred for I may venture. It is in the very fibre of your DNA. When I saw that a recently returned and invalided soldier had been brought to the Criterion facility, I used my famous brain and concluded it would be a waste to allow you to drift. Everything I bring to you is a proposal of course, I shall leave the decision up to you."

I was on the verge of sitting down, feeling slightly exasperated, when the omnipresent Mrs Hudson appeared again. "Inspector Lestrade is at the door Sherlock."

Sherlock's eyes locked onto mine, the smile never leaving his lips. "Here we go John. Admit him Mrs Hudson."

And that's where we are now. I'm listening to this policeman named Lestrade explain to Sherlock about a body found at the top of The Shard. Murder in a hundred and fifty year old tourist attraction, baffling, public and exposed. And I can understand why he has come here really. They can know everything about the building, its history and significance. Every entrance, every exit, the busiest place for visitor footfall in the structure. But even with all that information, they can't work out how someone could be killed in the place, and then have the assailant seemingly vanish into thin air. But Sherlock probably can. And I think I'll go with him to find out how the perpetrator did it.

==IM/SUFFICIENT DATA RECOVERED/BOOT ORIGINAL
SEARCH ATTEMPT==

==IM/2185AD/03/04/21:01GMT==

I got back to the flat this evening and found Sherlock in oddly pensive mood. The lack of a case may have set it off, as he certainly wasn't having one of his 'episodes'. I walked in and took a seat opposite. His violin was laid to the side. A couple of strings were broken.

"It is odd how people forget John," he said, "that while they all headed off into the stars forty years ago, the Earth didn't really change. Not really. New places to go and new battles of our own making to fight, but back here, crime stayed."

I nodded, wondering where this was going.

"I haven't been completely honest with you John. But I think tonight I should be."

I think it was around then my mouth went dry.

"John Watson died ten years ago tonight. It was not his fault, but it was mine. Or so I kept telling myself at first. In the end, there is no stopping a madman with a gun, just the sheer randomness of fate. James Winter paid for what he did though."

Sherlock paused. His face betrayed no hint of emotion. Instead, he steepled his hands together in front of his face, the finger tips touching, his elbows resting on the arms of the chair. Staring into the space between us, but not focusing on me.

"Before I knew him, John Watson had been in the army as a Doctor. He lent his very being to what they asked of him, which in effect created you and hundreds like you. Physically at least. He retained the essence of himself privately though, mainly due to protest from various parties about the ethics of the process. You were never meant to set foot on Earth as a result, and so when I heard you were in a Criterion facility in London two years ago I was of course baffled. Then of course I realised – Mycroft. Only he would have the clout to place you there, waiting for me to find, and in effect safeguard. So yes, as you may have suspected, our first meeting was orchestrated, but it needed to be. I used to operate alone, but my brother had realised your predecessor's death left a hole that needed filling. I instructed Mycroft to allow you freedom of thought, and gave you the memories of the original John Watson, before he and I met. Though there was the risk that scrubbing me completely from his memory would not be fully successful. I can assume that was the case, seeing how quickly and cleanly you accepted my trust that first day."

He paused after this long explanation, delivered without taking breath. "I hope you do not think badly of me."

I sat for what seemed like hours, possibly minutes, but in actual fact I am certain my reaction was pretty much instantaneous. "No Sherlock," I said through thick, dry lips, "I don't blame you. If you hadn't instantly pulled me into this entire crazy existence I would have been dead within days, or certainly purposeless."

Sherlock's eyes finally focused and locked onto mine over his finger tips. A wry, half smile came to the right side of his mouth.

"There are many constants in this world John, and things we take for granted are the result of those that came before us. Honey is a synthetic, sugary gloop we spread on our dry toasted bread, but in the past it was produced by remarkable insects that humankind used to care for and nurture. Now, even the bees are gone, yet their greatest legacy endures. I took John Watson's friendship for granted, and then one day he wasn't there. I do not intend to make the same mistake again."

I half snorted with laughter at the gall of him. A man who had somehow completely controlled my integration into society had the nerve to tell me all this. And possibly compare me to a dead insect. But then, that is his way.

"I don't believe in second chances," I told him. "But this entire city has no right to be here. Everything here should have been knocked down and redeveloped hundreds of times over, but it's still standing. And thanks to you, so am I." I leant forward out of my chair towards him, with my hand outstretched. The HL replacement one. Sherlock sat still as stone for a few seconds, then moved his hand and took mine, realising the irony of what I was offering him with a smile.

Back in training, our instructor said that the only constant is war. I disagree. The other is Sherlock Holmes, my friend.

==IM/END/DELETE SEARCH==

Vir Requiēs

by Kaylin C. Sapp
Ohio, USA

Cadenced scales and chords discordant
Coaxed from strings, more scrape than tune
Partner with the darkling twilight
Shrouding all in fog-wreathed moon.

Softly now the lamp-light flickers
Casting 'cross that pensive face
Shadows which betray the darkest
Perils of the human race.

A child's hope, a father's burden
A gracious lady's firm behest –
But L'art pour l'art, because the Master
Is not swayed by wealth or crest.

But then! The tuneful musing halts
As convoluted lies take flight.
Sophistry and misconception
Must give way before the Light.

Truth is Light, and his Conductor
Unassuming, strong, discreet –
Stalwart friend and chronicler, he
Guards the sleuth of Baker Street.

Scarlet studies, Games and madmen
Speckled bands but one close call.
Valleys change from Fear to Shadows
Heralding the Final Fall.

An Empty House stands still and silent
Monument to genius gone
But no true hero lies forgotten
While a chronicler lives on.

The Darkest Hour
by Peter Holmstrom
Oregon, USA

It is only through great determination, and the realisation of my impending death, that I have chosen to tell this tale, for it concerns the darkest hour of my life.

With the declaration of war in Europe, I volunteered my services in whatever capacity seemed fit. I do not deny at this late date, that I had believed my service to be one of medical training, or at the worst, tending to the wounded shipped back to England. But as the casualties wounded continued to piled up by the thousands, I was ordered to the front lines, straight into the inferno of the great Battle of the Somme.

This truly was the most horrific experience of my life. The medical station, located within an abandoned church, became less about saving lives and more about expediting death. Morphine was in short supply within the first few days; the most we could do was clean their wounds and direct them to God, for whatever good it did them. The air stank with death. The soil outside became tinted with blood, and the sound of screaming was never far away from our thoughts and minds.

It was on a particularly grueling day in late July, that I obtained the worst single memory I have of the war. I was tending to another of the many wounded men. A piece of shrapnel had punctured his right lung and was protruding through the other side. As I looked down at the young man who was all too young to die, the frequent, and somewhat comforting thought occurred to me that this boy would not have even been alive when I first met my old friend Sherlock Holmes. Our later adventures would have been nothing more than the meaningless screaming of the newspaperman, completely oblivious to the pains and evils of the world. And now here he was, dying on my makeshift-operating table.

My mind went to those years in Baker Street. The comforting fire, the easy chair, which I so often found myself in, and Holmes standing near the hearth playing his violin. A bell would ring, and up would come some poor devil to ask for the help of the great Sherlock Holmes. It seemed like no matter how dire, Holmes could defeat any evil. But Holmes was retired to his bee farm, where I had not seen him for over ten years; and now there was an evil, which even he could not best.

The boy on the operating table died. Screaming and panting as so many do, begging for a miracle that will never come. Blood dripped down my apron, as I watched the life drain from the boy's eyes.

I stormed out of the church, cursing the day that I ever decided to volunteer for this blasted war, when I saw something out of the corner of my eye. As I focused harder, my mind almost thought that I was hallucinating. Across the square that separated the former church from the battered village, stood Sherlock Holmes.

At least, I thought it was Holmes. The man across the way was dressed as an elderly beggar, hunched over and carrying a walking stick. But there was something in the eyes, and the way he walked which made me almost certain that was my old friend.

I could hardly believe my eyes. I walked over with the firm intention of confronting the man. Disregarding the rain and the crowd of people, disregarding the whole war, I needed to see him.

But by the time I moved across the square, the man had gone. I looked around frantically, no doubt attracting the attention of some of the soldiers lingering around outside, but I didn't care. I moved through the crowd and began down the nearest alley, which I thought would be his likely route. The shadows rose around me as I walked between the shattered remnants of the village.

I had just about given up the search, when a hand seemed to come out of nowhere and tug at my shirtsleeve. Turning, I saw the same derelict old man hunched over in the shadows. He spoke some words French that I didn't understand, but there was still that twinkle in the eyes.

"Holmes?" I must have sounded almost desperate, for Holmes began to chuckle almost apologetically.

"Why, my dear Watson, what are you doing in a place such as this?"

I let out a sigh that seemed to encapsulate the weeks of emotional torture undergone in this hellhole. The tension in my muscles fell away as I stared at my old friend, Sherlock Holmes.

"Holmes, you truly have no idea how good it is to see you!"

"And you old fellow, but please I beg you, keep your voice down, for this disguise is not for play." He motioned me to step further into the shadows as we both sat down on a pile of rubble.

I stared at my old friend as well as I could in this dim light. Even through the disguise I could see how the years had treated him poorly since last we spoke. The lines under his eyes and the grey in his hair did not need to be faked any longer. Yet as he spoke, I could tell that his spirit was still as strong as ever, and despite all the years, he was still Sherlock Holmes.

"I suppose you're wondering why it is that I have forgone my quiet life of bee- keeping to come here?"

"Frankly Holmes, you could have come for a cup of for the tea for all I care, I'm just extremely glad to see you. This war has been eating away at me like I could never have thought possible."

Holmes stared at me for a moment and let out a long breath, and after which he pulled out his familiar cherry wood pipe.

"I was sorry to hear about your wife Watson…"

The pain struck through me like a hot needle; on top of everything else, the reminder of my wife's death at the hands of a disease I could not cure, pained me in a way I thought not possible in that city of blood. I swept away a tear, almost feeling glad that I could still feel.

"Tell me the story Holmes. How did you come here?" Holmes smiled slightly and patted me on the knee.

"It was only a few weeks ago actually. I was situated quietly enough in my Sussex bee farm, content to let the war play out without my involvement, when a motorcar came up the drive… Do you have a match old fellow?"

I shook my head; it had been more than a few months since I had smoked anything.

"Ah well, as I was saying… The driver turned out to be my brother Mycroft. You will remember of course that Mycroft's position in the government would have made him quite indispensable through this war. So I knew that this was not a social visit. He came, insisting that I accompany him to the north of France, of all places, on a matter of some urgency."

I could hear the contempt in his voice as he spoke, it was clear that Mycroft had exerted some influence over him.

"We arrived in a small town near the front lines and proceeded to drive directly to an army hospital, without Mycroft letting me know anything of what was going on. 'All I can tell you Sherlock is that there is a situation which requires your experience.'

'The expertise assistance of the bee keeper, I rather think not.'

'Don't be flippant Sherlock, this is a matter of delicate importance.'

'I'm jittering with anticipation.' I sat myself back, as you can imagine Watson, with more than a little chip on my shoulder.

"Upon arriving in the hospital I was confronted with much the same scene as must be common for you, but for me it was more than a little sobering. We were shown through to a private room where lay a man, who had probably once been about five foot six, but now was missing his legs, with the rest of him hardly faring better.

'Why are we here Mycroft?'

'Wait... Lieutenant...Can you hear me?' The man fluttered open his eyes to stare up at the ceiling, but said nothing. I looked at Mycroft, expecting some explanation.

'This is Lieutenant Prendergast, Sherlock. He had been taken prisoner three months ago just outside of Verdunp. One week ago, he managed to escape back across the lines. We found him bleeding out on the fields of Flanders of Flanders, where we believe his most recent wounds were inflected there. Since then he has been in and out of consciousness, yet through his delirium, he has maintained one fact....' Mycroft leaned down to speak into Prendergast' ear. 'Prendergast, tell us your secret you told the nurses.'

"For a moment Watson, I felt that Prendergast might die right there, he was shaking and sweating profusely, but he somehow found the strength as he struggled to find the words.

'I heard em, they thought I was dead, but I heard em...'

'What did you hear Prendergast?.' said Mycroft. At this moment Prendergast lifted his head to stare directly into Mycroft's eyes.

'There's a spy sir... A German spy, on the Somme... We're being ambushed by a German spy!'

'How can you be sure?' said I.

'I heard em talking…Soldiers, passing by me, they didn't know I was there, but I heard em…They mentioned said how they got information from someone on the British lines. They knew when we'd attack… Even before the soldiers did… Thought that was funny they did… That they knew days before those who were gonna be doing the fighting. Who could know that sir? Who could know our own movements before we do?'

"We walked out of the hospital and back into the car; both of us knew to hold our tongues until then."

'Mycroft, I really don't know what you expect me to do?'

'Surely it's obvious, solve the case, find the traitor.' I let out a sniff at the absurdity of his reasoning.

'If what he's saying is true, that the German's know our plan of attack before it moves down to the masses of the common soldier, then there can surely only be four or five people that…'

'This is a delicate situation Sherlock! We have word every day of mutinies occurring on the front lines. Knowledge of an investigation into high-ranking officials might just push things into a massive widespread revolt! This needs to be done quietly, so no one will know. Should you find the culprit, there won't be Scotland Yard to bumble in and take him away. There will be no trial Sherlock, moral for this war is weak as it is. No one can know of this treachery. Do you understand?'"

I stared at Holmes, not really believing what I was hearing. "Was Mycroft asking what I think he was asking Holmes?" Holmes chewed on his unlit pipe steam and stared off into nothing.

"We're treading in extremely dangerous waters here Watson, and the destination might not be a pleasant one."

We sat there in silence for a time, neither of us wanting to speak the truth. The sound of the rain was indistinguishable from the sound of the bullets in the distance, and I wished to god we were still in Baker Street. After a moment, he turned to me.

"And so I ended up here Watson… It became clear with little investigation that the spy must be located at this location; the orders came in from too many different people for it to be from headquarters.

No, it has to be on the receiving end. I took this disguise and came here."

I barely heard this last sentence. A German spy… on our lines, passing information about troop movement and attack plans, could cost England thousands of lives.

"Can I help in some way Holmes?"

"I should like that Watson. I've determined the information isn't being sent via wires, or other more modern technology. So the last two nights I have held vigil over the front lines. Yet so far, I have seen nothing."

"Then I shall accompany you tonight."

"Thank you, my friend. Let us meet here, at around nine, and perhaps together we can stop a traitor, and save England in the process!"

I spent the rest of the day tending to the wounded, actually saving more than I watched die, which gave my mind some relief. I found my spirits to be much improved; the thought of once again chasing criminals with Holmes made even the war seem tolerable for a little while.

At the stroke on nine, I slipped out of the church into the dark, to find Holmes where I had left him a few hours before. He had abandoned his disguise, and was instead now looking more like the old Holmes I had in my memory.

We walked through the shadows, beyond the village, moving ever closer to the front lines. We ended our journey on the side of a hill, from where we could see both the village in the distance, and the trenches holding thousands of young English boys, most of them whom would probably never see come home.

We sat together for a time, finding cover in a outcropping of rocks as we stared out at the barren fields of Flanders. I remember the screams the most.

With the mass numbers wounded in every attack, the General ordering thousands to attack daily, most of the wounded were left where they were. Screaming for a help that would never come. But through all the faint screaming, there was an eerie, hollow silence in the air. The sky was uncommonly clear, and the moon shone down bright onto the battered landscape; dotted and scarred with innumerable puncture wounds from artillery rounds, once beautiful fields were now no man's land. Grey sections of earth probably to never see life grow on it again. I couldn't help but think these thoughts as we sat together, waiting for a sign of treason on that cold summers night.

"Is any of this worth it Holmes? Can any of this death and destruction have a purpose?"

"There is a point to it perhaps Watson, but it is not for us to see. The bleak landscape we see before us, and the horrors you have seen in the hospital, will be used as a symbol. A warning beacon for other generations, to remind them that war is not to a means for the politicians to achieve their ends. From the ashes of this war will come a peaceful, a more conscientious world. That is why we fight Watson. Not for the politicians in Whitehall, but for the well being of the all. And may a better world come from it."

"One can only hope."

Holmes suddenly leaned forward, looking intently into the night's sky, and the expression on his face growing deadly serious. I turned to see what he was looking at, but could see nothing.

"Holmes? What is it?"

"Of course. What a fool I've been!"

"Holmes? What did you see?" I could tell Holmes couldn't hear me. Even through the dark I could see the mind of the great man was moving faster than any others.

"What a fool I've been! Come on Watson! We're running out of time!"

We were sprinting off the hillside before Holmes had even finished the sentence. No longer concerned with lurking in the shadows, Holmes ran at the speed of a man half his age, and with double the determination. I somehow managed to keep up with him, all the while gripping the revolver I had placed in my pocket.

We ran through the night, approaching the village within a very few minutes, ending our return outside the same church which I had left mere hours before.

"Holmes, what are we doing here? Tell me! What did you see?"

Holmes beckoned me further into the shadows across from the church as to give us a clear sight of the entrance.

"I was a fool not to think of it earlier, and had it not been a clear night I would have missed it completely."

"I looked as well, but didn't see anything!"

"It was a mere instant, passing in the direct light of the moon. A bird Watson! A carrier pigeon. It must be painted black as to hide itself in the night. And where would the sound of a pigeon not attract notice?"

"In the tower of a church! Blast it all Holmes, are you telling me the traitor's been under my very nose the whole time!"

"Yes, and hopefully we haven't missed him already."

Our wait was not a long one. Within five minutes, the large oak doors opened, and a man strolled casually out.

"Holmes! It's General…"

"No names Watson! Not even in whisper. Quietly now, we must follow him."

We followed him through the night; right back to his own quarters. I stared at the man in front of us as we followed. The man who had ordered hundreds of thousands of men to their deaths. The man who I believed had our best interests at heart. The man who was a traitor.

There was a guard stationed in front of the General's quarters, but Holmes led us around to the back where a window had had its glass blown out. We stood on the other side of the street, staring at the window, knowing what lay beyond.

Even through the darkness, I could see the look of struggle in Holmes' face.

"I must confess Watson, I don't know what to do."

"Why don't we have him arrested? Surely the name of Sherlock Holmes would convince at least an investigation!"

"No, Watson, Mycroft was right. Were word of this to get out, the repercussions would be calamitous."

The next few moments seemed like an age. I could hardly believe what I was hearing. Sherlock Holmes, a murderer…

"Surely there must be another way?"

Holmes let out a long breath, which I wished to God would have been longer.

"Let me do it then…"

Holmes looked at me for a moment.

"No Watson…"

"He's my commanding officer! And when a commanding officer commits treason, the penalty is death. Forgive me Holmes, but some heroes need to remain pure."

We stood there for a moment, the air itself seeming to freeze with the weight of it. Slowly, Holmes began to nod.

Two days later, Holmes left the front, the General's death being put down to a heart attack.

I must have inquired as to the General's motivation at some later date, for I have Holmes' response specifically noted.

"I cannot know Watson. Perhaps in the end he saw all the death and destruction he himself was ordering, and felt the quicker end to the war was to support the enemy. When one man's sin is another's virtue, can we ever truly know? Can right and wrong ever be truly known?"

A Train Ride to London
by C.M. Vale
Bronx, NY, USA

I'd no reason to think over-much of the matter until, having disembarked from the train at Euston Station, I found the strangest thing in my pocket...

At the time I received word of my father's death in December of 1887, I had been, for nigh on six years, residing in a sleepy Scotland village. There I had taken up a country practice, far away from the grimy roads and venomous air so customary to the great cesspool that is London.

Thus it came to be that, being the eldest sibling and only living male heir to our negligible fortune, the morose task of settling the family's estate fell solely upon my shoulders. The chore promised to be an arduous one, as father's financial papers were always kept in a state of profound disorganisation. It was not so much the inconvenience of being forced to shut down my rather lucrative general practice to make some sense out of the confusion of bills and (in all probability) overdrawn bank accounts that nettled me about the whole business. The source of my irritation stemmed from being kept away from home and hearth during Christmas, which was, incidentally, to be the first celebrated with my lovely young wife, Violet.

She is as headstrong a woman that ever drove a husband to distraction, and so intent was she on coming along, no argument on my part could persuade her otherwise. It was my hope one of us could be spared from the tedious proceedings and spend the season with a proper Christmas dinner alongside a roaring fire in the home of one's closest relatives, but it was not to be.

We embarked upon our wearisome journey the day before, so that on Christmas Eve, arrived at the Oxfordshire railway station, which would take us directly into London.

It proved an awful wait for the blasted train, for despite our arriving promptly at four minutes past seven, the time indicated by our Bradshaw, it was bitterly cold, making the merest moments spent standing idly enough to freeze the very blood in one's veins. There also appeared to be some sort of a commotion further down the platform, as some queer – not to mention obviously disturbed – fellow got it in his head that now was as good a time as any to wander along the tracks. Of course, when the train did arrive, it was held up expressly because of this venturesome individual. Eleven minutes and thirteen seconds worth of hold up, which might have been spent thawing off inside, in the blessed warmth.

Somehow, these goings-on were finally put to rights, though I dare say hushed up is more like it. I cannot tell for sure how the thing was resolved, since despite the lateness of the hour a fairly large crowd was gathering, probably all with the intent of hurrying to their respective families before morning, and blocking my view in the process.

When at last we were allowed to board, I made it a point to ask the conductor precisely what had been going on.

"Strangest thing I ever saw," he remarked. "Some fellow who weren't right in the head was sifting through the dirt, he was, all the while going on about samples he needed for a monograph. I never heard the likes of it in all me days!"

"How irregular," said I, as he brought us to the last available carriage. "What have we asylums for if lunatics are allowed to wander freely?"

He did not know what to make of it either, and left us pondering over what this world was coming to.

It has ever been my preference to travel privately on railway sojourns, short or extended as they may be, for one never can be too cautious, what with all those of unsound mind among us. Our friend taking a leisurely stroll on the rails proved that much.

Thus, I was reasonably perturbed when, upon entering with Violet's cumbersome portmanteaus and my own humble carpetbag, (whilst she twittered with some lady or another) I was met with a scrawny fellow of substantial length already occupying a seat. Well, I say a seat, which anyone would take to mean that of the solitary variety, but this inconsiderate person was sprawled out in such a fashion that his feet had invaded the seat opposite. His confoundedly long legs were a terrible hindrance as I made several valiant attempts at heaving my wife's luggage into the rack. How someone appearing so wanting for a decent meal could overwhelm a space is beyond my understanding.

All the while, a cloud of malodorous smoke billowed out from underneath his cloth cap, which was tipped over his brow. "This is a no smoking compartment, my good sir," I informed him after having taken my own seat, though at least he'd the barest modicum of courtesy to remove his shoes from my side.

However, his reply to my grievance came in the form of a renewed puff of smoke.

It was here that my wife, all danger of having to assist me with her luggage having passed, joined us and my vexation with our travelling companion only compounded. The man, imagine his insolence, gave a most dismal groan upon her entrance, mumbling something or other about the intolerable proclivities of the fair sex.

I was in the very act of opening my mouth to form a defence on Violet's behalf when the fellow broke his silence.

"My condolences on the loss of your father."

"Why, thank... good heavens! How can you know about that?" My mourning band, of course, was concealed beneath my greatcoat.

If this uncanny knowledge of my personal affairs was not enough, to my utter astonishment, he broke out into a chuckle.

"Sherlock Holmes!" I ejaculated, for he'd raised his head and those angular features were instantly recognisable. "As I live and breathe, I never thought to see you again!"

Hoped it, in fact. Ever since I realised the full implications of what I had done to a poor, unsuspecting invalid in dire need of peace and normalcy to heal his strained constitution. It's all very understandable that the doctor would take an interest in such an intriguing fellow with so finely honed an intellect, but to endure his constant company was another matter entirely.

I do realise the man sorely needed to go halves to afford his lodgings, and I did suitably warn him, but how could poor Dr Watson ever know the full extent of the madness he should be submerged into until the two actually cohabitated? Most assuredly, he did not deserve to be thrust into confined quarters with a man who beat corpses to a pulp in the name of science and scoffed at most basic of human emotions. When I thought on the horrors Dr. Watson may have been subjected to in that man's company... well, I could but inwardly wince.

I imagine that, desperate as the doctor was, he was likely cursing my name for years afterwards.

"Nor I," said Holmes, and was that a hint of sincerity in his voice? The next shock of the night came in the form of Mr. Sherlock Holmes extending to me both a hand and a warm smile, offering what was, by his standards, an effusive greeting. Such cordiality was the last thing to be expected from so cold hearted a character. What on earth had warranted this?

"I see you are still up to your old tricks, though the devil knows how you do it," I remarked. "But yes, you are indeed correct. My father has passed on and my wife and I are headed back to London to settle his estate."

"The devil has nothing to do with it, Stamford. What you perceived as witchcraft was in fact my observation of the method by which you tied your left boot-lace and made quite the hash of your shaving this morning."

"Obviously," said I, content to allow him his delusions.

I then proceeded to introduce Violet to my old acquaintance, whom I could have sworn sneered at the mere mention of my marriage.

Never did much care for women, that one. It was no shock he was alone even now, no wedding ring on his finger and probably not a friend in the world. Not that the Sherlock Holmes of my memory had any great want for friendship. He was simply the sort of chap you might have admired for his astounding brain, but held humanity at such a distance, regarded his fellow man with such sheer apathy, that it was impossible to get on with him for any great length. Not the makings of anyone's friend, for who could ever care for such a cold-hearted reasoning machine?

"Tell me, whatever have you been doing with yourself all these years? We were always curious as to what line of occupation you intended on with such... unconventional interests you took."

Holmes gave a soft hum of amusement. "My profession is undoubtedly unique. In fact, I am the only one in the world."

Yes, you certainly are one of a kind, Holmes, you smug, arrogant...

"Oh, you mustn't keep us in the dark," my Violet chimed in. "What exactly is it that you do, Mr Holmes?"

He leant forward, snuffing out his cigarette stub on the windowpane. With no little pride, Holmes stated that he was a "private consulting detective", emphasising his independence from those "blunderers" at

Scotland Yard, mind you. At this self-aggrandising speech, I raised an eyebrow. The man caught my gesture and sniffed.

"A detective? Come now, man. Surely you jest!" I admit to a modicum of unintended cruelty, yet his haughtiness of old seemed to have sharpened.

"I most certainly do not," said he, crossing his arms in a petulant manner. "I have created my own profession, at which I am rather accomplished, or so my faithful chronicler shall attempt to convince you. He does tend to give me more credit than I am due," said he, eyes fairly glittering at the mention of this alleged chronicler.

Truth be told, I was a bit taken aback by all this. Who should take the pains to set down the biography of Sherlock Holmes?

"Really, man. You go too far! Whatever have you achieved to warrant such things?"

Of every possible reply I thought he might make to substantiate this claim, his actual response was what startled me most.

"Nothing." Then, with his usual bearing, continued. "My success is based solely on an elementary class of deduction which escapes the swift wit of the professionals. I've done nothing great, save to rely on a healthy dose of logic and imagination. In fact, I regularly invite Scotland Yard to apply my methods, but this seems to be a most painfully difficult task for that lot to grasp."

"If it is all so simple as you make it out to be, why the deuce would anyone take the pains to chronicle your exploits?"

"Oh, hush, dear. My husband is being unforgivably rude. Surely you have solved some important cases, then, Mr Holmes?"

"Some are of great importance, yes, though I prefer the most abstruse problems to challenge myself, and these are often of little interest to the Yard, or the reporters."

The thought had crossed my mind this was nothing more than a fancy of some deep rooted vanity, and was of a mind to say so, when another fellow burst into the carriage, bringing with him a blast of infernally cold air.

He was a dashing chap of medium height and build, fair haired and moustached, whose very demeanour suggested an amiable disposition. For all he seemed troubled by a limp whilst he struggled with two hands full of overstuffed valises and a medical bag, he ever retained a pleasant smile. It occurred to me this man was vaguely familiar, but I was hard pressed to place who he might be or where our paths had crossed.

"Awfully sorry," he apologised, as with a great effort, he heaved the bags into the rack, and I imagine had a worse time of the task than I had.

Sighing heavily, he slumped down beside the consulting detective, who was preoccupied with lighting a pipe procured from his greatcoat pocket.

"I take it the engineer was a trifle put out," said Holmes whilst he fiddled with a match.

"My dear fellow, he was livid!"

"Unreasonable man."

"Not to worry. Everything's been straightened out, though I think it best to mention he's threatened to set loose his three legged dog if he ever catches either of us on these rails again."

Propriety dictates I not record the response this drew from Holmes.

"I believe," said Sherlock Holmes as he turned his attention back to me, "that you already know my friend, colleague, and lately, chronicler, Dr John Watson. Doctor, you remember Stamford, do you not?"

The spark of recognition shone in those startlingly blue eyes once he gave me a proper look. They were dimmer, surely, the last time we met, but this was indeed the retired army surgeon I'd introduced to Holmes several years ago. Watson had changed considerably, for gone was the nerve wracked, gaunt shadow, his once haggard face glowing with health. He had put on a layer of weight, which bespoke of his former wellness, and certainly that sombre air prevalent that day at the Criterion bar was now replaced by a palpable cheerfulness of spirit.

How he came to manage this in the presence of the world's only consulting detective remains to me one of life's insoluble mysteries.

Impolite it may have been, my curiosity got the better of me. "Not sore at me for introducing you to Holmes?" I ventured, clasping his hand. Remarkably, Watson only laughed and was prompted to wring my hand more enthusiastically at I thought to be a most reasonable query.

"This must be your lovely wife," he gestured to Violet. The doctor always did have the lion's share of manners, which is more than I can credit to the other passenger, who smoked in silence, apparently weary from the exertions of condescending to converse with us mortals.

Over the next few hours, we exchanged pleasant chatter, until the topic of Holmes' line of employ was again brought up. Watson, I must admit, had us listening raptly to the tales of his companion's singular cases, and it was plainly evident what a natural flair for storytelling he possessed. Be that as it may, Holmes could scarce resist the urge to roll his eyes heavenward at regular intervals or criticise those same flourishes and romanticisms, which so piqued our interest, enlivened the tale. Even so, I fancied there were instances when I caught the ghost of a smile leak out from behind that abominable pipe, something I at first mistook for an arrogant enjoyment of having his brilliance flaunted to an audience.

At the stroke of midnight, the train ground to a halt in Euston Station.

"Merry Christmas, Holmes," said the doctor to his friend with an affectionate pat on the knee.

"Bah!" Was what he got for his efforts, though this curmudgeonly response seemed not to phase him in the least.

"What's the matter with him?" I enquired while tugging down my bags. Watson had meanwhile risen to assist me with the chore, never mind that leg appeared to be smarting him fiercely.

"Oh," said he, calm as you please, "He's only upset because the season seems to restrict the criminal element to misdemeanors."

Madness, it appears, is contagious.

Once we made our way onto the platform, Watson took me aside to offer his thanks for the chance introduction, claiming to have been more shattered by the Afghan campaign then he at first realised, that he was not so certain how else he might have survived those wounds whose mark was intangible.

Unspoken words heavy in the air, I confess to being grateful that Mr. Holmes chose that moment to emerge from the train and step up beside me, for Watson never did conclude that dismal thought. He proceeded to make some snide comment about bringing our eminently stimulating evening to a close, affecting a yawn to enhance his spectacular state of ennui. This led to the doctor fussing over his miserable sleeping habits, and we said our farewells soon after, having all four of us shaken hands with genuine fondness.

As I mentioned at the beginning of this long-winded account, once we parted ways with the doctor and that insufferable detective, I was set to consider the incident noting more than a (mostly) agreeable night of reminiscing with old acquaintances, a welcome way to pass the hours on a not so welcomed journey. And then I dug my hand inside my pocket, and found the strangest thing had been placed inside.

A rolled up edition of something called 'Beeton's Christmas Annual'.

On the front page was a bold advertisement for a story within, by one A.C. Doyle, literary agent of John H. Watson, M.D. The story itself was marked off with a note scrawled in a sharp hand. The contents were short and precise, and for some moments I stood rooted to the spot, staring somewhat dazedly at the words I'd read over enough times to have already permanently memorized. I saw then just a fraction of what the doctor must have seen all those years ago in a cocksure student at the lab, bragging over his haemoglobin experiment.

Taking Violet's arm, I read the note one last time, and before heading into a waiting cab, whispered to no one in general, "Merry Christmas."

Stamford,

Consider this a Christmas gift. If I am not much mistaken, in due time you shall find it a very valuable token of our mutual appreciation. Thank you, for having saved two lost souls.

- S.H.

The Adventure of the Exploding Moon
by Scott Varnham
Slough, UK

It was the year 1897 when Sherlock Holmes and I were called to the case of the ship simply called *Moon*, a tale, which has some small points of interest for fans of the art of deduction.

My friend was serenading me to sleep with a violin composition of his own after the conclusion of the Abbey Grange case. Just as I was drifting off into my slumber, my reverie was interrupted by the sound of flat-footed stamping up the 17 stairs of our Baker Street lodgings. Our old friend Inspector Lestrade opened the door to our lodgings and rushed in.

"Please, Lestrade, take a seat. It's a long way from the docks and the earliness of the hour suggests that there weren't many cabs to be had. I expect you're quite well exercised!" my friend remarked.

"Upon my word, Holmes, how'd you know I'd come straight from the docks?" Lestrade looked nothing short of astonished at my friend's casual deduction.

"The matter is simple enough. When I see a man coated in sweat on a cold London morning, I know he's made a great deal of exertion and travelled a great distance to reach me. And when I can detect a distinct whiff of sea air about you, Lestrade, then it's not too difficult to work out where you've come from." Holmes sat back and allowed Lestrade to absorb his deductions.

Lestrade gave me a smug look. "Simplicity itself!" Having played out this tired dialogue many times before, Holmes and I rolled our eyes. Lestrade finally took a seat and stated his piece.

"About two days ago, we received a telegram at Scotland Yard telling us about some strange occurrences on board the steamship *Moon*, which had recently departed from Newfoundland bound for the Docklands. Apparently the engineer had been taken ill after walking into his engine room one morning and seeing a strange white substance all over the walls. When they removed it, they found that more would be there the next morning, more than had been there in the first place. There had also been numerous small petty thefts going on at night.

Apparently they were laying a trap to catch the blackguard on the day before the telegraph arrived but it came to nothing."

At this point, Holmes interjected, "Might I see the telegram?" Lestrade fished around in a pocket before handing my friend a crumpled piece of paper, which he looked at briefly. He rubbed his fingers lightly across the paper before placing it on his desk for later examination. "Pray continue your tale."

"Well, apart from the substance in the engine room, it all seemed pretty run of the mill. This morning, I took a couple of constables down to the docks to await the arrival of the ship. We'd get the passengers to give us statements, maybe search one or two of the ones who looked good for it."

"But I take it that the ship never arrived?" Holmes turned away from the faithful policeman at this point to look for his Persian slipper. I was sitting on it and so said nothing.

"Oh, it arrived. We saw the ship pull in, Mr. Holmes, that is, until it exploded." Holmes turned round as quickly as I've ever seen him.

"It did what?"

"Aye, sir, it exploded. Plodding along into port, merry as you like, when it suddenly burst forth with fire and flame and started listing heavily to the side." Holmes looked rather troubled by this turn of events, so I subtly worked his slipper free and dropped it to the floor. His eyes immediately caught this and he motioned for the slipper. I passed it to him while he asked Lestrade some questions.

"Dreadful business. Were there any survivors?"

"None that we could see. There weren't many people on board anyway; it was a skeleton crew and one or two passengers seeking cheap passage to the Colonies. It's got us baffled. Who could stand to gain from such a thing?"

"I suspected as much. It should be easy enough to check; some manifests may have survived the explosion. Have you had a chance to conduct a proper examination of the ship yet?"

Lestrade let out a kind of half smile at this, something that was rare for him.

"No, I came straight to you. I know how much you like having fresh clues to look over."

"Quite so. It's a strange thing, Lestrade, but you may have presented me the riddle and the solution within the same story." Holmes sat back with a smile and let that one sink in.

"Come on now, man, don't play games! People have died!"

Holmes' manner changed in an instant. He wore a heartfelt look of sorrow upon his face, which was beginning to show his steadily advancing age.

"I assure you that when I make a statement like that, I speak from truth. I do in fact have a working hypothesis, but it will take time to verify. I will need to come down to the ship and take a look around."

"Excellent!" Lestrade ejaculated, "I was about to propose that very thing! Shall we head off now?"

Holmes gave an almost-unnoticeable look in my direction. I nodded my assent.

"If your search is awaiting my involvement, then we shall allow no delay. Watson! Fetch your service revolver, we shouldn't need it but it is better to be prepared, is it not? Ah, I see you already have it." He called our landlady in that loud but melodic voice that she'd grown accustomed to. "Mrs. Hudson? Kindly call a cab for us, post-haste!"

So it was that sometime later, we arrived at the docks. News of this terrible business had clearly travelled fast, and so we had to shove through a crowd of onlookers just to get close to the ship. Once we were out of the throng of people, Lestrade led us to where the remains of the ship lay. Most of the ship was essentially intact, as the explosion (although large) was confined to the one ship and the firefighters were quick to act. This allowed Holmes to have a brief look around the ship, although he had to tread gingerly in some areas. We passed some orderlies with stretchers as they carried bodies out of the ship. I stopped to chat with them about the nature of the injuries as Holmes and Lestrade pressed on. I ascertained that most of the bodies were found with massive burns, but the one they were carrying was found with a wound on the back of his head consistent with being hit by a lead pipe. I promised to pass this information to Lestrade, who wasn't aware of it because he was with us. I paid my respects to the man upon the stretcher and hurried to find my friends.

When I caught back up with them they were in the engine room, which I gathered was the room most affected by the blast. The room was truly a mess: the engine was completely devastated and would never run again, the walls were completely charred and any furniture that was within the room was nothing but cinders upon the floorboards. Holmes was in the centre of the room with Lestrade and a police constable, who was answering questions from Lestrade. Holmes noticed me out of the corner of his eye.

"Ah, Watson. Do come in. Constable Harrison here was telling us that they found a survivor. They're treating him for shock at the moment, but he should be well presently. Did you hear anything of note?"

"According to some of the men I spoke to outside, they've found one of the victims with his head bashed in, in addition to his burns. No doubt the former happened first."

"That would be a natural supposition, Watson. After all, there's no reason to bludgeon him after he's already burned to death. However, it is a capital error to theorise without data. We shall wait for the coroner's report before making the final judgement." I made a note to ask about the potential murder victim in a few days' time, in case it slipped his mind.

Lestrade issued a few orders to the constable, who left and left us to investigate.

"Any luck finding clues, Holmes?" I asked, knowing that he probably hadn't found anything yet. I was proven correct.

"Nothing yet, Watson. We got distracted by the constable. As this room was clearly the epicentre of the blast that took out this ship, let us see where we can get by examining it."

We then set about looking for some clue as to why this dreadful business took place. I had the slight feeling that Lestrade and I weren't going to find anything of note, as only Holmes knew what he was looking for. I tried my hardest to find something to go on, but the room was bare and hardly anything in it was intact. So naturally, it wasn't a surprise when Holmes showed us both up by giving a loud ejaculation where he was looking. We rushed over to look at what he had found.

"What is it, Holmes?" I cried with a tinge of exasperation in my voice. There are only so many times you can be surprised when your smarter friend proves to be better than you in his own field.

"Ah, gentlemen. See along this wall here, there are some slight bits of residue from the strange substance that Lestrade's telegram spoke of. Evidently, the fire didn't burn enough of it. Time to speak to your survivor, Lestrade!"

At this point, we took our leave of the ship and went to speak to the *Moon*'s survivor, a youth called Jack, who was recovering from shock at a local hospital. We called for a hansom cab and were there within twenty minutes. Once there, we were escorted to the youth. He turned out to be a strongly built boy of about twenty or so, no doubt a junior member of the crew.

"Jack, isn't it? You're in awfully fine condition, considering what you must've been through. Can you tell us how you survived this calamity?" Holmes ventured to try and coax his story out of him.

"Well sir, it's like this: I've been pretty down on my luck my whole life, so I was keen to make a change any way I could. I signed up for the ride over in Newfoundland in the hope of getting work in London. I wasn't fussy about how I got there so I just took a low paying, general cleaning job. About the second night, we heard a scream from the engine room. We all rushed down and saw the chief engineer shutting the door, gabbling something about ghosts and ectoplasm on the walls. We took a quick look in there, but our engineer was a dominating fellow and if he told us not to linger too long, you better believe we listened to what he said. He recovered his senses shortly afterwards, and got his assistant to help him remove the stuff from the walls. I'll be darned if there wasn't more there the next day, than there ever was in the first place."

"One moment! Who else had access to the engine room when neither the engineer nor his assistant was in it?" Holmes interrupted him to ask.

"Well, in theory nobody, but the room is unlocked in case the engine needs to be tended to in an emergency and the engineer's nowhere in sight. So I guess anybody could've got in there when he wasn't there." He looked at Holmes as if expecting another question and he didn't disappoint.

"I feel that if we concentrate on ghosts and so on, we're getting away from the real substance of the case. You see every crime must have a perpetrator. This one is no exception. So, continue with your story, but try to leave out the more…sensationalist material."

157

"I guess I can do that, Mr Holmes." The boy took a drink of water before continuing. "Apart from that, it was all pretty quiet. There were some petty thefts but nothing major. All was going well until we started to pull into port. I was standing on the deck, getting my first taste of English air and I heard what sounded like two men shouting in the direction of the engine room. Then the next thing I know, there's a massive explosion close by. I get hurled over the side by the force of it and must've landed on the pier or something. I guess where it counts, I am a lucky man. Then I woke up here."

At this, Holmes thanked the boy and we took our leave. We left the hospital and called for a cab. Lestrade couldn't quite contain his curiosity.

"What about it, Holmes? Are you any closer to catching our man?"

"I know exactly who did it, Lestrade. I just need to find some essential details that I am lacking. I'll be back in Baker Street at seven. Watson, you head back there and make ready for my return. The places I have to go are no place are not for civilised men such as yourselves."

He gave both of us a wry smile at this last comment and availed himself of the cab that we had called. Lestrade had duties to do, so we parted ways there and then as I headed back to Baker Street to catch up on my sleep.

I was fully refreshed by noon, so I spent much of the day writing up notes from old cases and solving Holmes' crossword in the paper (a habit that I developed one day when he was being particularly hard to live with). I was engrossed in this last activity when Holmes arrived, rushing up the stairs with triumph evident in his voice.

"Good news, Watson!" He bounded into the room with a small piece of paper in his hand. "The police have our man. I went down to Scotland Yard earlier and was present for the confession of the evildoer. Of course, it couldn't end any other way."

I took the telegram from him and read it. "'Holmes. Engineer is our man. Found him in local tavern. Thanks for tip. Lestrade.' The engineer is their man? Holmes, what the devil is going on?"

He sat back in his favourite armchair.

"I wasn't lying to Lestrade when I said I had the whole affair solved from the start, barring a few details. It was indeed a dark case." A touch of melancholy had crept into his voice as he began his summary of all that he had surmised. "My first clue came from the knowledge that despite being rendered insensible by a 'ghost', the engineer cleaned the engine room. Clearly he didn't want anybody else going in that room, except him and his assistant. This assistant was the same youth we met earlier today, by the way. Once I had that, the rest was easy. The substance on the wall was wax.

"The assistant got it from the hold in the form of a reserve of candles, while the engineer melted them down. Once the melted wax was ready, the two of them coated the room with it and turned off the boiling furnace for the night so the wax would harden on the walls. When they scraped it off in the morning, they collected it into buckets ready for the same thing to happen again, with more candles added so the process was quicker and covered more of the room. This continued until the last night, when they coated the walls in the largest load yet and then laid a bomb to blow up the ship. The engineer then hid in a secure area of the ship while the bomb exploded, then he was carried away upon a stretcher by some of his friends on land. The evidence of their misdeeds melted away with the fire. However, I found some samples of wax lining the floor at the bottom of the wall and this was enough to confirm my thoughts."

"Good God! The blackguard went right past me! I prayed for his soul!" I was left to sputter more indignant outrages as my friend continued with his story.

"Ghastly affair, Watson. The whole thing was done to kill one man: the Captain of the ship. It seems that the Captain had been a little too free with his affections when they were in America, and one of his targets was the engineer's wife. He took exception to this and started plotting a scheme for the Captain to meet his demise. Our friend the engineer is a most vicious and cold-blooded killer, one who considers ordinary people acceptable casualties. Unfortunately, his vile scheme worked perfectly."

"At least he was caught. He'll be judged in both this life and the next."

"Perhaps, Watson. Perhaps." He sighed heavily, and with extreme effort, drew himself together. "Life goes on. Pass me my shag tobacco. I'll have a quick puff and then we'll pop out to catch a performance of William Tell at the music hall."

That seems like a good place to bring this tale to a conclusion. And that, my dear reader, is how Holmes dealt with one of the vilest killers he met in his entire career on the same day that the crime was committed.

Dust in the Wind

by Daphne Vertommen
Mechelen, Belgium

To others, it might have seemed like an average English dawn. To us – the two figures marching through the green, dewy fields – the virtually alpine mist bore the scent of a fresh and intriguing mystery. We hadn't shared a word since our arrival, but didn't feel the need to. The unspoken excitement I had grown accustomed to over the years was palpable like a faint buzz in the air, thrilling us both to go farther.

During the walk I took a moment to let my eyes roam the breathtaking surroundings. There was nothing but green foliage and spacious heaths all around us, our peaceful solitude only disturbed by the occasional hare racing past. My breathing slowed down and I could hear the sound of birds, hiding in the fir trees just a short distance away. It seemed like such a peaceful, rustic place...

My thoughts were interrupted by a loud "Over there!" and I suddenly bumped into my previously silent companion, who now chuckled briefly. "Are you quite alright, Watson?"

"My apologies, I wasn't paying attention... just getting that London fog out of my throat..."

"Well, do try and keep up, for it seems we have reached our destination.'

Holmes then stretched out his arm to direct my attention to a point in the close distance. I leaned forward, squinting slightly.

"But there's nothing there."

That made the corners of his mouth curl upwards.

"Exactly."

He then dashed in a straight line towards the mystery location, not paying any attention to the aesthetically pleasing surroundings at all. I shook my head, smiling, before I followed him up a small hill that didn't seem to lead to anything but a clearing of the surrounding trees, and eight stone steps with sturdy handrails on each side that had somehow survived the test of time. By the time I reached the terrace, my friend was already investigating the remains of the building that had been there a long time ago, and crouched near the remains of what had quite possibly been a fireplace once.

I accidentally kicked a forgotten, rusty doorknob, which make him turn and give me a most irritated look. I offered him a half-hearted apologetic shrug in return, and made a mental note to keep quiet for a while.

As Holmes resumed his investigation, I made my way in the other direction to have a look at the rubble of various shapes and sizes. I saw dust covering crumbled stones and carelessly thrown graffiti cans, shards of coloured glass that might have been part of a coat of arms once, mouldered pieces of wood with flakes of paint that turned to a thin powder by my touch. I now couldn't help but keep a respectful silence, almost as if we had found ourselves in a church. This abandoned and forgotten sanctuary seemed to maintain a mystery novel aura, which I felt strangely drawn to. Any sound would feel like blasphemy. A look over my shoulder confirmed that my friend was working in an equivalent silence. There wasn't much to see, so I decided to sit and wait for him to finish. Soon I found a somewhat clean place in what had been the entrance hall of the house and sat myself down by the three steps that indicated there had been a sturdy wooden staircase once.

"I don't understand it."

"Hmm?"

It seemed like I had dozed off for a while. Time had passed: the sun had now finally managed to break through the clouds, its soft light intensifying the dreamy colours and turning our current location into a beautifully dystopian kind of painting. I looked up to see him sitting on the stone steps in the middle of the green mirage of a landscape. Holmes' dark figure with slightly hunched shoulders seemed as out of place as the fading brick stones of the long forgotten home. I stood up from my spot near the old staircase to join him, and I briefly surveyed my friend's worried frown before looking out on the picturesque mass of green that stretched out before us both.

"I genuinely do not understand why this happened. Why exactly the house was demolished. It's a mystery I cannot solve. This simply happened, and I can't determine why."

A sympathetic shrug was the only gesture I had to offer him. Every now and then this would still happen. Even after all those years of being a detective, the great Sherlock Holmes could occasionally be puzzled and remain in the dark when it concerned these slightly more complicated matters.

"I mean... didn't people care? Didn't anyone care?"

I looked back and tried to imagine what this house might have looked like once, a long time ago. The safe refuge it might have offered to its residents, the pleasant tales and memories that were now as lost as the house they had been born and lived in.

"I'm certain that some people did," I pondered, "but sometimes caring simply isn't enough. Without a sufficient amount of support you can't possibly achieve the things you want."

We sat in silence for a while, as he seemed to think that over. Then the words started to flow, with only a small hesitation after that first questioning phrase. "Does a residence lose its meaning, its importance, once its last inhabitants have passed away?"

I could only sit and listen as my friend slowly sunk into one of his more philosophical moods.

"I mean, didn't anyone consider the possibilities of this property? So many wondrous events could have taken place here. This estate could have been a place where time stood still, keeping the original design intact as an homage to the very first owners. A private home, serving as a peaceful escape to those who longed for it. Or it could have been a museum or a study centre, providing public access. It could have even been a hotel, or made into separate properties, anything. But now there is just... nothing. No one even cares. No developers' plans, no architectural enthusiasts or adventure-seekers to protect this house from demolition, no one at all. Only a thick layer of dust and silence remains."

His conclusion was nothing but a murmured whisper, barely audible and possibly not even meant for my ears. The words were most likely an accidental escape from his lips, but I caught them nonetheless.

"This house is now as dead as its owner."

I could only nod in agreement, as I couldn't think of anything to add to that. The brilliant mind next to me kept going in silence, providing itself with the rest of an undoubtedly most interesting discourse. I gave Holmes a few minutes before standing up with a loud sigh.

"We should head back," I announced. He looked up at me, now shaken from his thoughts and no longer locked away inside his own mind. I could see how a slow smile started to spread.

"Yes… yes, right you are. I believe we should."

And without looking back, we walked the fields until we both disappeared underneath the cover of the trees, vanishing silently like two ghosts. It was as if no one had been there at all.

The Adventure of the Family Heirloom
by Jo Lee
Leeds, UK

I have recorded many stories about the adventures of my close friend Mr. Sherlock Holmes, and I am sure you will all remember the terrible tale of how my friend met his end at the great Reichenbach Falls. It was three years after these events that I was finally reunited with him, and in that time I learned much, which I owe to the man, I then thought dead.

I have never before penned any stories of my own life in this time, due partly to the concern of my wife, that such activity would bring back unpleasant memories for me, and in some way increase my grief, and partly, I believe due to a sudden feeling of self-consciousness whenever I attempted to write them down. They do, after all, show myself to be rather cleverer than I ever realised before, and I often feared this might come across as pompous, or pig-headed when expressed on paper. Regardless of this however, I believe that in order for records of my time with Mr. Holmes to be as complete as possible, this story must be told.

It did not occur to me, in the first few months after that adventure I entitled 'The Final Problem', that regardless of the disappearance of my good friend the consulting detective, and with him having taken with him the consulting criminal, Mr. James Moriarty, that there would still be a call for Sherlock's services in his absence. It was mid-morning in late July when an elderly gentleman came to my practise, not as a patient, he said, but as a client. He was a tall, balding man, with a grey beard, grey suit, and large, thick lensed spectacles. He introduced himself as Mr. Herbert Morrissey. He said he had a case, which he required solving, and in the absence of Mr. Sherlock Holmes, wondered if I might be willing to help him. I only one further appointment that day, which was not difficult to postpone until the next, so I agreed I would hear his story, and attend the scene of the 'crime', but I was very careful to warn him that I expected I would be of little use.

The man was a bookbinder by trade. He lived alone, but was visited regularly by his niece, of whom he was very fond. She had been searching among the piles of books around his house for a particular Austen volume, and had stumbled across 5s 2d in small coins arranged neatly in a square, and sandwiched between Charles Dickens' 'A Christmas Carol' and Bram Stoker's 'Dracula'.

She enquired of her uncle as to why the money was kept in such a peculiar hiding hole, and he soon realised that in their place should have been a large volume of 'The Complete Works of Shakespeare' worth roughly 5s 2d. The book was of a highly rare edition, but in terrible condition. The front cover hung from the spine by exactly fourteen strands of 3 different materials, the book having been repeatedly re-bound and repaired. There was the small ring of a teacup stain on page 312, and pages 394 through to 427 were held together by an unidentifiable black substance, which had a tendency to stain the fingers of whoever tried to prise the pages apart.

Mr. Morrissey, realising the triviality of his upset, as the book had been paid for after a fashion, and was really worth very little, compared to pearls of jewels, decided not to bother the police with his difficulty, and, remembering reading my accounts of Holmes' adventures and tragic end, wondered if perhaps I could help him.

I pondered what my response should be for a long time, during which Mr. Morrissey patiently waited for my verdict, sipping his tea politely. I began to wonder what Holmes would think of my actions if I were to turn a man down. It slowly occurred to me that he would most certainly be disappointed in me, "Have you learned nothing of my methods?!" he would ask exasperatedly. That is why I agreed to accompany my new client to his home in the East End of London.

As we made our way along the winding streets of London, and our taxi wobbled and clanked, I did my best to recall as much as I could of what Holmes had taught me in our time together. The first thing he taught me at our very first crime scene (which I documented under the title 'A Study in Scarlet') was to be watchful for footprints or other ground mark as one came near to the area. With this in mind, I called to the driver to stop at the end of Mr. Morrissey's road, and we approached the dwelling place on foot. The street was paved, as was the path to Mr. Morrissey's front door, and there had been no rain recently, however I did notice a rather forlorn looking group of pansies under the ground floor window to the right hand side. The rest of the garden was spotless. The damaged flowers were a considerable distance from the path, so far that I conjectured that no man or animal would have been able to jump such a distance without causing damage at another point in the bed before the path. I did wonder for a short time if perhaps the mark were just there by some coincidence, and irrelevant to the case entirely, but the pristine state of the rest of the garden belied that surmise, and I was reminded of Holmes' words upon how rarely it would be beneficial to a case to put the greatest clue in one's arsenal down to coincidence.

"Oh!" exclaimed my client, as I enquired about the nature of the damaged flowers, "I have not noticed that before, and poor Miss Jackson (my niece) is usually so careful with the garden. The peculiarity of this business is surely affecting her more than she will show."

Leaving me to ponder his comments, he dashed inside, calling for his niece to come and greet me. I followed, perhaps a little more soberly than my flustered client.

Miss Jackson Mortimer was the second child of Mr. Morrissey's late elder sister, Irene. She was short, and of moderate build, with long blonde hair which reached almost to her waist when plaited. Her face gave an impression of pleasantry and kindness, but as we entered the room, I having caught up with the ageing bookbinder, she was leaning over a large photo album, and her face was contorted peculiarly in a mixture of grief, anger, and pain. She was clearly very absorbed in the object of her upset, for she did not notice our entering the room until my companion greeted her.

The girl looked startled, and jumped high out of her seat. She was quick however in rearranging her face, and a quick glance at her uncle told me that he had either failed to notice her previous expression, or was choosing to ignore it.

Miss Jackson had apparently been wondering if some time spent studying the family albums might distract her from the disturbance of the queer recent events. I decided not to query the matter at that time.

Mr. Morrissey showed me the room from which the book had vanished, and I asked for fifteen minutes of time spent there alone. He complied willingly, and I lost no time in leaning out of the window as far as I might, to closer examine the damage to the flowerbed underneath. It did not take me long to confirm my suspicion, the missing book was partially buried beneath a section of long grass cultivated, quite possibly especially for that purpose. Else it was an excellent chance for the thief that such a growth existed exactly where it was most convenient for them. I was quick to rule this out. Any ordinary thief would not have deposited the book in such a place so trustingly. Mr. Morrissey had mentioned before that Miss Jackson would usually be the one to tend to the garden, so it was logical to assume that she would have been able to set everything up which was necessary to complete her 'crime'. The main problem was that she was lacking in motive. I was not left to ponder this for long, as I heard the door open softly, and stood up to find Miss Jackson, staring in trepidation at the volume between my now sticky thumbs.

"I get the impression you have something to tell me?" I try to keep my voice calm, remembering the cool tones of my tutor in such business.

"Give me the book, and twenty four hours" she said, "I promise you will be understanding of my predicament, I have done no wrong... I only wish the keep the peace." A shine of gold about the young woman's neck caught my eye.

"Stand still, for a moment, if you will." I ask, trying to appear indifferent. Miss Jackson nodded silently, and I approached her, wearily. I replaced the book in the reeds first however, unsure where else would be suitable, as I was unsure of my next course of action.

As I replaced my sticky black handkerchief in my pocket, I used my left hand to lift the gold chain just visible around the young lady's neck, under the collar, and reveal a small, round locket.

Upon its opening, the golden shape revealed the pictures of two women. One, the elder, was on her own in a tall chair and holding a much newer version of the volume currently lying in the long grass below the window. In the picture it was in far better condition, with just a hint of yellow around the pages, and a few creases in its spine. The younger woman on the opposite side was accompanied by a tall young man at her shoulder, and a bundle of cloth, presumably a babe, clutched protectively against her chest.

"This is you?" I asked gently, pointing to the bundle on the left image. Miss Jackson nodded, mute from the tension.

The woman was presumably her mother, I could see the resemblance, and the man was her... brother perhaps? It was too young to be Mr Morrissey, by the time Miss Jackson was born, he would have been at least twenty, probably slightly more. It was difficult to judge, but further enquiry showed the elderly lady with the book to be Miss Jackson's grandmother, on her mother's side.

The value of the book was therefore explained, and as a family heirloom, I was satisfied that no further damage would be done to Mr. Morrissey or any other of his precious books within the day. I returned to the window, collected the book from the flowerbed, *again*, and placed it in Miss Jackson's tentative hands. Having informed Mr. Morrissey I would return the next evening with any further news, I retired to my home, and did my best to dwell no more on the matter. I did not want to come to any further assumptions, based entirely on judgement and conjecture. I was confident that tomorrow would bring before me all the relevant evidence.

I was right. At two pm the following day, Miss Jackson called. She was nervous, but healthy, she had clearly not slept as well as usual. I hoped she had not suffered too much anxiety by my movements.

I was of course, careful to have my revolver prepared in case of any trouble —my time spent with Sherlock Holmes had shown me how deceptive appearances can be- but I was careful not to make known that fact, not wishing to alarm my guest, who was clearly already on edge. Without any attempt at introduction, my guest began her story.

"My father was in the navy, he died about three months before I was born. Before that, he and my uncle had been good friends, *really* good friends. "More like brothers than in laws" grandma used to say. Anyway, when dad died, he left everything to my mother; Uncle M didn't get a single set of cufflinks. He didn't resent it, not at first.

"When I was in my teens, his money began to run out. His bookbinding business was failing, and he was forced to move house... He was too proud to ask for money, but he often dropped hints that he would accept a loan if it was offered him.

"Mum was never much good at subtlety, 'say what you mean and mean what you say'... it summed her up pretty well. I don't think she ever noticed Uncle M's hints. He thought she was ignoring him. He stopped visiting as much, and the family drifted apart.

"Shakespeare was Grandma's favourite author. I never understood why, like Uncle M, but Mum, and Tom both shares Grandma's passion. Tom's my brother. When Grandma died, she had written no will, everything automatically passed to Uncle M. Mother begged to keep the book, her only memento. Uncle refused; after all, she had never given him anything.

"For five years, mother forbade us to mention him, or his unkindness, and she died still missing her precious works. Uncle came to the funeral, and I spoke to him. He'd forgotten about the book, and was upset mother had not maintained contact with him. It was his way not to intrude or pester; he had assumed there was a good reason for it, and that she would explain when it was all over.

"I told him about the book. He got rather angry about it, said it was all very silly, and stormed out. I left it a week, and then went to visit him at home. Once I'd earned his trust, Tom said I should try and get the book back. The old man had forgotten it again, or appeared to.

"The thing is... when you spend so much time with someone, you get rather attached to them, and I knew he didn't forget about the book, not really. He missed mum far too much. I decided I'd take it, but I'd pay for it, buy it off him. I had it all planned: the hiding place in the garden, the money, I was just trying to keep the pile steady when he came in. I quickly made up a story about looking for an Austen, and finding the coins. I knew he wouldn't forget the book. He knew it was missing immediately. You have no idea how quickly he left the house. He came back a few hours later with you."

I sat back in my chair, unsure how to deal with the difficulty presented.

"OH! Please don't tell uncle M it was me who took it, it would so upset him! I would not want to lose his trust."

Suddenly the woman opposite me was in floods of tears and I had no understanding of what to do about it. I considered telling the old man his book was lost for good, and presenting it to Miss Jackson as the sort of rightful owner, but that seemed wrong somehow.

"I don't see that I have any choice" I did my best to be gentle, "where does your brother live?"

I left Miss Jackson with Mrs Hudson on my way to visit her brother. He was a tall man, young, but balding. I told him the whole tale, and asked if he would be willing to go without the book, for the sake of his sister's peace of mind. The boy refused, he had paid for a book that was already rightfully his, he claimed, and he was not going to give it up to his horrid uncle without a fight. I did my best to chastise him, but he would not stand down, and I was forced to take the whole news back to my client. I was saved such a difficult task however, as his niece had already explained everything to him. He was not upset, as Miss Jackson had feared, in fact, he was outraged. Not at her however, but at the brother. Once Mr. Morrissey had been calmed down, I retrieved the book from its place in the flowerbeds, it was now wet from rain in the night, and the pages stuck together.

One look at the volume's sorry state had Miss Jackson once again in tears. Mr. Morrissey's expert eye declared the book beyond repair, and with a short glance for confirmation at him, I took the book into another room, and left it on a table there, with a mind to return later to get rid of it.

There was no need however. Mr. Morrissey thanked me, and showed me out before I had chance, with the promise that he had plans for the heavy volume. I received a wonderful letter from them both a few weeks later, explaining that they had sent the original book by post to Mr. Jackson and purchased a new, readable copy of it for themselves. Mr. Morrissey promised me free service if I was ever in need of his literary help, and he became a close friend of mine, and his niece.

Upon reflection, I do not consider Holmes would have taken on this case, declaring it 'boring' and 'obvious'. For me however, it was one of my favourites.

The Owner of the Green Leather Gloves

by Michelle Erkers

Mora, Sweden

It was nearly ten o'clock in the morning when Holmes and I arrived back in London from our visit to Dulwich. The weather was superb for a morning in April, and I found my friend sitting with a satisfied smile on his curved lips. Despite the night's work all weariness left me as I caught some of his happiness.

"No doubt you have seen something I have missed," I remarked as the train rolled into the station. We collected our belongings and stepped off the train into the sunshine sparkling with the London dust.

"Now now, Watson, I have seen nothing you haven't. However, I look upon things with a different mindset than you do. The gloves, Watson!" he smiled as he drew out the two gloves in fine green leather from his coat pocket. He turned them inside out, and waved the intricately sewn initials R. M before my eyes.

"The victim's name was Gregory Barnes. There is no R. M. in his name. The owner of these is a fellow with these initials. He must have left them in Barnes' sitting room. Well-off, judging by the fine leather, and the perfect handiwork, and I doubt they are a gift."

"Well done, yes, I do believe you're quite right. They are not a gift. R.M. bought them himself less than a year ago, and values them highly. He has no children, but is without doubt pursuing a lady; the glove has the scent of a lady's perfume. Look, there are long coarse brown hairs stuck in the buttons, he must own a dog. Watson, I must ask of you a favour. It is of the utmost importance."

Holmes turned and stepped in front of me, blocking my way. The look in his eyes was intense. I immediately knew he was very keen to follow this lead as soon as possible. Without hesitation I asked what it was he required me to do.

"I need you to follow a man for me, while I work elsewhere. He ought to be here somewhere. He has a blue riding jacket, looks quite shabby, his long hair is streaked by grey, and he walks briskly for a man of his age. I saw him several times in Dulwich. It could take some time,

172

perhaps all day. Are you willing to do that?" Holmes asked, clutching the bag in his hands quite fervently.

With no desire to decline, as I had little else to do, I accepted the task. Holmes nodded, and told me he would be away for quite some time. Without a word of good-bye he strode off in the opposite direction, heading back to the railway station.

Keeping the description fresh in mind I sat down on a bench and let my eyes wander over the faces of the people passing me. It wasn't long before I finally spotted a shabby man in a blue riding jacket heading my way. He fit the description to the letter. I did my best to look inconspicuous as I watched him take a seat on a bench quite far from me.

After watching him read the newspaper for some time, I found myself relaxing in the warm sunshine. My mind began to wander back to the room in which poor Detective Constable Barnes had been poisoned the day before. His rooms had been searched, but since the mess was minimal the perpetrator must have found what he was looking for quickly.

The old man stood unexpectedly and my eyes followed him as he dashed across the busy street and into the telegram office. I pursued, keeping my distance, yet fearful that I could lose him. To my relief he showed no sign that he had noticed me, and was blissfully unaware of my intentions.

As I slipped into the telegram office behind him, I heard a few snippets of conversation between the man and the clerk.

"Thank you again for your assistance, and I need this to be sent to him immediately. Thank you," the man said in a loud burly voice.

He waited impatiently as the clerk sent the telegram, paid, and then left with me at his heels. I watched him turn down a side street then I halted at the corner for a while to give him some distance.

This particular man was not very easy to tail. He made plenty of twists and turns on his way throughout the City, Westminster, and into Camden, and I had the feeling he thought he was being followed. Precisely as Holmes had described he had a brisk pace for an old man. At a corner of Acacia Road he walked into an employment office. I felt it best not to seem too keen to follow closely at his heels into the second shop he passed, and decided to wait outside.

Tied to a lamppost outside was a large brown dog. It sniffed friendly at my legs, and I stroked it between its ears. I noticed it had a fancy green collar, and stooped to take a closer look. My hand stilled as I saw the familiar initials. R. M.

Understanding dawned on me. The man I was tailing must be R. M., owner of the green gloves found at the scene of the murder in Dulwich. The scene of the seemingly motiveless poisoning, of a Detective Constable of the Yard. I finally understood the urgency of my job.

The bells chimed noon and not long after a young man walked out of the office. He untied the dog and walked away down the street. I felt slightly disappointed that my theory had proved itself to be faulty. A few seconds later the old man came back out from the office, stretched his back like a cat waking from a nap in the sunshine, and walked off briskly in the same direction as the previous fellow.

The third place he entered was a pleasant Italian restaurant near the south corner of Primrose Hill. Once again the dog stood outside waiting for its master. By now I was feeling hungry and decided to have a bite while I observed him.

An hour passed, and another. Suddenly the old man waved his hand at a fellow sitting alone at a table next to him. I recognised him as the owner of the dog outside. The other man joined him, and they conversed quietly for a while like strangers until they seemed to relax into each other's company. By now I had finished my meal, and felt I had to order a pint to make my stalking less obvious.

I started feeling that there was something here I did not fully understand. Perhaps the dog did indeed belong to the old man, and the young man was simply out walking it. But why would they have sat apart while eating?

Before I had emptied my drink the two men stood up and left together arm in arm. My curiosity peaked. This case was turning out more intriguing that I had at first anticipated.

The men walked at a leisurely pace through Regent's Park, talking closely. I started to feel silly, and my distance to them grew, as I feared discovery amid the open landscape. Most of the day had now passed, it was nearing four o'clock in the afternoon and I had not yet received any important information that could distinguish this R.M. as a criminal.

We stopped at a gentleman's club some distance east of Regent's Park. I was running short on cash and only just afforded admission. I found the two men sitting quite close to the ornate stage, on which a group of striking young women were dancing ferociously, their vividly coloured dresses flowing graciously around them as they danced to the frankly abhorrent violinist.

I watched the dog owner clutching his walking stick tightly. The old man was grinning as he leaned over and whispered something in the young man's ear. The remark made them both chortle.

By now I found myself wondering what Holmes was doing, and what exactly it was he wanted me to find out by trailing around London after this old man. I had noticed no criminal behaviour; in fact, he seemed like a perfectly ordinary gentleman.

Inching closer I managed to catch snippets of their conversation but neither said anything peculiar. The old man made the occasional dry comment about the loveliness of the dancers, but he lacked feeling and seemed distant, while the other sounded very excited. This was not unusual in itself and did not attract my interest for more than a moment.

The time was nearing six when we finally left. I was starting to feel weary. Lack of sleep and the rather vigorous walk was tormenting my leg, and my thoughts wandered to the comfort of our sitting room in Baker Street. How lovely it would be to have a glass of brandy and a nap.

I hauled my bag off the floor and turned to follow the men out, but as I looked around they were nowhere to be seen. Hurrying outside I looked everywhere for any sign of them. The dog owner was walking down the deserted street, but I had lost my target. Oh, Holmes would never forgive my carelessness!

Just as I was starting to head back to Baker Street I caught a glimpse of a blue riding jacket. I sprang into the darkness behind a pile of crates just in time to avoid being spotted by the old man passing mere feet away from me.

The man hurried along down the road and I followed closely behind. I knew he had discovered me but I was intent on not losing him again. The vibrant riding jacket was a stark contrast to the murky brown and grey of the city and I found it easy to spot in the dusk. To my great disappointment however the man was very nimble and agile, and led me down many a deserted alleyway until I no longer knew where I was.

I followed him over a high fence with great difficulty. On the ground a small distance from where I had landed I found a small piece of paper. Picking it up, I scanned the alley, but the old man had vanished.

'*Well done, Watson. You will be rewarded when you return to our rooms. S'* the note read, in Sherlock Holmes' familiar handwriting.

Glad for the hunt to be over I picked up my bag and retreated down another alley. Subsequently I found my way back to familiar territory.

Before long I unlocked the black door to 221b Baker Street and walked up the stairs into our rooms. Holmes was not there yet; he must still be chasing the man. My leg was aching and I stretched myself out on the sofa, not bothering to remove my dusty coat. I removed my hat and ran my fingers through my grimy hair, as I pondered what had become of the old man whose identity I was no longer sure to be R. M.

Just as I had poured myself a small glass of brandy the door flew open and the ragged man in the blue jacket stumbled across the threshold.

"You!" I yelled as I scrambled for my pistol. The man froze and started to chuckle. I stared as he removed his hat, then his hair and beard...

"Holmes! Was it really you?" I said, so astonished I fell down on the sofa. "I spent all day chasing you? Why?"

Holmes hastily took off his disguise, and I was pleased to see the man I knew beneath the appearance of a strange old man. "I will explain, I just need to wash my face first."

I helped Holmes rinse the dirt and glue off his face revealing his weary self. We had just sat down on the sofa, each holding a glass of brandy, when Holmes started narrating his incredible story.

"Believe me, I did not do it out of spite, I merely felt you needed some exercise in following people. Your skills have grown somewhat crude lately. While you have been following an old man, the same old man has been following R. M. His name is Richard Moss, an accountant with a villa in Camden Town, a dog you befriended, and a lady who does not return his affections, no matter how hard he tries to buy her heart with trinkets and splendour."

He took a pause in which he gulped down half his brandy and I stared at him in amazement.

"Mr. Moss is the man we're looking for. Lestrade is across town on a fool's errand; he seemed to think the letter from Ms. Dawson was something to go on. Mr. Moss has murdered three people over the course of two years. In the telegram office I asked them about him, and apparently two years ago he was destitute. Apparently he had, and still has, a proclivity for the drink, and pricey companions."

Holmes proceeded to recount how Mr. Moss had talked the poor Detective Constable Barnes into changing his will. The poor soul had no idea his will left all his worldly possessions to his accountant, Mr. Moss.

"He has done this twice already before Barnes? That's horrible. How did you know?" I gasped.

"Remember that poor old woman in Hampstead who was poisoned nine months ago? She had recently changed her will, but it was nowhere to be found. Same thing with that retired navy captain nearly eighteen months ago. That is how he has earned his living and his villa in Camden. I told Mr. Moss to come here tonight for his gloves. He will indeed..."

A single ring on the doorbell almost made me jump. "Fetch the handcuffs, quickly! Here he comes!" Holmes strode over to the window and peered out.

I hurried into Holmes' bedroom and fetched the handcuffs. Upon my return to the living room I found Holmes sitting on the sofa and our guest lying prostrate and unconscious on the floor. Our guest was unmistakably the owner of the large brown dog. Richard Moss, the accountant.

"Wait here while I call on Lestrade. He would put up a terrible fight so you must restrain him," Holmes said as he drew on his coat and left.

The Adventure of the Broken Book
by Pamela R. Bodziock
Monroeville, PA, USA

I have never known my friend Sherlock Holmes to hold a grudge, nor to bear any ill will towards those who may have wronged him. Given his position as the foremost consulting detective of the age – a position which, by its very nature, resulted in an ever-increasing number of enemies and rivals swearing revenge of the blackest sort – it would be unsurprising, and perhaps understandable, if even a mind as coldly logical as his would, on occasion, turn to thoughts of resentment for any of his myriad foes. And yet, in my long years of association with him, nothing seemed to be further from the case.

Therefore, my surprise was considerable that May morning when I accompanied Holmes to a small village in Surrey to meet with our newest client. It was somewhat unusual for us to be seeing a client outside of London without ever having first received them at our Baker Street rooms for a consultation – but such was the nature of Holmes's quietly black demeanor during our journey that I knew this to be an unusual case in many respects.

Our destination was Undershaw, a private residence that proved to be of stunning and unique design. We awaited our host in a sumptuous entry hall, some two stories tall with a grand fireplace. "Holmes," said I at last, ignoring the dark look my friend had been stricken with since we'd set out from London, and was now turning in my direction. "Who is it that we –"

But before I could finish the question, our client had entered the room. There was a moment of silence, and I watched with some surprise as a flicker of quick-changing emotions passed over my friend's face – recognition, hesitation, something akin to uncertainty – before his features settled into an expression of oddly cold anger.

"Good day to you, Mr. Holmes," the gentleman said, casting a nod in my direction. "It has been a long time, has it not?"

"Eight years," said Holmes, as I raised an eyebrow in surprise. "Or three, depending on one's reckoning."

"Indeed," the other answered, with a curious note of sadness in his voice. Our client was a great giant of a man, his height rivaling that of Holmes himself, with a thickness of limb and body that far exceeded that of my friend. He was finely dressed in carefully tailored attire – though his most notable feature was that of a great walrus mustache, which was neatly groomed and hung across his face like a banner of honor. Or at least, it would have been such if the man's face had not been set in such an expression of utter disconsolation.

"I must confess, receiving your summons surprised me considerably – a feat which you, of all people, should appreciate the difficulty of," said Holmes.

"And I must confess myself still somewhat surprised at having asked you here," said the gentleman quietly.

"Holmes, you know this man?" I asked, glancing between the two of them with some small confusion.

"'Knew' might be the operative word, my dear Watson," returned Holmes. His eyes remained fixed on our client, and there was a chilling fury quite unlike anything I'd ever seen on my friend's face. "Our acquaintance with one another has lessened considerably in recent years."

"Perhaps I should introduce myself," the gentleman said to me, coming towards us with hand extended. "My name is –"

"Please, allow us to skip such pleasantries," said Holmes coldly. "Tell us why we've come."

Our host hesitated but a moment. "Very well, sir. I have requested your presence here because I ... need your help."

A long silence greeted his words. "Surely you are not serious," said Holmes at last.

"Would I ask you here, after all these years, only to make a jest such as this?" the other returned. "It's no joke, I assure you."

"Then I regret to inform you that my associate and I are taking on no new clients at this time." Holmes was already making for the door. "It was a pleasure to see your lovely home –"

"My dear Holmes." Our host clasped his hand upon Holmes's arm, and though my friend's expression did not waver, I who knew him so well could see the flicker of emotion buried deeply in his eyes. "Perhaps I've no right to come to you asking for help, but I simply do not know where else to turn"

"And I tell you I cannot help you!" Holmes cried, with a passion that would have surprised me had I not been measuring the growing fury in his eyes. "The bond between us has been severed by your own hand, doctor, and no amount of speeches will repair that damage."

"Holmes, who *is* this man?" I said, unable to bear my friend's anger without understanding its cause. "How come the two of you to know each other?"

"How I know him, and who he was to me at one time, is of no consequence," said Holmes, shaking off the other's grasp upon him. "Know him now as who he has become to me – the man who contrived with Professor James Moriarty to fling me into the depths of the Reichenbach Falls!"

I gaped at my friend's declaration. "This man was in league with Moriarty?"

"It was he who set Moriarty in the center of his criminal web, who gave him the tools and resources he needed to control his empire – and who led Moriarty on the path to find me. The man you see before you, Watson, is, if truth be told, the mastermind behind the mastermind. I would not be guilty of exaggeration if I were to proclaim him the creator of a madman!"

The reason for Holmes's unaccountably dark mood had become clear. There had been some deeper relationship, that of acquaintance or colleague or even, perhaps, friend. Our newest client was not merely a criminal, but a traitor. "And now you, sir, an associate of my friend's greatest enemy, come to Mr. Sherlock Holmes asking for help?" I demanded.

"I come not knowing where else to turn," said the gentleman whom my friend had called a doctor, before turning to Holmes. "We have had our differences in the past, but surely you will not deny that I have attempted to make amends. To, if I may be so bold, resurrect you from the fate I had so coldly laid in store for you?"

"No doubt," said Holmes, but his face and voice were stone. "Then I suppose you will suggest that listening to your request is the least I can do for the man I owe my life and career to, even if you remain the very same man who once attempted to solve the 'final problem' of both?"

I understood little of what Holmes may have meant by such words, but our host seemed to relax just slightly. We soon found ourselves seated in the gentleman's study, a spacious room which nonetheless appeared to be closed in on all sides from the endless bookshelves surrounding us.

"You may be aware that I commissioned Undershaw to be built several years ago," began the doctor, smoothing his mustache to either side in a well-practiced gesture. "It has become home to myself and my family, but our true attachment is to its Surrey location. The dry weather and healthy climate are a requirement given our current situation." His mustache seemed to sag slightly at his words, as if the man was plagued by some internal thought, before he continued. "I need not dwell upon the subject; I only wish you to understand the necessity of my family remaining at Undershaw at all costs."

"I understand, to be sure. Pray continue, doctor," said my friend, his tone unreadable.

"Quite, Mr. Holmes." Our client cleared his throat, shifting slightly in his seat. "The trouble began several weeks ago. I was in my study alone when I stepped out of the room to retrieve a pipe which I had left in the drawing room. I could not have been gone for longer than three minutes, and yet, when I returned, it was to find a dozen of these books, their covers slashed and pages torn, strewn in piles upon the floor.

"This would have been a baffling incident in its own right; someone's idea of a cruel joke, perhaps. But of further disturbance was the impossibility of the event. I was gone, as I say, but a very few minutes, and I was alone in the house at the time."

It was Holmes's turn to shift slightly in his seat. He was not a fidgety man by nature, and I took his movement as a sign that his interest was being drawn into the unusual development quite against his own wishes. "As the damaged books were editions of your own work, I expect you kept the volumes despite their ruin?"

"Yes, I thought –" Here our client broke off, starting slightly, and then gave my companion a half-smile. "And yet I did not mention to you that the books in question were of my own writings. Though I should not go so far as to say that such a deduction from yourself is of any great shock to me."

I looked at our client in surprise, wondering now at his apparent status as both doctor and author.

"It is the most elementary of deductions; had they been someone else's work, you would have described their destruction as vandalism, not a prank," said Holmes, with a carelessness that I knew to not be entirely legitimate. "But as you mentioned that your trouble 'began' several weeks ago, I take it that this is not the only unusual circumstance of the past fortnight?"

"Indeed not," said our client, looking grim. "Two days later, the fireplace was found stuffed with the worst kind of rubbish, the flue closed behind it to trap the smoke. The stink proved impossible to rid the house of easily. And it continued. The doors and main staircase have both been defaced, although fortunately the staining did not prove permanent. Perhaps the worst damage has taken place in the drawing room – the game trophies have been slashed, and the walrus tusks on display are cracked. Some of the windows, which are of particular pride to myself and my family as they bear our coat of arms, have been smashed –"

"Have you any clear theories as to suspects or motive?"

"There is no one to suspect," said our host, spreading his hands. "The servants were either out or otherwise occupied when each of the incidents have taken place, and there has never been any sign of forced entry."

"You are not – forgive me for asking – considering a supernatural cause?" asked Holmes, with a peculiar sharpness.

Our host managed a small smile. "I am not ruling anything out, good sir. Is it not you yourself who have often remarked that, when all impossible explanations have been eliminated, the remaining improbability must be the truth?"

Holmes raised an eyebrow but said nothing. After a moment, our client sighed. "I do not know what to think, Mr. Holmes. I can only say the damage seems to be coming from inside the house itself – yet there is no one within these walls to suspect."

A gleam appeared in Holmes's eyes, an expression quite familiar to me. "Allow me to examine the house more closely."

We started, at Holmes's insistence, with the drawing room, working our way through the rest of the house in turn. Holmes examined it all with his usual attention, running a hand over the stains of the doorways and examining the gashes torn into the game trophies. He spoke not a word until we arrived back at the study, and then only to request a closer inspection of the damaged books.

I had just taken up our client's offer of a cigar and was in the midst of lighting it when Holmes gave a shout of triumph. I turned along with our host to see Holmes, standing before the shelf with a book in his hand.

"I have had my suspicions from the beginning, but this marks such conjecture as fact," said Holmes. He held the broken pieces of a book out towards us, and I had time to glimpse only the word *Return* upon a shard of its cover before he had snapped it back upon the shelf. "Let us proceed to the lowest level, shall we? As it is the only remaining area of the house we've yet to search, I believe we'll find our answer there. We'll most likely require a candle – and, Watson, be sure to ready your revolver."

We made our way into the basement, Holmes holding a finger to his lips for silence. As we reached the bottom of a narrow staircase, out from the silence came a sudden dull thump. As one, we whirled to see an ominous figure crouching in the corner. Before the intruder could make a further move towards us, I had stepped forward with revolver raised.

Our quarry froze in the half-darkness, and I gestured with the revolver for him to take a place against the wall. Our host raised his candle higher as our prisoner complied, and my heart leapt as I took in the cruel blue eyes beneath the deep-lined brow – the face of a man I remembered all too well.

"As I expected," said Holmes serenely. "May I present Colonel Sebastian Moran, right-hand man of the late Professor Moriarty?" Moran's eyes flashed with murderous fire – not for Holmes, but rather for our client.

"How did you know, Holmes?" said our host, gazing in astonishment at the colonel.

"And how is it possible?" I asked, my revolver still trained upon Moran. "The doctor – forgive me, sir – was himself once in league with Moriarty. How did you know the vandal was another of Moriarty's gang?"

Holmes gazed with a steady intensity upon the snarling ruffian. "Because, while our client may have had dealings with Moriarty, the doctor's tenuous loyalty to his partner-in-crime extended no further than that – certainly not to a thug such as Moran."

"But the villain could have been anyone," said our client, his face set in an expression of utter bewilderment. "What made you suspect —?"

"You said it yourself," said Holmes, speaking over his shoulder to our host. "The crimes could only have been committed by someone within the house. If not the servants, only one possibility for a culprit remained who could pull off an 'inside' job – a character of your own creation, sprung from within the pages of the very book he was so eager to destroy."

I gazed at Holmes quizzically, but our host seemed to understand my friend perfectly. "But, to know it to be Moran?" the doctor asked.

"I had my suspicions the moment I saw the state of the game trophies in your drawing room," said Holmes. "Moran considers himself, first and foremost, a hunter. A man who so values the joys of the hunt would see it as the ultimate insult to destroy another's prizes. But my theory was confirmed when I examined the row of defaced books. All were damaged, but only one was torn in twain: *The Return.* The book in which Moran's fate was born – and in which my own was returned to me."

"Moriarty trusted you!" Moran spat the words out at the doctor. "You'd hatched the perfect scheme to rid the world of Holmes forever. And then you had to go back on your word! You had to resurrect the thorn in the side of every criminal in the world!"

"But why attack my home?" said our host, and there was more perplexity than anger or fear in his eyes. "If a hunter such as yourself truly meant to kill me, surely –"

Moran's snarling fury cut him off. "I meant not to kill you, Dr. Doyle. Merely to ruin you – as you have ruined me!"

"You thought to destroy the tranquility of Undershaw, and so to sabotage the peace of mind and inspiration which, as an author, our friend Doyle has found in this place," said Holmes, and I realized, with a start, that it was the first time Holmes had referred to our client by name.

"I thought to end that inspiration before he can bring about the death and ruin of any more honest criminals, Mr. Holmes," said Moran. "Would that I had acted more swiftly."

"Would that you had, indeed. And now, friend Watson, perhaps you would assist me in leading the colonel upstairs as we await the arrival of the local constabulary?"

Later that evening, as we were readying ourselves for the return to Baker Street, Holmes turned once again to our host. "I must ask, Mr. Doyle – were you disappointed to learn your mystery was not the work of a formerly-known departed spirit after all?" And in his words, I heard some deeper, unspoken challenge within, as he leveled his gaze at our host.

"You mock my beliefs, Mr. Holmes," returned our client, but there was a gleam of something like affection in his gaze. "But surely you judge me too harshly. After all, one never likes to think ... that one has completely lost a friend."

Holmes studied the author, and I saw a moment of understanding pass between them.

"I was wondering if you and your associate might be available for future consultations?" Doyle went on, a small smile playing beneath his mustache. "There is another most peculiar case which has come to my attention, concerning some unusual circumstances in Norwood ..."

"I should be most eager to look into the matter for you, Dr. Doyle."

We took our leave then, but I am pleased to be able to say that, from that day forward, my friend Mr. Sherlock Holmes and I were not infrequent guests at the house known as Undershaw.

A Case of Murder
by Carla Coupe
Silver Spring, Maryland, USA

Sunlight streamed through the windows in our chambers as Holmes and I sat reading and smoking post-luncheon cigarettes.

A brisk rap sounded on the downstairs door.

"Are you expecting someone?" I set aside my newspaper.

Holmes glanced up. "No."

A moment later, Mrs. Hudson ushered in our visitor. A lady of middle years, she displayed an intelligent expression and air of competence.

"Mr. Holmes?" she asked as we rose.

Holmes bowed. "This is Dr. Watson, my Boswell as well as my colleague. Please take a seat and tell us of last night's tragedy."

Her hand pressed to her heart, she grew pale and swayed. "Do you already know of it?"

Alarmed, I joined her. "Please, madam, sit down. I will have Mrs. Hudson bring tea."

"Thank you, Doctor." She sank into the chair with a sigh.

Holmes resumed his seat and crossed his legs. "I know nothing more than the fact that you are widowed, that you succored an injured man last night, and that you caught an early train to London this morning."

She nodded. "You are quite correct in all respects, Mr. Holmes. I know of your reputation, and should not be surprised at your perspicacity. But first thing's first. My name is Mrs. John Maurice. I must confess that I have very little money, but I will find a way to pay you..."

As Holmes dismissed the need for payment, I rang for Mrs. Hudson and requested tea, then returned to hear her tale.

"I am housekeeper for Dr. Henry Undershaw. He is a decent man and dedicated physician. Several years ago, Mr. Dennis Velope, an old friend of Dr. Undershaw's, offered to purchase the doctor's home and land. However, the doctor refused to sell, and they had a falling out.

"Until yesterday, Mr. Velope would not let the matter lie. He uttered constant threats against Dr. Undershaw."

"How did the doctor respond?" asked Holmes.

"It distressed him greatly, for they had once been quite close."

Mrs. Hudson entered with a tray, and Mrs. Maurice accepted tea with a grateful nod. I watched her colour return, and indicated to Holmes that he could resume his questions.

"What happened yesterday?" he prompted.

"The doctor received a note, and he informed me that Mr. Velope would call that evening to mend relations."

"Was Dr. Undershaw surprised at this news?"

"Stunned, I would say. Mr. Velope was not known for changing his mind. In fact..." She hesitated.

"Yes?" I said with an encouraging smile.

"Well, speaking plainly, he is a stubborn man with a vindictive nature."

Holmes looked pleased. "My investigations would be much simpler if all my clients were as truthful. Pray continue."

"Last night, I met Mr. Velope at the door. I scarcely recognised him, he was that changed. His face was sallow and drawn, and his eyes deeply sunken. I showed him into the study, and as I walked away, I heard the door being locked."

"What did you do then?" asked Holmes.

"I returned to my sitting room. It was late, but I did not feel comfortable going to bed. Not while Mr. Velope was still in the house." She pressed her lips together. "A good thing, too. Not a quarter hour had passed before I heard a terrible clatter and a series of thumps coming from the doctor's study.

"I rushed to the door, but it was still locked. I heard raised voices, then a scream. I tried to use my keys to open the door, but my hands shook, and it took several tries to fit the key into the lock. I finally got it open."

I sat forward. "Good gracious! What had happened?"

"The room was a shambles. The mahogany reading table overturned, chairs tipped on their sides, papers strewn across the carpet." She shivered. "I saw the doctor, lying still as death before the hearth. My heart stopped, I was that stunned! Then I saw Mr. Velope face down across the window seat, a knife in his back and blood everywhere." She paused, hands clasped tightly in her lap. "The sight gave me a turn, it did."

"No wonder!" I said. "It must have been dreadful. What did you do?"

"I ran to the doctor. When I saw him take a breath, I was so relieved!"

Holmes held up his hand. "Please describe the state of the doctor's clothing."

With a puzzled expression, she said, "It was wrinkled, but otherwise unremarkable."

"And his hands?"

"I noticed nothing unusual about his hands."

"Thank you. Please continue."

"I called to Cook, who was in the kitchen putting bones to boil. She roused the boot boy and sent him to fetch the constable.

"I checked Mr .Velope's pulse, but he was gone. " She wrinkled her nose. "I've seen death before, gentlemen, and I know it's not pretty, but he was a sight! His face all contorted, and he smelt horrible."

"Horrible in what way?" I asked.

"It was a sweet odour, almost sickly."

Holmes rose and crossed to the hearth. "Did you notice the odour when he arrived?"

"Yes, I am certain I did."

"I see." He nodded slowly. "When did the constable appear?"

"Within the half hour. While we waited, I had the gardener carry the doctor to the front parlor." She looked at me. "I could not leave him on the floor, Dr. Watson. Not with Mr. Velope's body still there."

I nodded. "I'm certain you were very careful. Had he regained consciousness?"

"Well, not to say regained. He was agitated, mumbling, and when I spoke to him, he didn't respond. He had a lump here," she pointed to her right temple, "and bruising on his face.

"I sat with the doctor once the constable arrived. Goodness, there was such to-ing and fro-ing, with telegrams to this person and to that, the arrival of more police, all traipsing in and out of the house.

"It was almost dawn, and the doctor was stirring, when there was a knock and a man entered. He said his name was Athelney Jones and he was from Scotland Yard." She made a soft sound of disgust.

"From Scotland Yard he may be, but he is no gentleman. He brushed past me and shook the doctor's shoulder.

'Wake up,' he said. 'I have questions for you, my man.'

"Well, I soon sorted him! He left the room with a flea in his ear. Imagine, trying to bully an injured gentleman, policeman or not!"

"Quite right, Mrs. Maurice." Holmes' lips twitched as if suppressing a smile.

"We should all be fortunate enough to have such a protector," I said.

Her cheeks flushed. "Of course, once the doctor could speak coherently I sent for Mr. Jones. He would not allow me to stay while he questioned the doctor, and Dr. Undershaw, soul of kindness himself, told me everything would be all right."

Her eyes filled with tears, and she withdrew a handkerchief from her reticule. "But it isn't, Mr. Holmes! I had not been out of the room for more than five minutes when Mr. Jones came out holding the doctor by his arm. The doctor told me he was under arrest for murder.

His face was as white as milk, save for the bruises. He said he didn't recall anything of last night, but had faith in Scotland Yard's investigation. He also asked me to send a message to his family solicitor. And then that Mr. Jones took him away, still unsteady on his feet with a terrible headache, I'm certain."

"Why did you decide to come to me?" said Holmes.

"I have read of your skill in matters of detection. I told the maid not to tidy the study when the police were finished with it and took the first train to London, determined to consult you. Surely if anyone can prove the doctor's innocence, it is you! And now," she said with a nod, "I put the entire matter into your hands, Mr. Holmes."

The three of us caught the afternoon train from Waterloo. Although a trap waited for us when we disembarked, the journey was so quick we could have easily walked to Dr. Undershaw's house. Holmes gave the lovely Georgian building and well-tended garden a cursory glance before hurrying inside. I offered Mrs. Maurice my arm, but she gestured for me to follow Holmes.

I found him in the study, kneeling beside the hearth, studying a corner of the brass fender. I glanced about the room, still in disarray, and crossed to the gory window seat, where Velope's body must have lain. Rusty brown bloodstains covered the cushion and pooled on the floor. The window itself was fastened shut and flanked by heavy shutters.

As Mrs. Maurice appeared beside me, Holmes rose, his keen gaze sweeping the room. He went to the sideboard and bent over two wineglasses, still sticky with their dregs. After studying the Tantalus, he strode to the window and subjected cushion and shutters to several minutes of intensive scrutiny before clapping his hands together, a brilliant smile illuminating his expression.

"Mrs. Maurice, you were quite correct: The good doctor is innocent of murder, and thanks to your prompt action in consulting me, I shall prove it." Ignoring her cries of surprise and pleasure, he continued, "Do not move so much as a particle of dust in that room." He turned to me. "Watson, we must catch the last train. Tomorrow we shall return with Inspector Athelney Jones and reveal the truth of the matter."

That evening, Holmes refused to discuss the case even in the most oblique manner, so I quashed my annoyance and enjoyed the splendid food and drink at Simpson's. The following morning, I met Holmes and the inspector at Waterloo. I never did discover what inducement Holmes used to persuade Athelney Jones to accompany us, but it was effective.

After we settled into our compartment, Althelney Jones scowled at Holmes, who stared out the window and quietly smoked his pipe. The inspector turned to me.

"Come, Doctor! The man was found practically driving the knife into the murdered man. He is obviously guilty. Surely you will drop me a hint about what you have discovered. Mr. Holmes insists on remaining mum, but I know you are a fair man and will not leave me in the dark."

I smiled. "I'm afraid I can't help you, Inspector, for I know no more than you. You know how Holmes enjoys his surprises."

Despite the inspector's near-constant grumbles, it was a pleasant journey, and I enjoyed the walk from the station to the house.

Mrs. Maurice greeted us at the door. Holmes declined her offer of coffee, although Jones looked as if he would have been glad of a restorative. Leading us into the doctor's study, Holmes paused in the middle of the room.

"Now, Inspector," he said with great good humour, "oblige me with your reconstruction of last night's events, based on the evidence and your interview with the doctor."

"You brought me all the way from London to tell you what I already know?" He snorted. "Very well, Mr. Holmes. I shall give you facts, despite the doctor's supposed lack of recall. The victim arrived around ten and was shown into this room. As stated in his note, he had come to make amends, and the two gentlemen enjoyed a friendly glass of wine. Note the empty glasses on the sideboard." He pointed to the goblets. "They talked, but the doctor would not accept Velope's apology. Their talk turned to argument, blows were exchanged, and in the course of their struggle, furniture was overturned and papers scattered.

"Angered beyond reason, the doctor grabbed the knife that served as his letter opener and plunged it into Velope's back. Velope's outflung arm hit the doctor, who fell back onto the fender, striking his head and losing consciousness. Velope expired almost immediately."

Jones gave an emphatic nod. "Those, gentlemen, are the facts."

"Excellent, Inspector! Really, a remarkable reconstruction," said Holmes.

"That is the sort of skill experience grants," said the inspector with a pleased smile.

"Of course, your conclusions are almost entirely wrong, based as they are upon preconceptions and superficial observations."

Ignoring the inspector's indignant reply, Holmes continued.

"In one instance you are correct: Velope did arrive at ten. But he did not come to make amends; he came to place his old friend in the exact situation he is in at this very moment. Consider, Inspector! Mrs. Maurice states that Velope was a changed man: gaunt, with bad colour. Watson, would you hazard a guess at his condition?"

I started at Holmes' question. "Not without more data; though it sounds as if he suffered from a chronic, debilitating illness."

"The exact nature of his illness is immaterial. Suffice it to say, Velope was not a well man and in considerable pain, for he had chosen to smoke a small quantity of opium before arriving."

"Opium?" Athelney Jones shook his head. "You cannot know that he smoked opium."

"The smell, Inspector! It is quite unmistakable. Mrs. Maurice commented on Velope's sickly-sweet odour, and indeed the smell is still perceptible in the cushion on which his body lay. He did not smoke enough to fall prey to the lassitude that characterizes heavy opium use, but used an amount sufficient to ease his pain and allow him to proceed with his plans."

"And what plans would those be?" The inspector crossed his arms over his chest and glared at Holmes.

"To have Dr. Undershaw falsely accused of murder."

Athelney Jones' befuddled expression was almost comical, although I shared his astonishment.

"But Holmes," I said. "There was a fight, the evidence is plain. And you cannot get past the fact that Velope was stabbed in the back, he could not do that himself."

"Indeed!" cried the inspector. "The facts support my theory!"

"Ah, but he *did* stab himself in the back," said Holmes. "Dennis Velope was a cold-blooded killer who wanted Dr. Undershaw hanged for a murder he did not commit."

"Then what actually occurred?" I asked.

"The evidence clearly tells the tale, gentlemen. Velope arrives and is greeted by Dr. Undershaw. Velope asks that they not be disturbed, so the doctor locks the door. Almost immediately Velope stuns him with a blow to the head. The doctor falls by the hearth, and Velope is free to continue his arrangements."

"Why not kill Dr. Undershaw while he was incapacitated?" I said.

"That would be far too straightforward a revenge. No, Velope was a vindictive man. I suspect he discovered that he would die of his illness soon, and he wanted the doctor to suffer. So he waited until the household grew quiet, occupying himself with reading the doctor's private correspondence and drinking wine."

"But two glasses were used," said the inspector.

"One man may drink from two glasses," Holmes said. "Remember, Inspector, that he wished the police to believe that the two men were having an amiable chat. Once the household grew quiet, he took the letter opener and wedged it, blade pointing out, in the shutter bracket—you can see the scratches where the handle rested—and then proceeded to overturn the furniture and shout, as if a fight had erupted.

"This is the point where the man's true nature displayed itself," continued Holmes, his expression grave. "For he stood with his back to the window, the point of the knife resting against his jacket, and threw himself backward onto the blade. With his last breath he raised himself high enough to free the handle from its cradle, then collapsed onto the seat, dead. If you study the shutter, Inspector, you can see the dried droplets of blood where it sprayed during that desperate thrust."

Athelney Jones hurried to the window seat. He frowned at the shutter, and then turned. "This is all very well and good, Mr. Holmes, but I will need more evidence if you wish to prove the doctor innocent."

"That is easy enough," said Holmes. "First, a close inspection of the letter opener's ivory handle will reveal scratches that correspond with those made by the shutter's bracket."

"How did you know of the ivory handle? Did the housekeeper tell you?"

"There was no need," said Holmes. "Traces of ivory remain on the shutter hardware. He must have adjusted the letter opener until it was in the correct position for his purposes. Second, you saw Dr. Undershaw last night; did he have any blood on his hands or his clothes?"

The inspector's frown deepened. "No."

"Given the pattern of blood spray on the shutter and the position of the letter opener in his back, it was not possible for the doctor to stab Velope and remain unmarked. Velope committed suicide in such a way as to condemn his former friend to death."

"Good God," I whispered. "The man was mad."

The inspector stared at the window seat for a long moment, then drew a deep breath. "Mad or not, Doctor, he received the fate he deserved. I don't like to admit it, but you have convinced me, Mr. Holmes. I shall return to London on the next train and see that the charges against Dr. Undershaw are dropped."

"Mr. Holmes, Dr. Watson!" Mrs. Maurice clasped my hand again as we stood at the door. "I cannot thank you enough for all you have done." Holmes bowed, and then started down the drive.

"It was our pleasure," I replied, freeing my hand with no little difficulty. "And I shall be forever grateful that you gave Holmes the opportunity to save Undershaw."

The Doll and his Maker

by Patrick Kincaid □
Coventry, UK

> So please *grip* this fact with *your cerebral tentacle.*
> *The doll and his maker are never identical.*
> - ARTHUR CONAN DOYLE

When Herbert proposed to me, I had to put on a little act of
astonishment, replicating a girlish squeal I'd once heard in the theatre. It
made him gape with laughter, and I saw the silver in his molars. Who, I
wondered, had given him that sweet tooth: the medical father or the
dead mother? More likely, it had been some menial, charged with
bringing him up. Anyway, it was what he said next that made me cry out
in earnest.

"Steady on, old thing," he said. "I shan't be leaping for joy
when you drag me along to meet your mother."

"But she's not a famous author."

"Famous or not, the old boy's hardly interesting. That's rather
the point of him, isn't it?"

We drove into the South Downs the following Friday, chasing a
late summer sun. I laughed dutifully at Herbert's jokes, bellowed out
over the engine's roar, and clung to my seat as he tore into the country
lanes. The crooked ways straightened beyond Rotherfield, and for a time
we cut through sculpted fairways, before plunging into a forest of new
pine. And at the crest of a hill we found the mock-baronial pile for
which we here headed: an Arts and Craft confection in crimson brick,
with a crest above the oaken double doors.

"The house a spectral hound built," said Herbert, hopping from
the car. "Not at all what we firstlings were used to."

"You didn't live here as a child?"

"Certainly not. I grew up in a house, with bay windows and
gables, not a bally castle!"

A man of rich complexion came out to carry the cases, and
Herbert called him Billy. I looked for some trace of the innocent
pageboy he'd once been, but only saw signs of a middle-aged

debauchery. Beyond the double doors, in the high hallway, we were greeted by a boy of thirteen in knickerbockers and a jersey. "It's Bertie and his girl," he cried and dashed through another oaken door, deeper into the fastness. We followed him, entering a modern mead hall decked out with divans. The hearth alone might have housed a family from the London slums.

"This ragamuffin's Edward," Herbert said, clipping the boy's ear. The boy winced and punched at Herbert's belly. "What's that on your cheek, ragamuffin?"

There was a purple mark there, corresponding in shape to a flattened hand. "Papa did it."

"And what did you do, ragamuffin?" Herbert made to clip the boy's other ear.

The boy ducked. "We were waiting in the car for Mama, outside the vicarage, and I saw a lady come out of a shop who looked exactly like a pig. Honest, Bertie, she had a snout and everything! Well, I said to Alexa, 'Look at that ugly woman.' And Papa turned in his seat and swiped me. 'No woman is ugly,' he said."

"He really is a terrible old Victorian," Herbert told me. "Not that you didn't deserve it, ragamuffin. By the way, this is…"

"I know who she is," the boy yelped, and shot out another door.

Herbert shook his head. "His mother's spirit, I'm afraid. Now, I suppose you'll want to tidy up, old thing. I've a telephone call to make, but Billy will show you up to your room. See you back here in half an hour?"

And with a kiss he left me to the superannuated boy in buttons. As I was led up red-carpeted stairs and along a dark-panelled corridor, I listened out for signs that the man of the house was home. All I heard my guide's wheezing. He left me at the door of a room as bright as the rest of the house was dismal: not an item of furniture or inch of wall in it, but wasn't festooned with pink and cream flowers. When I'd counted to twenty, I stepped into the dim passage again, and stood with my head cocked, like a spaniel's. It was foolish of me: I'd read that my quarry still favoured pen and ink, and so I knew there'd be no clack and rasp of a Remington to lead me to him. But within a minute I heard a light cough. I followed it to where the corridor branched, and found a door ajar. There was more dark wood inside, upholstered with red leather now, and cases of neatly ordered books, and an ornate desk with a green-shaded lamp on it: I was put in mind of a Harley Street consulting room. My host was sat with his broad back to me, and I watched him dip his pen in the inkwell and write the last lines at the bottom of a leaf of foolscap. His hair was white, soldier-short at the neck and thinning at the crown. When he laid down the pen and opened a draw, I assumed he was after more paper—but he pulled out a revolver instead, and calmly turned it my way.

"My children learn from an early age to avoid me in my study," he said, "my servants always knock, and my wife is not due home until five o'clock. You will slowly push the door open, young lady, and step inside."

I did so, and saw my shadow move on the wall to the right of his desk. "I didn't wish to disturb you."

He rose from his chair, and the gun remained steady, as if it were on a tripod. "Then you have not been successful."

"I should have introduced myself."

"On the contrary, you should have waited to be introduced."

He was exactly what I'd expected: a progression from those images I'd studied as a girl in The Strand Magazine. Tall, moustached according to the fashion of an earlier epoch, and bound from knee to throat in bespoke tweed. Though age had given him bulk and had hooded his eyes, he remained handsome in a solid sort of way.

"But the formalities are dwindling," he said. "And besides, I know who you are."

I nodded at the gun. "In that case, is the museum piece really necessary?"

A shadow smile passed over his lips. "Forgive me. I have reason to distrust those who would approach me unseen." He returned the revolver to the desk draw.

"A Beaumont-Adams point 442," I said. "The commentators have pronounced it a Webley, you know."

"Nothing so modern. Pray sit, so that I might, too."

I took the armchair he indicated and he returned to his desk chair.

"So, when did you plan to tell my son that your engagement to him is a sham?"

I'd known, of course, that he would prove cleverer in life than he was in his writings. "I thought it best to simply disappear," I said.

197

"Now?"

"Tomorrow morning at six. A taxi from Rotherfield will meet me at the gate."

The hooded eyes surveyed me closely for about a minute. 'A steady income, I should think, but meagre.'

"You can't be more precise?"

The ghost smile flitted across his face again. "Your spatulate fingertips," he said, "suggest that you use a typewriter, but you hold a pen as often, as is indicated by that callous on the middle finger of your right hand. The red marks either side of your nose show where your spectacles rest, and since you do not wear them now, and do not squint, it is clear you need them only for close work, such as reading and writing. Your pallor tells me that you spend even these sunny days indoors. I conclude, then, that you are a scholar, and one who keeps the wolf from the door by typing up the work of more senior colleagues."

I, too, controlled the impulse to smile. "Spatulate fingers may be an inherited trait," I said. "Drawing with a pencil can disfigure a finger as easily as writing with a pen. Eyesight may be destroyed with needlework. And I may suffer from anaemia."

He raised his eyebrows. "Then I was wrong?"

I smiled openly. "Not in any particular. May I try the trick on you?"

He shrugged. "I am too well known."

"That might be disputed. But if you like, I'll only tell you those things I know you've tried to conceal from the public."

He nodded, still unsmiling. "You have my permission."

"Your Christian name," I said, "is James, not John."

Another shrug. "A slip of the pen, made early in my career. But it has been noted before now. Go on."

"In Afghanistan you were injured in neither the shoulder nor the leg, but in the groin."

"Better," he said. "My literary agent suggested the first lie out of delicacy, and I invented the second because I had forgotten it. Anything else?"

"You were raised a Roman Catholic."

That surprised him. "Was I indeed?"

I nodded. "When inventing aliases, you often draw Christian names from Catholic translations of the Bible — Elias and Isa — and surnames from Catholic Ireland — Moran and Moriarty."

"Bravo," he said. "Though the last was no alias. Anything else?"

"Yes," I said. "Your first marriage wasn't happy."

There was a long silence in which he did nothing but examine his hands. They were swollen with rheumatism, and when clasped together, as they now were, resembled some huge, tropical nut. Then he stood and made for the door. I'd blown it—the interview was over! But when he reached the door, he only pushed it shut.

"You are impertinent," he said, "but you are not wrong. When my first wife and I met, we were both free as air, and were quickly overtaken by the most romantic circumstances."

"I read about them," I said. "Like a million others."

His heavy eyes brightened a moment. "But only you read rightly. You and another."

The implication thrilled me.

"I see her dullness in Herbert. It is a blessing that his constitution has kept him from service. He could not have survived it, even in health. Indeed, I wonder how he will weather a broken heart."

He was trying to distract me. "Why did you ignore my letter?"

He stared at his fingers, entwined again. "Why should I not? I receive a hundred such in a year."

"But you knew mine was different."

He shook his head. "There was nothing empirical to distinguish it."

"And still you knew."

He straightened his back, looked me in the eye. "What you asked was impossible and remains so. Your feelings in the matter are not my first concern. Your..." He stopped, tried again. "The gentleman of whom you wrote..." But then he stopped entirely.

"I understand," I said. "Such abuses of mind and body must have consequences. But I also know you protected him: that you were a friend even when he didn't seem to want one. I read all that between the lines, too. And I read your new article, about his service in the present conflict..."

Now it was he who resisted distraction. "You are confusing James with John. The delicacies I was forced to observe at the beginning of my career have been displaced by new ones. It is impossible now to depict vices no longer allowed in law. As for the article to which you allude, you must consider its purposes: though it contains no outright lie, I was obliged to emphasise the continued powers of my..." he stumbled again, but only for a moment, "of my colleague, and pass over his present failings."

I made to speak again, but he held up his hand.

"Oh, I wish I could have protected him as successfully as I imply. But in truth, reality and my records began to diverge years ago. I am afraid it is always so: the doll and his maker are never identical."

"And is that what he is to you?" I said, angry now. "A doll?"

It was so patently unjust that he knew he needn't reply. Instead, he returned to his chair. He even managed another smile. "You resemble your mother," he said.

"She told me I resembled him."

He took another close look at me. "Your hair is dark enough, it is true. May I ask your age?"

"Twenty-two," I said.

He shook his head. "I had no idea that the ... the liaison had persisted so long."

"Fits and starts."

After a moment he said, "I never stopped following your mother's career. It seems she can still draw a crowd to the concert hall, or could before the war, anyway. Do you see her often?"

"Almost never."

Another moment passed. "What surname have you adopted? It cannot be the one you appended to that letter you sent me. Herbert would have remarked on it: as a boy, he read my work as assiduously as any other."

"I usually go by my mother's real name," I said. "But I often use the alias you created. And I sometimes use my father's."

Then we lapsed into a longer silence. He looked out the window and the sunlight gave definition to the scores and ridges on his forehead. I thought I might have calculated his age to the second.

Finally, he said, "I do not doubt you are his. You have intelligence and wit, and you treat your own person with a rigour that is

200

not entirely healthy. You are also disdainful of the property and feelings of others."

I smiled: it was his best bit of deduction yet.

"But I am also his," he said. "I was once accessory to his mock-betrothal, under an alias, to an innocent housemaid. I have helped him break into houses on several occasions. And I have witnessed him act as judge and jury, pardoning men who might otherwise have gone to the gallows."

"As I said, you are a true friend to him."

He smiled at that, before turning very grave. "I am something other than his friend now. Not his brother, either — I might be called his keeper. His body has become a cage to him, and at times his mind is one, too. Oh, he writes his monographs on bees, and will sometimes speak sagely on current events, but too often his thoughts are all turned inward. He used to emerge from such fits unchanged, but now they exert a heavy toll. We grow old, after all." He looked at me closely again. "You hold yourself like an athlete. Do you fence?"

I nodded. "My mother would've liked me to sing, but I inherited other talents."

"You do not play a musical instrument?"

I shook my head.

"Well, that is a relief, at least."

We had strayed from the point, but I was wary of being pushy. My best advances had been made in silence, after all. "Your house is splendid," I said, "but very isolated."

"I have my family."

"And friends?"

He considered a moment. "My literary agent is a near neighbour. But you shall find, as you grow older, that family acquires much more importance..." He stopped himself again, and I tried not to smile. And then he allowed himself a bout uninhibited laughter. "You have indeed inherited other talents!" he cried through it.

"But I didn't put the thought in your head: it was yours, and I know you believe it."

His whole aspect had changed, the heavy eyes wide now, and clear. "Of course I do," he said. "Family, comradeship, and courtesy: we neglect these things at our peril. And hospitality, too. You shall stay the weekend."

"You invite me to?"

"We cannot have you creeping away at daybreak. On Monday morning I shall make telephone calls and see what may be done. You have my word that I shall do all in my power to help you in this matter. My attempts to obstruct you were motivated by care, but I see now that it was misdirected."

I didn't know what to say: 'thank you' seemed inadequate. But the sound of footsteps from the corridor, and of a voice calling my name, saved me from embarrassment. My host rose again and opened the door: "In here, Herbert." My fiancé appeared in the frame and stopped there, dead still: I saw then the power of a long-standing injunction, and knew how far I'd been honoured. Herbert—an insubstantial figure next to his bullish Papa—goggled at the two of us in turn. "Getting acquainted, what?"

"Indeed," said his father, taking him by the elbow and coaxing him across the threshold. "You know, Herbert, a friend of mine once demonstrated to me his contention that life is infinitely stranger than anything the mind of man could invent."

"A friend of yours?" Herbert could barely hide his scorn. "You mean the friend of yours."

His father recognised the scorn, but didn't admonish it. Instead, he moved his hand from Herbert's elbow to his shoulder, and so embraced him. The look on Herbert's face showed how unexpected this was: it contained bewilderment mixed with a little terror.

"Herbert, I must tell you straight away that I cannot agree to this marriage. I shall give my reasons later, but for now let me commend this young lady to you as a friend. And one to keep for life: she has the pedigree for it. No, there must be no questions, Herbert. We shall talk after dinner."

Herbert looked to me for explanation. The bewilderment had grown, pushing out the terror.

"I'm afraid it's true," I said. "We can't marry. There is a... What do they call it? There's an affinity between us."

My host nodded. "Yes," he said, "that's it precisely. This young lady is already family. Now, let us go into the garden while the sun still shines. No sulking, Herbert. We must not waste a minute of the day that is left to us!"

The three of us left the room — two, at least, thinking on another.

The Ghost in the Military Machine
by Graham Cookson
Kent, UK

September 1st 2011: United States Department of Defense 'The Pentagon', Virginia.

The preparations for the anniversary of the September 11th 2001 attacks were finalised. General Patrick Mendoza sat in his courtyard-side office, watching as a small selection of the 23,000 employees at the Pentagon meandered from one side of the sunlit, pentagon-shaped courtyard to the other, some stopping to talk to others, some busy in their own reverie.

General Mendoza faced the mounting emails in front of him.

"Blast!" He uttered to himself, opening one particular email.

The contents told him that one of the main routes for the President's carriage was being altered and he would need to ensure that all military personnel involved were aware of the changes. "Damned Secret Service," he muttered to himself. "A little more warning would have been appreciated."

He hit the intercom button on his phone, contacting his secretary. "Jamie, hold all incoming calls please. And call my wife, I'm…" General Mendzoa was cut short.

The lights in the office started flashing like mad and his computer screen began flickering, new windows opening and closing at random and the silent alarm light in the corner of his office started flashing bright red.

"What the…?" The general looked around, bewildered by the electrical chaos.

"What is it?," Jamie asked from the other end of the intercom.

General Mendoza didn't respond to her question; he was looking at a new window on his computer, which remained open – it had a timer on it.

Five, Four... the general could do nothing but watch as the numbers flashed on screen... Three, Two... One. The counter reached zero.

Jamie strained to hear what was going on over the intercom. A loud click and then a grinding sound could be heard.

"Hello? Who's there?" She heard the general call out.

There was the sound of some movement, possibly a chair being moved and footsteps. Then nothing. She waited patiently for a minute. Then a loud bang and click could be heard down the line.

Jamie rushed into the joining office. "General?" she said in soft despair, looking around the empty room.

As head of security, Major Powell was trying to calm the situation. It must be a computer virus. He didn't know how, but it had slipped through the firewalls and was now causing havoc in the building's military-grade security system; doors were locking and unlocking at random, and alarms were being tripped all over the vast building.

The entire building was put on lockdown, no personnel in or out, until it was resolved – everyone in the building needed to be accounted for and searched, section by section.

By 0200 hours, only one member of staff was unaccounted for, General Patrick Mendoza.

September 12th 2011: 221b Baker Street, London.

"Well it looks like the Twin Towers anniversary went well," Watson said. Folding up his paper he looked over to see Sherlock staring at a stuffed beaver on the mantelpiece.

He had been studying it ever since Mrs. Hudson found it in a parcel left on their doorstep. There was no note or address, so (as

Sherlock had pointed out) the parcel was obviously hand delivered and there could be no mistake that it was for one of the occupants of 221b.

But the beaver had come as some surprise – it was set in a position where it was standing on its hind legs, its front right paw held a pipe to its mouth, with a monocle on its left eye, and a small, beaver-sized deerstalker hat adorning its head. It had left Sherlock baffled, much to Watson's initial amusement.

"I said the September 11th anniversary went well," Watson said out loud again, trying to raise some response from the catatonic Sherlock.

"Hmmm?" Sherlock mumbled.

"Forget it, just forget it," Watson tossed the paper to one side, landing front page up, the headline bearing the legend, 'America Remembers'.

The doorbell rang. Watson paused, to see if this would bring some sign of life from the 'great detective'.

'Ring. Ring' The doorbell sounded again.

"Oh I'll get that shall I?" Watson suggested sarcastically.

"Hmm?"

Shaking his head, Watson made his way to the front door.

The bell rang again. "Yes, yes. I'm coming." Watson said impatiently.

Watson opened the door and was confronted by four men, dressed in black suits, with white shirts and black ties.

"Sherlock Holmes?" one of the men said, with an American accent.

"Let them in John." Sherlock's voice came from behind Watson.

Watson stepped to one side, watching as the men walked in past him into the living room.

Sherlock, still standing at the mantelpiece, looking at the mysterious beaver turned to face the men. Watson watched as Sherlock's keen eye looked to each man individually.

Before any of the men had a chance to speak, Sherlock began. "You are from the U.S. government. FBI? No, no. Definitely not CIA, that much is obvious. You're manner, attire and those small badges on your lapels would suggest Secret Service. But why would Secret Service be in Britain? The President is not visiting, so there would be no need for your presence here."

Sherlock's gaze landed on Watson's discarded newspaper. "Ah, something to do with the 9/11 anniversary perhaps. But what?"

"Sir!" The man said with some urgency. "We are pressed for time, our flight leaves in an hour."

"Oh, very well," Sherlock snapped. "I take it I am to come with you?"

"Yes, your presence has been requested. We can de-brief you both on the fight."

On the eight-hour flight to America, Sherlock and Watson were de-briefed on the situation. The men were indeed from the Secret Service, as Sherlock had deduced, on a special assignment from Homeland Security as part of a National Special Security Event (NSSE).

While it had not been reported in the papers, the Pentagon was subject to a suspected terrorist attack in the lead up to the 9/11 10th Anniversary. After the attack on the Pentagon, one member of staff disappeared, and it has now been determined that it could be a kidnap situation.

The agent explained that the general was on the intercom to his PA at the time and that she said it sounded like he began talking to someone else, then she heard some strange sounds, possibly a struggle.

But during the incident no one entered or left his office. Yet he was gone.

Sherlock and Watson arrived at the Pentagon in a stereotypical unmarked black sedan. The duo was escorted to one of the entrances and led inside.

Just inside the building, they were greeted with a security check point, not unlike one would find at an airport, though the security personnel were more heavily armed. Staff and visitors had to go through a metal detector, while bags were scanned through an x-ray machine.

After being allowed through security, Watson and Holmes were met by Major Powell, who led them to the security control room, just a little way from the entrance check point, with two more military officers escorting them.

After some brief introductions, the second de-briefing began, though more in-depth than the one given on the journey from Britain.

Sherlock had been specifically requested by a government official, (though they were not told who), and they needed his help to work out how the attackers had managed to infiltrate The Pentagon and kidnap General Mendoza – without being noticed by any security camera.

One of officers working in the control room explained that the system monitored and controlled the alarms, cameras and the electromagnetic security doors.

"What happened during the attack?" Sherlock asked.

"Well, we lost control of the alarms and the security doors," the officer said.

"And the cameras weren't affected at all?" Sherlock questioned. "No chance of even a momentary blackout? You have to be very specific here."

"All footage from the cameras can be accounted for - no known glitches, blackouts or anything out of the ordinary detected," Powell answered.

"Excellent," Sherlock responded, much to the surprise of military personnel in the room. "And what about the virus' source?"

"We found the source of the attack; turns out it was a disgruntled former employee. He was part of security programming and knew our system. He has been detained - but is refusing to tell us what happened to the General Mendoza, or who he's working for," Major Powell replied. "Would you like to question him?"

"No, I don't need to question him," Sherlock said. "But I do need to see the general's office," he added.

Watson and Sherlock were, once again, escorted by two officers and led by Major Powell, down some of the many corridors of the Pentagon. Each corridor and hallway appeared to have a theme; some were memorials to different conflicts, humanitarian missions or branches of service. They turned down one corridor which had its walls practically covered with quilts and memorabilia.

The major told them that this was one of the corridors that had been hit during the 9/11 attacks and all the articles lining the corridor had been donated by families of the victims, schools, and communities; they remained there as a permanent reminder of the tragic day.

They walked to a hallway just off the 9/11 memorial corridor and into an ante room, Powell explained that it was Mendoza's PA's office. Her desk was empty, on leave after the incident.

Mendoza's office was something that one would expect of a high-ranking military official. The room was lined with oak panels, a bookshelf on the wall immediately to the right as they entered the room. A long window opposite the entrance gave a picturesque view of the central courtyard. Along the left side of the office, sat General Mendoza's old, yet sturdy wooden desk, behind it adorning the wall was a landscape photograph, showing a birds-eye view of the Pentagon.

"Nothing has been changed since the attack happened. Even the computer has been left on, as it was found," Powell explained.

Sherlock remained silent, mentally reconstructing the scene as he had done so many times before. He walked around the room, investigating the bookshelves, the area around the desk and the view out of the window.

"Looks quite antiquated," Watson commented, trying to break the silence. "Not quite what I was expecting of the U.S. military."

Watson had intended the comment to be light-hearted to ease the moment.

"I can assure you anything old in here has been selected," Powell responded tersely.

"The Pentagon underwent a major renovation between 1998 and 2011," Sherlock stated, still inspecting the room. "Everything was updated to modern standards, including security, decor and even the windows. As a military man, I would have expected you to know that, my dear Watson."

Sherlock pushed against the tough, double-glazed windows. All the windows had been replaced during the renovation, sealed-shut for both security and energy efficiency.

"Lovely," Sherlock commented. "I'll need to see the security control room, one more time."

Stopping outside one of the many bathrooms the Pentagon held, Sherlock let out a small exclamation. "Did you know that the Pentagon has more toilets than it should?"

Watson, Major Powell and the two officers looked bewildered at Sherlock.

Sherlock continued, "Yes originally the architect had designed the building to feature segregated facilities, with separate toilets for 'blacks'. But when President Roosevelt looked around before its opening he demanded the removal of the 'whites only' signs. The Pentagon was the first and only building in Virginia where segregation was not allowed at that time." Sherlock then promptly walked into the lavatory. "Watson will you join me? This is a piece of American history right here," Sherlock said as he disappeared into the lavatory.

Watson hesitantly looked at the American officers beside him, shrugging he followed Sherlock into the men's room.

"With those accents, you can never tell which side they bat for," one of the officers jested.

"Sherlock! Have you lost your mind?" Watson said sharply. "What are we doing in the bathroom?"

Sherlock began talking in a fast, hushed tone. "I need you to remain here and then make your way to General Mendoza's office. Once in there, wait and see if anything unusual happens."

"Why?"

"Because I have a feeling that what I'm about to do could potentially have me detained, and without you in the office, I won't be able to solve this case."

"You never make things easy do you?" Watson said despairingly.

Sherlock walked calmly out of the bathroom and explained that Watson was otherwise 'occupied'. Leaving one of the officers to escort Watson back once he'd finished, the major guided Sherlock back to the control room.

Back in the control room, Sherlock turned to Major Powell, "Right, we need to recreate the events of the day."

"Excuse me?" Powell said incredulously.

"I need you to sound the alarms and unlock the security doors," Sherlock requested.

"Absolutely not!" Powell said.

"Do you want to find out what happened or not?"

"Mr. Holmes, I have been patient enough with you, you will tell me what is going on, or I will have you escorted from the premises," Powell demanded.

"Well, it's patently obvious that this was no kidnapping," Sherlock said intolerantly.

"What do you mean?"

"No threats or demands had been made on the Pentagon or General Mendoza. Your security cameras were not disabled, the office windows have not been breached - no one could have possibly entered or exited that office without you knowing," Sherlock said as he casually strolled around the control room. "Which means that General Mendoza is still in his office."

Sherlock finished speaking and then, without another word, suddenly flung himself at a nearby control desk and hit several buttons he had studied earlier.

Watson was waiting in one of the cubicles of the bathroom when alarms started sounding in the corridor. "Here we go," he thought to himself.

Cracking open the restroom door, Watson peeked out. The officer left outside was now running away from the toilets towards the direction of the control room.

Watson made his way to General Mendoza's office. All was quiet within the room, the thick wooden door muffling the sound of alarms outside. Nothing looked out of place – it was just as it had been earlier.

Moving around the office, Watson made his way to the desk and sat down, to wait for Sherlock or some angry military personnel. Suddenly, the computer monitor flickered out of sleep mode. A new window opened and a countdown timer appeared. Watson stared as the numbers hit zero. There was a loud click and then a grinding sound.

Watson turned around to see a segment of the wall behind him, near the window, sliding to one side. Inquisitively, he approached the previously hidden doorway and gagged as a pungent smell emerged. Covering his nose, Watson found himself in front of a thin side room. He stepped across the threshold.

The room ran along the back wall of the office, behind where the painting hung. It appeared to be some form of panic room. Finding a switch, the lights flickered on with a buzz, as though they hadn't been used for a long time.

Now able to see the room more clearly, Watson reeled as he spotted the body of a middle-aged man dressed in a military uniform.

Moving closer, Watson saw the name badge bearing: 'General P. Mendoza'. Giving the body a very quick check over, he deduced that suffocation was the most likely cause of his demise.

As Watson turned to leave, the sliding door suddenly slammed with a bang.

Trying not to panic, Watson pulled out his mobile phone. There was no reception; either the panic room blocked out the signal, or it was to do with the Pentagon's security. Watson knew that certain high-profile military buildings used signal-blockers to prevent any un-monitored communications.

"Damn it!" he exclaimed.

Looking around, he finally saw a small panel with coloured buttons on the wall above Mendoza's body. Relief set in, and he pressed the buttons, one by one. There was no response, either they had been disconnected or were so old they had stopped working.

"What?! No!" He yelled out.

Watson reduced himself to banging on the door. A loud metallic sound echoed in the room, hopefully someone would hear. But then Watson looked back to General Mendoza's body; he had suffocated, which meant that this room was airtight and most likely sound proof.

The air, already stale with the smell of Mendoza's rotting corpse, was becoming increasingly harder to breathe in. Watson sank to the floor, knowing that asphyxiation could set it at any time – he would become dizzy and blackout. There was nothing he could do.

His breathing became increasingly laboured and he could feel the dizziness setting in, he was losing consciousness...

Then the panic room door slid open. The silhouettes of two men moved forward, dragging Watson from the room.

Watson found himself lying in General Mendoza's office. Major Powell and four officers were standing around him, Sherlock stood by the door to the panic room, in handcuffs.

"You're lucky to be alive," Powell said, helping Watson to his feet.

"We'd have been here sooner if you hadn't stopped me," Sherlock churlishly mumbled.

"Don't push me Mr. Holmes," Powell snapped. "You're lucky that we only handcuffed you. Now, perhaps you could explain your actions in full. Otherwise, I will charge you."

Sherlock sighed, "As I'm sure are aware, the Pentagon was built during the Second World War. It is likely that certain offices for high-ranking personnel, such as this one, had extra security features built into them – such as a panic room like this," Sherlock said, pointing at the hidden room.

"When the incident happened earlier this month, the alarm systems were activated and certain security doors unlocked – including this panic room, and while General Mendoza was talking to his secretary, the door automatically opened.

"Like you, I'm sure that the general had no idea that this room existed, and thinking that someone had opened the door from the inside, he went to investigate," Sherlock explained, looking around to see if everyone was following his deduction. "Now, following you're procedures, you set the building into lock-down. This, I believe, locked off the panic room's door and shut down the emergency supply of air, meaning that the general was unable to open the door and ultimately asphyxiated."

"It seems absurd that something like this could have been overlooked," the major said.

"Is it?" Sherlock said wryly. "It's highly possible that in renovating the building and updating the security software that something could have been overlooked.

"I would imagine, that the Pentagon's original blueprints would have some exclusions. Remember, it was built during the biggest war history has known; the U.S. government wouldn't have wanted exact plans detailing its newest and biggest military building to be potentially leaked to Axis forces."

"So the general's death?" Powell asked.

"Was all an unfortunate accident," Sherlock said. "Your former employee is guilty of the virus, but had no malicious intent towards General Mendoza. And I suspect he was just working alone.

"This unknown panic room should not have been affected in the lockdown, it is an anomaly in your system; a ghost in the machine, if you will," Sherlock finished with a dry smile.

September 18th 2011: 221b Baker Street, London.

"Sherlock, it's your brother, dear." Mrs. Hudson's kind voice could be heard from the hallway.

Sherlock made a rude sound under his breath at these words. He picked up the stuffed beaver from the mantelpiece and sat down in his armchair, pretending to be engrossed in studying it.

Mycroft Holmes walked into the living room, giving a smile and a nod to Watson, sitting on the couch, reading the paper. Watson politely nodded back.

"Sorry to intrude, Sherlock," Mycroft began. "I was on my way home and have been asked to pass on a message. The US government send their thanks for your help the other day."

Sherlock shifted in his chair, giving a childish grunt, not looking away from the beaver.

"Well then," Mycroft smiled once more in his awkward way. "I won't interrupt you any longer." Mycroft turned to leave and stopped, looking back to Sherlock. "Oh, I'm glad to see you are enjoying your present."

Sherlock looked up to his brother quizzically.

"I was sure it would fascinate you." Mycroft smiled again and winked at Watson, then left.

Sherlock looked down at the beaver that had been puzzling him for so long. "Bloody hell!" he exclaimed, dropping it to the floor with child-like fury.

The Adventure of the Second Mantel
by Jack Foley
Sunderland, UK

Upon recollecting the more than 120 cases I have had the pleasure of documenting during the 23 years I spent working with the great detective Sherlock Holmes, not one presents such an unusual chain of events as the adventure of the Second Mantle. It was to be the last case of Sherlock Holmes, where Holmes' methods of deduction were used against him.

It was the winter of 1904 and I was living out in the country with my second wife, Violet. After vacating my lodgings at Baker Street I had made myself a good living through my country practice. I had not seen Holmes in several months and, upon my return, I was apprehensive as to the state in which I would find him.

When I arrived at our rooms Holmes was his usual self. He was sat in his armchair, facing the fire, glancing over a pile of documents.

"Ah!" he exclaimed, barely looking up from his work, "My dear Watson, pray take a seat, I trust you had a good journey."

"Holmes, you haven't changed a bit, what have you been up to?" I enquired as I took a seat, noting the scars upon his face. He threw down his papers and looked up at me.

Holmes told me that he was on the verge of bringing to justice the most dangerous criminal gang in Europe, an organisation responsible for no less than seven brutal murders in the past year. That Friday, they intended to murder a wealthy Scottish medical practitioner and author living in London. It was Holmes' intention to be waiting for them.

Holmes and I had only been speaking for several minutes, when we were interrupted by Mrs. Hudson, who brought us Inspector Lestrade. My friend, as usual, seemed uninterested by the Inspector's arrival and imprudently asked him,

"What trivial matter do you wish bring to my attention today Inspector?"

"The murder of Lord Ashdown," replied the inspector, stepping into the flat.

216

"Why do you feel the necessity to concern me in this matter?" rebuked Holmes.

"There was a letter accompanying the body, a letter addressed to you."

"Watson," Holmes began, leaping from his chair, clearly intrigued by the case, "As you are in London for the day will you be good enough to join me on this case."

Having been away from Baker Street for some time I had long wished to accompany Holmes on another case. I joined my friend and the Inspector in the four-wheeler that was waiting outside for us. On the way I told them how I had met the victim just one week earlier, at a dinner hosted by my friend and former superior officer, a Mr. Charles Harding. He was a rather jovial gentleman who took great interest in myself, and my stories of my work, with Mr. Holmes.

Lestrade informed us that the body lay in the middle of the room, the blood stains from a single bullet upon his shirt. The room had also been completely emptied, save for the furniture, in what Holmes described as a desperate attempt to hide the group's motives.

We arrived at the empty house in North London finding the body exactly as described, in its possession, a letter addressed to my friend. He glanced over it once and passed it onto me.

Dear Mr. Sherlock Holmes,

We trust that you will find this letter. It was your involvement in our affairs that has forced us to push forward with our plans. We have learned much about your methods over recent months and we thank you profusely for your help in arranging this matter.

"Whatever does it mean Holmes?" I asked, placing the note down on the table.

"Last November, in the light of a ghastly triple murder I became knowledgeable of a criminal gang working in London, the Second Mantle, one of the most dangerous organisations I have ever encountered in my career. I had reason to believe they were planning to orchestrate one of the largest robberies this country has ever seen. In order to bring them to justice I needed data and therefore, over the successive weeks, I posed as a homeless man in need of employment. I gained their trust, carrying out minor errands for them, eventually becoming part of their organisation, meeting regularly in a disused tunnel under the Thames.

"They took me into their confidence," he continued crouching down beside the body, "They told me what I wanted to know, they informed me of their plans; that this Friday, they were to murder Lord Ashdown, a wealthy Scottish author, living here in London. I intended to be ready for them. However, it appears they were aware of my involvement and have pushed forward in their plans. All my work has been in vain. I have been duped; I cannot trust anything I have been told. I have learned nothing while they now know everything they want about me."

"What do you intend to do?" I enquired, observing Holmes pacing round the room, looking for any evidence he could.

"They know everything about my methods, I cannot trust any evidence they have put before me. They know exactly what I will be looking for."

Holmes explained that all he could deduce from the little convincing evidence available was that there had been five people here last night. They all came and left different ways, taking different things. Examining the room he saw that there were droplets of water around the fire. It had been put out in haste. This fact, combined with the fact that Lord Ashdown couldn't have seen his killer and the position of the bullet in the body pointed to the fact that he was shot from the window, while he was sat by the fire.

Holmes wrote a short letter addressed to my friend Mr. Harding, he asked me to return to Baker Street to collect some documents and take the documents and the letter to him. Holmes and the Inspector were to go to Scotland Yard. The Inspector was, under the orders of Holmes, to ensure a police presence around the home of Mr. Harding. Holmes gave me clear instructions to meet him at the British Museum after delivering the letter.

I returned to Baker Street to pick up the documents and took them, along with the letter, to the home of Mr. Harding. As Holmes had requested there was a visible police presence around the house. I gave Mr. Harding the letter as I was instructed to.

It was just after six when I arrived at the museum. Holmes was waiting for me inside and he showed me through to a store room at the back, asking whether I had been followed. Inspector Lestrade was waiting in the store room with about a dozen officers. Holmes gave us his instructions.

"I expect them to arrive at around eight," Holmes began, "This is a risky crime they are committing tonight, so I very much doubt that the leader will be with them. However, as for the other four, I feel I can pinpoint their movements with reasonable accuracy. Two members will enter through two different windows on the West side of the building, on the ground floor. Their aim is to get any security or police over to that side of the building. They will only be here for a short time, very unlikely to steal anything. Lestrade, if you wish to catch them you must ensure your men stay hidden until the gang members enter and when they do, you must be quick."

"Another member will enter through the store room door, the door through which we entered. I have a feeling he works here and he will make his way through the museum, making his way to the other store room on the second floor on the East side of the building. He intends to find the object he is after and open the window; the final member of the group will be waiting below for the object. He is a young athletic man, he will take the object back to their hideout."

"Now Inspector," Holmes looked sternly towards Lestrade, "I suggest you organise your men, in order to catch these criminals before they know that they are walking into a trap. Do you believe yourself capable of doing so?"

"I'll most certainly try my best Mr. Holmes," he replied.

My friend and I remained in the storeroom and when eight o'clock came the group arrived exactly as Holmes had anticipated. Lestrade was able to arrest them and take them to a four-wheeler that was waiting for them. We bid the Inspector good night as he drove off to the yard. Holmes began to fill me in on the details of the case.

"Although the Silver Mantle's upmost priority was to feed me false information to put me on the wrong line of enquiry, I have been able to piece together the majority of the case from the little information I have been presented with. Firstly, my dear Watson, you mentioned that only last week you had dinner with Lord Ashdown and your friend Mr. Harding. I know that Mr. Harding enjoys reading your accounts of our work and you often take him unpublished manuscripts; documents detailing my methods and cases. Last week you took him several accounts, one of which documented our work recovering a priceless Egyptian artefact, the Mantle Staff, you may recall that the piece was travelling to the British Museum from a museum in Cairo and was stolen in transit. We recovered the staff and returned it to the British Museum. Your account then goes on to document the security measures placed upon it."

"Last week you gave these accounts to your friend. Presumably, after you left, he gave some of these documents to Lord Ashdown who you said took an interest in your stories. He took the accounts home to read them over. The Second Mantle knew that he had these documents and they wished to see them in order to gain further knowledge of my methods. The group had studied my methods for a while and attempted to remove any evidence and also use my methods against me, planting evidence to lead me down the wrong track. We know that he was shot from the window while he was sitting by the fire, it seems he was reading the documents. The body was moved onto the floor in order to hide this fact. They took everything in the room to further hide what they had stolen, however, the fact that they wanted to hide everything must have meant they were taking something I would know about."

"The fact that he was shot from the window also told me about the group's plans. The person who shot Lord Ashdown will have been the main member of this organisation, the one also trusted with carrying the precious cargo, the documents. He would have took the most direct route back, he headed South-West, meaning their hideout was somewhere near Tavistock Square, near this museum. It became obvious they wanted the documents for details about the security of the artefact, as it seems doubtful they would go to such lengths to discover things about my methods, especially as they met with me on a weekly basis. I felt that their next step would have been to kill Mr. Harding but I believed that they might have anticipated me working this out. I sent you with several documents to Mr. Harding, documents I believe they may have wished to see. I also organised the strong police presence to give the appearance that I expected the group to try and kill Mr. Harding. In actual fact I was one step ahead."

"I expected the group to push forward in their plans seeing the large police presence outside the home of your friend. I made sure that myself, Lestrade and the police, entered the museum unnoticed through one of the store room doors. I was able to anticipate the groups movements as in your documentation of events you had .conveyed my concern to various holes in the security. By reading your account they could piece together the best way to steal the staff."

"Fantastic Holmes!" I exclaimed, "Now only one step remains, to find the leader of this organisation." We decided to go to the storeroom on the second floor where the artefact was being kept. It was in a rather small wooden crate. Holmes lifted the lid and to our surprise the Mantle Staff was not there. In its place was a letter. Holmes read it once, threw it to the floor and left the museum in silence. I shouted after him, picking up the letter.

My Dear Mr. Sherlock Holmes,

I must take this opportunity to congratulate you; over the past few years you have proved yourself to be a formidable opponent. On several occasions you have successfully foiled my plans. However, I regret to inform you that the artefact you came here tonight to protect has left the country, and I with it. Last night, after the murder of Lord Ashdown, the others took rather long diversions to our meeting place. This gave me a lengthy window during which I was able to steal the artefact. I knew that the men coming here tonight were walking into a trap.

I have always wanted to meet you in person, however now I doubt if I will get the chance. My communications with yourself have always been in disguise or through agents acting on my behalf. Several years ago you met an agent of mine, posing as me, in Switzerland. Believing this agent to be me you defeated him and allowed him to fall over the Reichenbach falls.

After that event and the capture of Colonel Sebastian Moran, I was forced into hiding. My vast criminal empire falling apart. I have spent the years since then gaining knowledge on your methods, creating a plan to finally defeat you, to use your own methods against you. I have succeeded in eluding you, the game is up. I have left the country with the artefact, never to return.

Professor James Moriarty

After reading the letter in shock I left the museum. It was late and as Mrs. Hudson had not had time to prepare my room I decided to spend the night in a nearby hotel.

The next morning, as my hansom pulled up outside 221b I was worried about the state of my friend. He had been beaten, outwitted, and situations like this usually only called for one thing. However, much to my surprise, I found Holmes sitting beside the fire, two large suitcases to his side.

"Whatever are you doing Holmes?" I enquired.

"My dear Watson," he looked up from the floor, "I have always feared that one day I would no longer be able to continue in my unique profession. A nagging doubt I would one day find a criminal astute enough to use my own methods to my disadvantage. Professor James Moriarty has proved to be just the man. He has defeated me on several separate occasions and proved to be a dangerous adversary. It is with that thought in mind that I have taken the decision to retire from my role as the world's only consulting detective."

"For many years now, my brother, Mycroft, has owned a small farm on the Sussex Downs, five miles west of Eastbourne. A cosy little place, looking out over the Channel. Mycroft has, this morning, handed the farm over to me, so that I can use it as my permanent residence. My hansom should arrive on the hour to take me from London."

Precisely on the hour, Mrs. Hudson alerted us to the presence of a cab outside. Holmes put out the fire, rose from the chair and picked up his luggage. He went over to his desk, and from the top drawer, took the most precious item in his possession. A single photograph of Miss Irene Adler. Holmes donned his deerstalker hat, turned, and left the flat.

I stood for a moment, thinking about all the cases that had begun in this very room, the dancing men, the speckled band, the Copper Beeches. All of the people who had visited Holmes here for help, from Sir Henry Baskerville, to Miss Violet Hunter, to the King of Bohemia. Sherlock Holmes had always been someone the people of

London, and beyond, could turn to if ever they had a problem to which they couldn't find a solution.

I took a final look at our rooms, at my empty desk, where I had rather frequently sat and documented the singular gifts of my friend. Where I had written my sixty or so accounts of my adventures with Mr. Sherlock Holmes. Tales such as the terrifying case of 'The Hound of the Baskervilles.' I felt saddened to know that the place where all these stories had been written now lay dormant and was to eventually fall into disrepair. I followed my friend out.

Holmes was sat in the hansom, although I have frequently noted that my friends cold, abhorrent mind, seemed devoid of emotion and compassion, he appeared deeply saddened to be leaving Baker Street behind.

"I would like you to have this, I no longer have a need for it," he said, handing me his photograph of Miss Adler.

"Holmes, I cannot possibly accept!" I rebuked.

"I intend for my retirement to be a permanent one, I do not have need for reminders of my cases. I would like you to have it, as a little memento of our time working together. Farewell, my dear Watson."

Holmes drove off in the hansom, driving out into the fog of an early morning in London. Leaving London for the last time, one final adventure. Leaving 221b Baker Street, Sherlock's home, the empty house.

Links

Save Undershaw   www.saveundershaw.com

Sherlockology   www.sherlockology.com

MX Publishing   www.mxpublishing.com

You can read more about Sir Arthur Conan Doyle and Undershaw in Alistair Duncan's book (share of royalties to the Undershaw Preservation Trust) – An Entirely New Country.

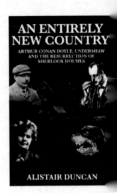

Alistair won the 2011 Howlett Literary Award (Sherlock Holmes Book of the Year) for *'The Norwood Author'* and is one of the UK's leading experts on Sir Arthur Conan Doyle.

Thank You

A huge thank you to Jules, Emma, Leif, David, Jacquelynn, Graham, Alistair and Steve whom without their help this book would have not been possible.

Lightning Source UK Ltd.
Milton Keynes UK
UKOW041016300512

193616UK00001B/1/P